HOOD LUVIN' FROM A DETROIT GOON

By: Londyn Lenz

DISCLAIMER:

This series is about 8 high school/college freshmen characters. The actions of them are from the mind of eighteen and nineteen-year-olds. Before you leave a negative review about immaturity, please keep that in mind. If you prefer older characters, then stay tuned for my next project.
Thank you.
-Londyn Lenz

Londyn Lenz Catalog (in order)

In Love With A New Orleans Savage

Married To A New Orleans Savage

I Gave Him Loyalty He Gave Me Lies: Brandon and Tiff

Karlos & Kylee: Crazy In Love With A New Orleans Savage

A Royal Valentine's Day

Karlos & Kylee: Finding Our Way Back To Love

Giving My Heart To An Atlanta Street King

Ty & Ashley: The Heart Of A Street King

Ronny & Kori: A Giving My Heart To An Atlanta Street King Spin-Off

His Gangsta Love Saved Me (1-3 Completed Series)

A Bad Boy Stole My Heart (1-2 Completed Series)

She Got It Bad For A Detroit Hitta

Shorty Still Got It Bad For A Detroit Hitta

Cursed Andreas & Annabella

Finessed By A Detroit Boss (1-3Completed Series)

Seduced By A Heartbreaker: A Miami Scandal

Fallin' For A Detroit Rydah (1-3 Completed Series)

Tis The Season To Fall For A Thug

She Fell In Love With A Real One (Spin-off of Fallin' For A Detroit Rydah)

Lucas & Paige (Spin-Off of Seduced By A Heartbreaker: A Miami Scandal)

In Love With A Las Vegas Outlaw (1-3 Completed Series)

Keep up with me:

My Facebook Reading Group: Londyn Lenz Besty Bratz Reading Group

Facebook Author Page: Author Londyn Lenz

Please SUBSCRIBE to my YouTube channel: Through The Lenz Of Londyn

Email: Londyn_Lenz@yahoo.com

JURNEE ARIEL WHITE

Tick-Toc

Tick-Toc

Tick-Toc

I watched the wall clock like a hawk, it felt like 1pm was taking forever to come. A normal full school day ends at 3:15 but today was early dismissal. I'd finished my work and Mrs. Crook, my chemistry teacher, was even ready to hear that sweet sound of the bell. I pushed my glasses on my face and took the scrunchy off my wrist, placing my long curly hair in a low ponytail.

I pulled the sleeves of my hoodie tighter around my waist and then zipped my bookbag all the way up. I should have worn a jacket instead of a hoodie. But then I remembered in the morning it was like forty-nine degrees. Don't you hate that? Chilly in the morning but hotter as the day goes on? I had a basic short sleeve v-neck shirt, so I was fine; my jeggings and baby doll shoes were basic as well.

This was how I dressed all year unless it's wintertime, then I wore Uggs or some Bearpaw boots. But I always kept on leggings or some jeggings with a basic t-shirt or graphic tee. I always and I mean always wore a hoodie around my waist. It made no difference what I wore because I couldn't hide my body to save my life. I mean, I wasn't trying to, but I damn sure wasn't trying to show it off.

I guess you can say I was a nerd as far as how I dressed and what my interests were. Anyway, I was ready to run out this door and get summer started. Summer in Detroit was so damn fun but the best part was not having to get up every morning and come here. I looked back at the clock and it was a matter of seconds now.

5, 4, 3, 2 1!!

Everyone darted to the door when Cooley High School bell rung. The school year was officially over! As soon as I walked in the hallway there was loose-leaf paper thrown all in the air. Lockers were slamming, everyone was smiling big, running down the halls and shouting. It was like the bells were a sign of freedom.

"Ayyyyeeeee!! Aparecer!!(Turn Up!!)" My best friend Toni walked out her English class excited and waving her arms, speaking Spanish.

I laughed because she was always so silly and her wild curly hair was all over. Her dad let her put golden highlights through her chocolate brown curls. It brought out her honey-color skin.

Putting her arm around me she said, "I thought the bell would never fucking ring."

I was about to agree when someone jumped on both of our backs.

"Free at last, free at last!" Coya yelled in our ear as she jumped off us. She was my other best friend.

"Yo' heavy butt always jumping on somebody." I laughed and mushed her head, making us both giggle.

"I have to make my presence known always, quote by the one and only Ms. Bassett herself." She joked back then took a bow. This was the actress of the group; Coya lived for being a top actress one day and her idol was Angela Bassett. This woman wrote a five-page letter to the Oscars stating why Angela Bassett should have been gotten an award. It was crazy, but I loved her passion.

"Oh Lord, look at this girl." Toni chuckled and pointed to Brinx.

The entire school was in the hallway and outside, but she was inside her French class taking pictures with her camera. Not a camera phone, I mean an actual Nikon zoom-flash camera that she took just about everywhere. We walked in the empty classroom laughing and just watched her take pictures.

"What are you doing crazy girl?" I asked her.

"Look how the chairs are scrambled; I'm going to develop these in black and white. It will look nostalgic when we look back at them in about ten years." Brinx's eyes were actually glowing when she talked about it. My third best friend and our photographer of the group. This girl was always taking pictures of any and everything.

"Girl let's bounce," I said putting my arm through hers after she put her camera around her neck. "Take pictures outside of our happy faces."

"Hell yes! We are officially seniors! Whooohooo!" Coya yelled out as soon as we stepped outside in the bright sun.

Toni played *Act Up* by *The City Girls* on her phone and both of them started twerking and acting silly. Me and Brinx were cracking up shaking our heads at our crazy friends.

"It feels so good to say that. Bye-bye 2020 seniors and hello 2021 seniors." Toni said, turning the music down

"Oh bitch, don't act like you won't miss your boo Adrian." Brinx teased.

"Don't play with me, y'all know I can't stand him." We all smacked our lips and waved her off.

"Yeah right, that hate is really love in disguise." I teased, getting in her face making kissing sounds.

"I hope y'all got some ruby red slippers in your bookbags because y'all about to be clicking your way home." Toni hit the alarm on her Ford Escape. It was a present from her dad when she got her license. She was the first of us to get a car and we were so excited for her and ourselves because we were done with riding the bus unless our schedules didn't sync.

We put our bookbags inside and leaned against it. This is what we did when school let out unless it's too cold to be outside. No one just went straight home, you'll miss any action that went down. Like right now, we were looking at Casey cuss out LaRon because once again, he was caught cheating. They were like the soap opera of Cooley; always fighting, cussing each other out. She'd fuck his locker up and cry all day over him. By the next day, they'd be back caked up like nothing ever happened.

"Jurnee I'm coming over your house to burn every hoodie you own," Coya said, trying to pull it off from around my waist.

"Will you stop!" I yanked it from her. "You always playing, punk." Playfully shoving her, I tightened it around my waist even tighter.

"You know I love you best friend, but I hate them hoodies too." Brinx added and Toni nodded her head in agreement.

I smacked my lips. "Forget y'all."

"2020 IN THIS BITCH!! 2020 OUT THIS BITCH!!" Those loud ass varsity football players came out the school loud like they have been all year.

I'm not going to hate and say these seniors weren't lit because they were. I think it was just tradition to just not like upperclassmen. While they were loud and twirling their football jerseys in the air, a black 2020 Suburban truck with chrome wheels turned the corner. The music was loud as hell coming from it and it parked right behind Toni's car.

Everyone knew who was inside because all the girls started licking their lips, twirling their hair and grinning wide. The driver's door opened, and August Legend stepped out. He had the black Suburban, so I wasn't surprised when he got out. His brother Adrian Legend got out the passenger door and Austin got out the back door.

"Sup ladies, what up doe, Brinx." August spoke to us but made sure to speak personally to Brinx.

"Hey August." She spoke back and her high cheek

bones got red.

Me and my girls weren't mean, so we spoke as well.

"Who borrowed their grandma car?" Adrian asked laughing and August shoved him, laughing too.

"Shut up asshole, you know damn well this my car. It's the same one that rides past your flat foot girlfriend, Brittany, while she's walking." Toni was quick with the clap back.

"You just made yourself look stupid because ain't no bitch of mine walking."

While they did their usual, some of the varsity team walked towards August's truck. Audrey Legend was a year older than his other three brothers. He graduated this year and he was Cooley's best quarterback. Audrey was fine as hell and he had dark brown neck length dreads that he kept in a high ponytail. The rest of his hair was faded out and he always had a design cut in it.

He had a short full beard and stood about 6'3. Audrey was a yellow boy with toned arms and tattoos all over him like he wasn't in high school. I'd be lying and also blind if I said he wasn't fine, hell all of the Legend brothers are, but they weren't my type.

Too many girls go crazy over them. Even if they

just spoke to you, these girls would melt. But what topped it all off was those blue eyes. All four of them had some crystal blue eyes and even if they glance at you for a second. I guarantee you will get hot and bothered.

It was sickening and I didn't want to be a part of the Legend train. Like now, Audrey couldn't even get to his brother's truck without girls crowding him asking his summer plans. I just shook my head chuckling and taking out my phone when I felt it vibrate. It wasn't nothing but notifications from Instagram.

"What up, y'all coming to my party tonight?" Audrey asked us once he finally got away from his groupies.

"Didn't you make it clear that class of 2020 only was invited?" Coya asked, putting her hands on her hip. Austin was looking at her from head to toe like he was starving.

I mean that's for the niggas, for women, as long as they fine then it's a go," Audrey said then he gave his brother Adrian a pound.

I scoffed and mumbled, "So shallow."

"What was that?" Audrey asked me with his eyebrows bunched up.

He didn't scare me but I wasn't like Toni, so I just

waved him off and went around to the car and opened her back door.

"Make sure y'all leave her mean ass at home." Audrey said, still giving me a mean glare.

I laughed and shook my head. "I don't give a damn about your party, *Aubrey.*" I purposely said his name wrong.

"You better get'cho ass in that car while you still can." He spoke in a threating tone.

I put my middle finger up and got inside, closing the door behind me.

"Well damn, that was intense." Brinx said when she got in sitting next to me.

"Fuck that little boy." I turned my nose up.

Toni and Coya got in the front.

"Girl what the hell did you say? Whatever it was got that nigga in his feelings." Coya looked back at me laughing and asked.

"Hell yeah bestie, he was bent tight as hell." Toni giggled, starting her car up.

"All I said was he's shallow, which I wasn't lying."

"I died when you called him Aubrey." Brinx cracked up. All of them started talking about it.

I just shook my head and looked out the window

while Toni drove each of us home. She and Coya stayed on the same block, me and Brinx stayed on the same block behind theirs. Four westside girls who were as tight as any friends can be.

"Ok, so I'll pick you both up at seven." Toni said when me and Brinx got out the car.

"Pick us up for what?" I asked, putting my bookbag on my arm.

"For Audrey's party."

"Umm weren't you just there a few minutes ago? That boy is not letting me in his party and frankly, I don't want to go." I folded my arms in a pouting manner; you'll have to excuse me, I'm a spoiled Pisces.

They all laughed at me and Coya said, "Girl, he ain't about to tell you to leave; it's going to be so packed he probably won't see you."

"Come on Jurnee, you know we all have to agree." Brinx said, poking her lip out.

Coya and Toni did the same, making me laugh and huff. "Ok. Ok, I'll be ready at seven."

"Yasssss! Oh, and no hoodie!" Toni yelled, then she took off down the street.

"I'ma slap her." I giggled, shaking my head. "What are you wearing?" I asked Brinx as I walked towards my porch and she walked towards hers. We stayed next door to each other.

"It depends, I ordered some stuff from Fashion Nova so if it's here, then I'll wear something from there but if not, then I'll look in my closet and find something."

I pulled the sleeves around my waist tighter.

"Jurnee." Brinx called my name and I looked up at her.

"Your body is bomb as hell, you don't have to be ashamed of it in any way."

"That's easy for you, Toni and Coya to say, y'all have bodies of models." I admitted because my friends knew how I felt about my body. I wasn't a big girl, but my thighs rubbed together, I had a big booty and my stomach wasn't washboard flat like theirs. I did everything from diet to working out. I blamed my mama because I was shaped just like her.

"I swear I hate that you don't see what we all see. But do me a favor, don't pick out anything or get dressed until I come over at six. Ok?" Brinx was talking to me but she was looking through the lens of her camera.

I laughed. "What are you doing?"

"Taking pictures of my beautiful best friend in the whole wide world."

I kept laughing, shaking my head and rolling my eyes as she clicked away. "You're crazy! Oh my gosh!" I ran on my porch laughing and hurrying to unlock my door because this girl was actually taking my picture like she was the paparazzi.

"See you at six!" She yelled out when I got inside.

"Crazy girl." I mumbled to myself, getting my last few laughs out. "Daddy!" I called his name, taking my shoes off and throwing my bookbag on the couch.

"Hi Gizmo boy, aww come here." I squatted down and showed my dog some love. Gizmo was my and my dad's bulldog. We've had him for about five years now and he was a big baby but his brother was worse. "Where are Daddy and Bear, huh?" I asked him while smiling then standing up.

Walking through the kitchen I saw some food containers. I could smell it and I knew what it was. After I washed my hands I opened the four containers and it was food from *Taste Of Love*. My dad's childhood friend, Tina, and her daughter, LaShawnta, sell dinners and desserts. When I tell y'all it is the best damn food on the westside.

They cook some of everything and I loved when Daddy would order from them. Before I could dig in, I walked downstairs where I heard music and smelled weed. Anytime my dad didn't want me to come down he would have the red light lamp on that was at the top of the stairs.

"Hey daddy." I said once I got down there all the way.

Our basement was where my dad was pretty much all the time. When you got down there it was a big steel pool table, bar and two stripper poles. Then in the far-left corner there was a long leather couch that had light up cup holders facing a seventy-inch curve TV. The carpet was a plush chocolate black and my dad kept it clean.

"Fuzzy-Wuzzy." Dad got up and hugged me. That name he'd been calling me since I was two years old always warmed my heart. "My official senior as of today! How was the last day of school?"

We both sat down on the couch and I noticed he was watching *Blue Hill Avenue*. Bear came and put his head in my lap. I of course rubbed his face and back.

"It was pretty good, I cleaned out my locker and found out I had more than enough credits for my final year." I looked at him with a grin so wide I felt air on my gums.

Dad put some gum in his mouth. "Why are you

looking at me like a creep, my child?"

I smacked my lips with an open smile. "Daddy! Stop playing, you remember what you said!"

He got up laughing hard and shaking his head. "I don't know what you're talking —"

"Daddy! You do!" I jumped up pushing on him playfully. Me and my dad were super close, that's who raised me. I was an only child and the apple of his eye.

Blake White was the dad that all girls needed but regretted at the same time. He was overprotective and always thought boys meant all kinds of trouble. But we had a bond that was father-daughter and friends. My mama was in my life, I loved her and wouldn't trade her for anything. Her and Dad broke up when I was one and she moved to Lansing.

They were young when they had me and Mama wasn't fully ready to have a child full-time. I don't fault her for it because she never missed a beat of my life. When I was ten she got married and of course she asked if I wanted to move with her.

As much as I loved her, I would never leave my dad and she understood. They get along good and Dad even gets along with her husband, but this was home and I loved it here. Right now, he was annoying me acting like he didn't remember his promise. We were both laughing hard and I was pulling on his arm.

"Oh I remember, I said I'd get you a new bike if you finished your junior year above credits. You want a 10 or 20 speed?!" He joked and ran around his pool table because I was chasing him.

"Daddy stop joking!"

Bear and Gizmo started barking when they saw me chase Dad. They weren't about to do anything, they just hate when we horse play.

Finally, Dad stopped running and was out of breath. He wasn't overweight but he wasn't skinny, kind of medium build, light caramel skin, a round bald head with a jet-black beard on the top and the bottom of it was a smokey grey. He was handsome in a gross way in my eyes. He stood at 6'5 and held a stature like a tree.

"Thirty-six is catching up to you, old man." I laughed and joked. Bear and Gizmo were all on me making sure I was ok. Bear was 28 inches and about 130lbs, his fur was a shiny black and he was healthy. Gizmo made everyone laugh because he was so fat and lazy and as much as he loved sleeping in my room, I hate when he does because he snores like an old man.

"You keep talking mess and I won't keep my

promise." Dad laughed as he walked back over to his couch.

"You've never broken a promise, so I'm not worried about that, besides, I kept up my end of the deal."

"Yeah. Yeah. Yeah. First thing tomorrow we will go car shopping."

"Ahhhh!! Yayyyyy!!" I was so happy, I gave him a big hug and a kiss on the cheek.

Laughing he said, "I'm very proud of you Jurnee, go call Mama and let her know."

I jumped up excitedly taking my Galaxy Note 10 out. Then I remembered I hadn't asked him about tonight. I could lie to my girls and tell them Dad wouldn't let me go, but they will just come here, beg him and then I'll be caught up in a lie. Besides, anybody who is anybody will be at Audrey's party tonight.

"Um, one more thing, daddy." I said before I went upstairs.

"Aw shit, them eyes all big so I know you're about to ask me something that I'll say 'no' to." He stretched his legs out while still sitting on her couch, crossing them and his arms he waited for me to ask.

Dad never intimidated me because even when he was mad, he would become extremely soft when I cry or even look sad. "I want to go to a party with Brinx, Coya and Toni—"

"Whose party and where at?"

"Um, Audrey Legend." I held my breath because of what my dad did for a living. He knew all about The Legend Brothers.

I saw his chest go in deep and then out, his eyes were on me and he had that thinking expression on his face. "You know I trust you, right? it's them and the people who they hang with that have me on edge."

I nodded my head and then poked my bottom lip out with my hands pressed together like I was about to pray when really, I was begging.

"School is out, so what time is curfew?"

"Midnight." I answered quickly with a big smile.

He chuckled and let off a sigh. "Ok, but if some shit goes down and you're hurt, I'm blowing the entire house up."

We both laughed and I hugged him again. "Thank you, thank you, Daddy!"

"Yeah, yeah, yeah, you know your Dad loves you and I want you to enjoy your life, just use good judgment, always listen to your first mind and—"

"Know you're just a phone call away and you'll

fuck the world up." We both said in unison and laughed. Dad had been telling me these same three lines my entire life; it was embedded in my head. My phone vibrated and I rushed upstairs when I saw what it was. I turned my ringer up because school was out for the summer, so I didn't have to keep it on vibrate.

Once I closed my door to my room, I took my clothes off, put on my pajama shorts and t-shirt then got in my Queen size bed. My room was a typical girl's room. I had posters on my wall of my favorite movies *Hairspray*, *Twilight* and the TV show *Stranger Things*.

Also, by my bed was a giant poster of Chris Brown. That was my man in my head, and no one could tell me any different. There was a pink see through desk with a matching chair and I had my awards from school on there. Science fair, honors society and some girl scout badges and awards for high sells in cookies. Moving my Mac Book from under my pillow, I turned my TV on and unlocked my cell phone.

So let me catch y'all up. About four months ago my teacher from my writing class told me about this story board site. People would post their fiction, non-fiction, short stories and poetry writing. You can choose to stay anonymous or announce who you are. I post all the time and I chose to stay anonymous. I just didn't want to be known, especially because of the type of stories I write.

But when I posted my first one, I never thought it would get shown so much love. Now, I am kind of a popular being on there. Anyway, I had a picture of a Pisces and my screen name was PenQueen. It's almost like Facebook but with more words and no status making. Just story posting, you can leave comments and you can IM (Instant Message) someone. Well one day I went on there and I saw someone went through all nine of my stories.

They liked them and left comments telling me their favorite parts. The screen name was SwagWordz. I went on the profile and they were anonymous as well, but it was a boy who was eighteen and according to his profile picture, he was an Leo. I noticed we were the only two who had zodiac signs as profile pictures. He had ten poems up and he had been a member on there about a month longer than me.

The poems were amazing, some sexual and the others were just about love. I won't lie, the sexual ones turned my virgin ass on all the way. In my mind, I knew what this guy looked like and he wasn't only reading me his poems, but he was acting them out on me, too. Still,

I'm not the kind of girl to make a move so I kept posting, he'd read, comment and like.

Then he would post, and I would do the same to his work, then I got an IM from him. I was so damn excited but when I opened the message it said, 'You're either a freak or a virgin.' I felt so exposed because I didn't know I wore my virginity so damn clear. Was it an odor or something coming from me? Anyway, I responded 'I'm neither, just a fan of good writing.' I wasn't about to tell a stranger my business.

That day on for the past four months, we have been sending each-other IMs. It's crazy because we haven't exchanged pictures or numbers, we just sent IMs to each other every day and all night. The conversation was endless, even if I thought we would run out of things to say, it never happened. What I did notice was, we both wouldn't mention anything that could pin-point a location.

I believe we were each other's escape, like a perfect fantasy and including anything in the real world would mess everything up. My friends knew about SwagWordz and they teased me all the time about it being a fifty-year-old man in prison or a big ass hairy dyke Coya would joke and say. I wasn't stupid, I've seen the LifeTime movies and my dad has had the safety talk with me, so I knew better.

This was just conversation. I wasn't hurting anybody or putting myself in danger. I had a few hours before the party, so I got up taking my phone with me, and headed to the kitchen to eat and keep talking to SwagWordz.

AUDREY 'CHAOS' LEGEND

PenQueen: Are you excited to be done with high school?

SwagWordz: Hell yeah I am, are you excited to be officially a senior?

PenQueen: I am extremely excited, I still have my youth. Old man Grandpa LMAO (laugh my ass off)

I chuckled to myself once I read her message. As I typed a witty response, my name was called.

"Damn Audrey, how bad is the bitch you talking to? I called yo' name three times." My brother, Austin, pulled me out of my private world.

"Shut up nigga, it ain't none if your business who I'm talking to." I put my phone in my pocket, glaring at him.

What up doe, I'm Audrey Legend aka Chaos. That name was giving to me when I was two by our Pops. I was bad as fuck but only if I was provoked, which having three little brothers made that always. I just went too far and didn't know how to stop, for example. I'm a year older than my brothers. Pops wanted to try for one more boy and him and Mama got three at once.

I don't know what the hell I would do if a chick gave me three kids at once. Pops always said he shoots golden sperm which made me and my brothers laugh. Anyway, I was five and they were four, we were at McDonalds playing in the little play area. A kid was having a birthday party which we didn't give a damn, as long as we could play.

Well, the little boy whose birthday it was started messing with Adrian. I got so much of my father in me so I issued a warning first, but he didn't listen. He pushed Adrian and made him cry, so I socked his ass in the face. But that wasn't enough for me, I went over to the table where his cake and shit was at.

I pulled the Spiderman tablecloth and the food, cake and gifts fell on the floor. Fucked his cake all up and I remember it looking all fancy. I didn't get in trouble; Pops' favorite thing was 'boys will be boys'. Our job was to look after each other, our Mama and our little sister, Ava. I took that job serious and caused all kinds of hell if I felt something wasn't right. Hence the name, Chaos, but believe it or not, I wasn't the wildest one out of my brothers.

"Damn, you all in your feelings, it gotta be a bitch."

Austin continued, joking.

We were standing outside of August's truck. After they scooped me from school we rode to get something to eat. Then once it got to be 3:00 we headed to Central High School so we could pick up Ava.

"You gon' make me fuck you up." I told him as the school bell rung.

It was hot as hell and I was ready to head home so I could make sure everything was tight for my party tonight.

I was finally done with high school, graduated with some good grades and tonight I was celebrating. Hell, I was celebrating all damn summer, plus I got into Wayne State University on a football scholarship. My goal wasn't to go pro, I just liked to play football and if it gave me a zero payment in college then why not.

"Central ain't got shit but hoes, I got half these bitches on my phone getting ran." Austin's nasty ass laughed and said.

"As long as you strap yo' dick up twice fucking with these skeezers, then have fun my nigga." I told him while shaking my head and chuckling. Now granted, it was hoes in every school, but Central had the top spot. That's why we were on Ava's head tough; her dumb ass mama made her go here because they stayed on Web and Dexter Street.

"Why the hell you had to be rude to Jurnee? I was hoping to chill with Brinx tonight but now they might not even swing through." August asked me, putting his red fitted hat on.

My face got hard. "I wasn't mean to her, she always got a stick up her big ass booty. Y'all know I don't like nobody talking shit. Female or not."

"Jurnee ass is big, like stupid big and it look soft as fuck." Adrian cracked, making us laugh too.

"Hell yeah, she keep them hoodies tied around her waist like it's really hiding something. I can hide a penny between some big ass titties better than she can hide that booty." I then joked and gave Adrian a low five.

"If her and her girls show up tonight will you let them in? Don't cock block me, bro." August asked me. He had a thang for Brinx's goody-goody ass.

Truthfully, Jurnee, Brinx, Coya and Toni were the finest girls in Cooley. Brinx and Jurnee were the uptight ones and I hated an uptight bitch.

"If they come through I ain't blocking shit, I don't have no beef with them but Jurnee better watch her attitude," I said getting serious now.

"Man that girl a damn scared puppy. Her Pops may be the truth but she ain't no gangsta. Actually, none of them are, especially Toni's smart mouth ass," Adrian said as he tied half his long dreads up.

Me and him rocked the dread life. Mine stopped at the end of my neck and were dark brown. His touched the middle of his back. Austin was the 'pretty boy' of the group. He had long hair that he kept in cornrows, and August had a low cut with waves bangin' hard as fuck. All four of us had a nice grade of hair because Mama had some Indian mixed with her from our grandfather. We didn't give a damn about all of that because whether light, brown or dark, we were some niggas.

"That's facts, but I still don't tolerate no disrespect. Next time I'ma flip her thick ass inside out," I said referring to Jurnee.

"Aw hell naw, look at that shit." Austin said and pointed. We looked in the direction he was talking about.

Ava was coming out the door with Duran's arm around her neck. Naw see, this ain't the shit we about to have. Before we head over there, let me put y'all on game. Duran, Simon and Bishop were cousins. Dexter boys we called them. They ran Central and sold dope with their uncle, who is Bishop's Pops. Now we all live on the westside of Detroit but different sections were ran by different niggas.

Me and my brothers ran Fenkell, 7 mile and Schoolcraft, or that's what was said in the streets. But wherever me and my brothers went, we demanded respect and got it easily. We weren't really wild for no reason. The same way that we can shoot a gun, believe me, we can throw a fist. Pops made sure of that. He would even have me beat my brothers' ass if they act out of pocket.

It was either that or Pops would beat my ass for not having them in check. We were close because he always said if we stay tight, then none of us will stray off with strangers. Nothing came between me and my brothers. Whoever was my friend was also their friend and vice versa. Pops was in the dope game heavy and so were we.

Before you judge, remember what I just said. Family stays tight and no outsiders. He raised us to be a jack of all trades, but the streets were where he really gave us all the tools. We sold to everybody as long as they had money. Teens, whites, blacks, teachers, some cops, it didn't matter. The only thing we didn't do was go get the dope. Pops took care of that every two months; he'd head out of town and come back with a reup.

I guess you can say he was our connect. Regardless of what you call it, we get money. Duran, Bishop and Simon' uncle used to work for our Pops back in the day. He went on his own, but Pops' buyer only wanted to do business with Pops. Their uncle felt Pops should have put in a good word for him and when he didn't, they fell out.

Instead of killing each other, they agreed to just stay out of each other's way. Everything was smooth until our dope made its way over to Dexter and further in their space. Now, how the hell can you blame us because our dope is better?! They lame assess stayed in their feelings. Always crying and lately it's been tension between us. Not to mention, Ava goes here and won't seem to stay away from Duran.

"What up doe Cooley boys? Y'all know there is no need to keep coming up here. A man got Ava." Duran said and he had a smart-ass smirk on his face.

"How the hell you call yo'self a man weighing less than 200lbs?" August laughed and said. "She ain't got no man, you's an overgrown toddler."

We cracked up hard as hell when he finished his joke.

"Don't disrespect my damn cousin Taz, he didn't

say shit out the way to you." Simon's black ugly ass spoke out. He looked like a pile of throw up with some tiny shit locks in his head and tattoos on his neck. Grimy looking as fuck and every time he spoke, his breath smelled like two months ago.

"Fuck yo' respect and fuck yo' cousin," I said, stepping towards Simon. Shitty-Boo Boo breath or not, y'all know I hate fuckers talking crazy.

"Stop." Ava intervened, standing between us. "It's not that deep, let's just go." Ava started pushing me towards the truck.

"Aye Kid, make sure you kiss my son good night for me." Bishop yelled to Austin. He was fucking Bishop's baby mama Nicole, which I didn't understand why.

"I dope the lil nigga up so I can fuck Nicole's throat!" Austin yelled back at him laughing and grabbing his dick.

All three of them stood there with their bitches looking heated as hell.

"Why do y'all have to start stuff all the time?" Ava asked after we were all in August's truck.

"The question is why are you fucking around with Duran? He a second-year senior. Meaning he's a straight idiot, Ava." Austin told her. "Bro, would you please tell this damn girl." He leaned his head to me while I sat in the front seat.

"I'm not saying shit to her right now because y'all know my temper goes from zero to life in prison in two seconds." I looked down at my phone; I was sending IMs to PenQueen.

August turned down Ava's block and we saw her mama's car in the driveway. We were cool with her; she always knew Ava was protected since we were kids. We all got out the truck to speak and make sure Ava got in the house straight.

While my brothers ran in the house, I was sending another IM and then I put my phone in my pocket. Ava walked in front of me with her blue eyes matching ours, looking at me all sad. Ava had the same tawny skin complexion as Adrian. Since she was small, she hated seeing me mad, but she mostly hated if she was the one who got me mad. Now, baby sister may have been young. But she doesn't carry herself like a sixteen-year-old and I'm not talking about physically. I still didn't let that stop me from overprotective.

"I'm sorry Audrey, I know how y'all feell about Simon, Bishop and Duran."

I was way taller than her, so I was looking down at

Ava with my face still tight. "Then why the hell do you continue to have Duran in your face? Ain't shit good about them Ava and you know that."

"That's not true, Duran doesn't be with them that heavy. He actually studies with me, doesn't pressure me to do anything and he's real cool. Can you please just trust my judgment?"

"Hell no I can't, the three of them are fucked up, plus, you are a junior now. You got to get serious about your shit because senior year will sneak up on you. Duran doesn't have shit coming his way and he's a repeated senior. Ava you are way better than that, what the fuck is wrong wit'chu?" I felt like I was talking to my daughter or some shit.

"I'm not sleeping with him, I haven't even thought about that. We are only friends, he doesn't mention you or any of our brothers. We don't even hang with Simon or Bishop, it's always just the two of us." Her face was pleading with me to understand but naw, I wasn't.

I breathed out hard and shook my head.

"Look at this." She said and unzipped her bookbag, pulling out an envelope. When she opened it, she handed me the paper that was inside.

I read over it and smiled big as hell then looked at

her. "This shit is A-1 Ava, I'm proud of you." I said and then I hugged my baby sister and kissed the top of her head. Straight A's on her final report card and officially a junior.

"So, does this mean I can come to your party tonight?" She asked me as we walked on her porch.

"Yeah you in there, but don't show up half naked." I told her for real.

Ava looked just like *Saweetie,* the rapper, with the same body shape and she was only sixteen. Smacking her lips, she just laughed and opened the door.

**

"So what's this shit I hear about Ava messing with Duran?" Pops looked at me and asked.

After we dropped Ava off and chilled with her and her mama for a second, we went to the warehouse to meet Pops for a reup. Apollo Legend didn't just sit on his ass while we made money, aside from him flying out and picking up dope, he also sold too. Minnesota and Tennessee were his number one spots where he moved a lot of weight.

We handled Michigan because we were still in

school and he always made sure that was of priority before the game. What I loved about Pops was he didn't play us. What we sold was our money and ours alone. The crew we had was paid from us but that was all. He always said we ran the show. If he ever had to step in then that meant shit was hitting the fan.

In other words, because I was the oldest, I needed to be on top of my game. If I wasn't then I would have to deal with him and that ain't shit I wanna fuck with. Pops wouldn't kill us or anything, but he'd fuck me up even with me being only two-inches shorter. It was a respect thing, he was Alpha and we didn't challenge him but we never had a reason to. The nigga was a good ass father to us.

"I been getting in her ass about that shit for two months now. Ava's stubborn and won't listen. She thinks Duran is different from his two pussy cousins." I told him while his boys put duffle bags in the back of August's truck. Suburban trucks are mine and my brother's thing, August had a black one, Austin's is white, Adrian has a grey one and mine is red.

"Let me holla at you in my office." Pops said to me in a way that wasn't like I had a choice.

The warehouse was just a gigantic space: one

floor, three rooms and a dingy basement. Pops' office was on the left and the door was made of bulletproof glass. Once we got inside, I closed the door and stood next to the chair in front of his desk. Pops leaned against the front of it and took his phone out his pocket, sitting it on his desk.

He looked like all of his kids, but the blue eyes were how you knew you came from his nut sack. He was light skinned with a Detroit 'D' on the front of his neck, a goatee, and a bald head. That gold cross necklace he has had since I was three was around his neck. No matter the weather or occasion, Pops was always in all black. He could dress it down or dress it up. Right now, he was in some black jeans, a black Polo and some white and black Jordans.

"You know I hold you responsible for your brothers and sisters, but I hold them accountable for their own decisions as well. Did you get at Ava one on one?"

"Yup, I came calm then I came hard. She's feisty as hell and won't listen. I feel like I should just kill Duran." I was getting so heated because my sister was better than that fool.

"Ok." Pops said then he walked towards me until he was in my face. "That sounds like a loud ass crybaby move. A quick way to get thrown in jail or in the grave. Did I raise you boys to move like that?"

"No."

"No what?" His eyes were locked on mine.

"No, sir."

"Good, don't let me hear you say that shit again." He stepped out my face and leaned back against his desk. "I would have been had you and your brothers kill them and I would have killed Bishop's father a long time ago. That ain't what we on. I'll go holla at Ava tomorrow and I'll talk to his uncle. I don't want you to push so hard. If we all do, she'll keep running to his ass."

I nodded my head agreeing with him.

"But keep a sight on it and if anything, I mean *anything* is off, then kill him."

That's the shit I like to hear, and I was doing that shit in a humiliating way. "Got it."

"Also, I got word from my friend who's a cop. You and your brother need to be careful when y'all make them suburb sales. The city cops ain't the same out in hunky town and I don't wanna destroy this whole state over y'all, but you know I will." He gave me a stern glance.

"I know and I'll make sure we are careful. I know we are supposed to stay away from Dexter but the feigns are coming to us. That might be a problem."

"If it does then we will handle it accordingly but if custos coming at y'all then make that money," Pops answered and I was glad he said that.

"Good, now off business for a second." He smiled wide. His blue eyes shined like ours when we get happy. Then he hugged me and kissed my jaw. "I'm so proud of you boy, full ride to State and a B average on your final report card."

I was grinning too as I hugged him back. "Thank you Pops, I'm so glad that shit is over. I wanted to take a year off but I'd rather utilize that free money them hunkies giving me." I may have been laughing, but I was for real.

"No doubt son that's smart, you know you were covered either way. You, your brothers and sister, right?" He asked me then walked behind his desk and opened the drawer.

"Oh yeah, I know." I scratched the side of my full beard. I was going to cut it but I actually like the way it brought out my eyes and my dreads.

"Here." He gave me a folder.

I opened it and read what looked like an itinerary over. I laughed into my closed fist. "Myrtle Beach, for real

Pops." Hugging him I looked at it again.

"Of course, my son graduated, I was going to pick a place out the country but y'all Mama threatened to kill my ass." We both laughed.

"Naw, this is perfect. Thank you, Pops." I was so geeked I hugged him again.

"Five suites at Sea Crest Ocean Front Resort, I know y'all will want to take Chill. Ava cannot go; she better be lucky I'm letting her go to your party tonight." It was funny because when Pops got serious, we looked like twins.

"This shit is so damn lit and it leads into my 18th birthday." I said once I took notice of the four five days trip. I couldn't wait to tell my brothers.

"Have fun son, you deserve it, but not too much fun. Be smart no matter where you are."

"Always Pops." I told him hugging him again.

He opened his door and I walked back out with my brothers.

"August, bring yo' ass in here. I gotta talk to you about the wild shit you on."

When Pops called out to my brother, me, Adrian and Austin lowly snickered because we already knew what Pops had to talk to him about.

While I sat where August was at, I started counting money, so we knew how much we were getting a piece. It wasn't much to go so when we were done, I put all four of the duffle bags in the truck. One of Pops' workers whistled loud as hell inside the warehouse.

My brothers and I stood up; Pops opened his door with August behind him. We walked outside of the warehouse and saw a green old school at the end of the gate. Pops' three shooters were there and when it got back to us that Bishop's father, Darius, his son and his punk ass nephews wanted to speak to us, Pops told them to let them through.

"Well got damn, you'd think I was trying to see a celebrity!" Darius said out loud when he opened his door getting out the car.

Simon and Duran were in the back seat and Bishop was in the front, all of them got out.

"Not a celebrity, more like a King and his Princes. Now, what can I do for you Darius?" Pops folded his arms and waited to see what he wanted.

My eyes scanned the three cousins because I knew Pops was handling Darius.

"I hear we got a few problems and I wanna see if we can come to a middle ground." Darius rubbed his hands together with a sneaky ass grin. He looked just like Diddy and had that arrogance like him.

Pops still stood in his hard stance. "Ain't no middle ground, custos want good shit and they know where it's at. My boys don't fuck with Dexter, Dexter fucks with them. What the hell you want us to do, turn down money? I'd be a fool to do that or tell my boys to do it."

"You wouldn't be a fool, you'd be smart, old friend. If the custos come to you and they are from our area just send they ass back to us. Simple. We'll know you stopped dealing to ours because we won't see those green bags all on the ground." Darius shrugged and laughed, dabbing his big head ass son up.

Our dope was in a dark green baggies. It was how you could tell our good shit apart.

"What the fuck you think we about to interview every feign that comes to us? You sound like a drunk tryna give a speech. If you get better product then you'll get all the custos."

I knew Pops struck a nerve because all four of them fools' faces got heated. My fingers were itching for some shit to pop off, then Darius started laughing.

"No need to throw shots, all we are asking is to respect each other's turfs—"

"We been doing that and for me that's growth. Like I said, we can't help our shit is better. Now if there is nothing else, y'all can leave the way you came." Pops said and he wasn't backing down.

"Man Unc, fuck these mutha—"

"Shut up, Simon." Darius said but his eyes were hard on Pops. "No need for all that hostility, we came here, talked reasonable and got a response. Let's head out."

Everything about what he said rubbed each of us the wrong way; the nigga basically declared war.

"I got a date I need to get ready for." Duran said, turning around but not before he winked at me.

I was like a bull but Pops put his arm out in front of me, stopping me in my tracks.

"You'll have the chance to kill that lil nigga soon," he said to me.

We watched Darius' car drive off and once again, my hand started itching. I was ready to get rid of them niggas.

Block Party by Sada Baby feat. Drego was blasting so loud that even from the inside of the house it could be heard. I had a DJ outside in the backyard throwing the fuck down on the spins. Everyone here was here by invite; I didn't play muthafuckas in the house, so everything needed was outside. Three porter potties, all the food, I had tents set up outside with booths and cushion made chairs all around. Only people allowed in the crib were me, my brothers and Chill.

He's been me and my brother's friend since fifth grade and he was as real as they come. Me and him were the same age and we both graduated from Cooley and had a scholarship for football at Wayne State. I was glad his fat ass picked the same school as me. That was big homie and I would have actually missed him if he went out of state. Chill wasn't his real name, but only those close to him knew that; he played offensive tackle, the nigga was 6'3, 325lbs solid.

"Nigga, did you eat all the dip?!" August asked. Chill picked up the bowl in the kitchen that had Mama's cheesy pepper dip in it.

"Oh shit, I thought it was pudding." He chuckled and then picked up his Corona.

We fell the fuck out as we all headed back outside.

"Fat ass muthafucka!" August yelled out, cracking up.

Our backyard was spacious as hell; we had a crib

on 6 Mile where a lot of the big homes were. In case you haven't figured it out yet, me and my brothers have our own house together. It's a three-floor crib with two bedrooms upstairs, two on the middle floor with a big ass finished basement and four bathrooms with one of them in my master room.

Pops put the crib in his name when I turned seventeen and my brothers turned sixteen. You'd think because we lived together, we were wild and irresponsible. Well hell naw, I mean we make our own rules, but you saw how Pops is; he doesn't play that shit and he damn sure doesn't play about us making him look bad. It was dope as fuck having our own crib, fully furnished, tasteful and well kept.

"Brittany, Regina and Nicole came in this bitch like they wanna get fucked by every nigga in here." Austin said and we looked in the area they were at.

They were sisters and the same age as my brothers. As y'all know, Nicole is Bishop's baby mama and Adrian messed with Brittany. I dabbled in Regina's jaw a few times. Last week, and she topped me off with some good dome.

Regina wasn't ugly, she had some big ass lips, light skin and wore her hair in this black short style that stopped at her neck with the middle part, or the "hood rat" part we called it. All the nasty freaky bitches wore a middle part. Anyway, the three of them weren't our girls at all but in their mind, it was more to it.

"Ayeeee! Congratulations, Chaos!" All three of them came our way loudly yelling.

I had my dreads in two big French-braids to the back, a Reebok fitted t-shirt on with an iced-out chain that said 'Chaos'. My jeans were denim faded and I had a new pair of Yeezys on my feet. My brothers were fresh too with some Yeezys on in different color and their iced-out diamond chain links with their nicknames on it as well.

"Y'all loud for no damn reason." Chill said after he passed me the blunt.

"And you big for no reason." Brittany said laughing and sticking her tongue out.

"Wasn't that same tongue in my ass while my mans was fucking you from the back?"

Now, he was lying but it still made all of us laugh so fucking hard. He had no damn fucks given what came out his mouth. Even her sisters were laughing and of course, Brittany got steamed.

"Fuck you Chill. Play, you'll let him talk to me like that?!" she asked, putting her hands on her hips.

"AbsoFuckinglutely!" He answered her, cracking the hell up.

Brittany was shocked, pissed off, but still was gonna be in his face. I was scooping our gigantic backyard out and saw everyone having a good time. It was some fine ass girls in here and I knew at least two of them were going to be in our basement tonight. I looked over by the big wooden entrance fence. I had one of our security doing the door and of course I had some shooters scattered around the outside of the crib in case some haters come this way. Coya walked inside after security cleared her; she had Brinx behind her along with Toni and Jurnee.

"Hell yeah, Brinx fine ass just stepped in." August said, narrowing his eyes on her.

Me being me, I made my way over there just to fuck with Jurnee's mean ass.

"Hey Chaos, here you go." Toni gave me a bag that was black and red, Cooley colors, and had 2020 on it.

Damn, I wasn't expecting a gift, most muthafuckas were here just because it's a Legend party.

"It's from all of us," she continued to say.

"I appreciate it ladies." I said then I looked at Jurnee. "Don't you have something special for me?"

Her eyebrows went in. "Special like what?"

"Like an apology; you didn't think I was going to forget about that did you? I mean my feelings were hurt." I was fucking around but she didn't know that.

"Chaos, leave my friend alone!" Coya said, putting her arm through Jurnee's.

"I'm sorry I spoke facts about you and your feelings got hurt. Maybe next time I won't be so honest and call you out." Jurnee replied, rolling her eyes and then they walked further in the party.

I swear the weed had me on chill because I wanted to yank her by her neck. I should snatch that hoodie from around her waist. I did notice she wore some skinny jeans and a top that showed a little of her stomach but like always, that big hoodie was around her waist.

I did notice she had her curly hair up in this high ass bun with long curls hanging in the back. Jurnee's hair is always down or in a low ponytail, bushy curls sprouted in the back. It was one thing she did have on that I wasn't feeling but I'll get in her ass about that later. Right now, I was about to party a little.

Me and my brothers were having a good ass time, dancing, opening bottles and they each got on the mic and showed some love for me and told me how proud they were of me. It was a good ass time. Now Regina was twerking on me while I sipped on my bottle of Moet. It was normal as hell to see her and her sisters twerking.

It was all they asses did to be slim with little booties. I looked over under one of the tents and saw Jurnee sitting down with Brinx and Coya. They were laughing, talking and drinking. I was shocked to see Jurnee drink. Even though it wasn't shit but a fruity wine cooler. I looked on the dance floor and saw Toni dancing on Miles; he had a thang for her and everyone knew it.

"Come with me over there," I said to August and Austin, nodding my head towards the girls.

Once they agreed I put my hand on the side of Regina's head and pushed her ass out the way, walking off. I could hear her smacking her lips and talking shit with her sisters.

"Seriously, y'all just gon' slide all up in our space?!" Coya asked with an open smile looking at me and my brothers.

We purposely boe-guarded the curve booth they were sitting in.

"Y'all picked to sit in the furthest tent in the corner of the backyard; fuck y'all over here doing?" August asked then he looked at Brinx.

"We are over here minding our business; we were dancing but we wanted to eat and chill now." She answered and her light cheeks were turning red because of how August was looking at her. Brinx rested her cheek in her hand to hide it.

I looked a Jurnee who was next to me; she was looking at everyone dance but I knew it was so she wouldn't look at me. I had two classes with her my senior year; they both were electives and I had one with her my junior year when I had to retake a sophomore science class. Jurnee was smart but she was mean as hell.

Aside from her talking to her girls, she never talked to any other people. I swear she owned every hoodie in every color and designer, and every damn day it was around her waist. I don't know what that was about; her personal style or if she really was trying to hide her booty.

What I did notice was if you spoke to her, she did speak back and gave a smile but everything else about her was mean and serious. I'd be surprised as hell when she comes to swing outs(high school events given outside of school) Cooley gives and parties like ours. This is the most I've ever talked to her and the nearest I've sat to her as well. I will say this though, I enjoyed fucking with her.

"You know damn well ain't shit interesting that way," I said, sitting my Moet bottle down on the table.

My brothers were having individual conversations with her girls.

Jurnee rolled her eyes hard as hell then looked at me. "There is nothing interesting to the right of me, either."

See what I mean? A mean ass muthafucka. The way I was built, I would have literally tossed her over the brick wall that traced our backyard. But naw, I'd rather keep fucking with her. I looked at that bullshit she had on and calmly peeled one off her. Jurnee gasped so hard she probably swallowed her own tongue.

"Why you got these long ass mice coochie hairs on your eye lashes? Who put these on you because I know damn well it wasn't your idea?" I said looking at the ugly lash in my hand.

"Yooooo bro wild as fuck." Austin said laughing.

I was looking serious and waiting for Jurnee to answer me.

"I'ma kick yo' ass nigga! Why would you pull my lash off!?" Jurnee hit my arm with her closed fist then pushed me in the same spot.

Silly ass probably thought she was actually doing

something.

"I swear Chaos you are so damn rude, what would make you do that to my friend?" Brinx asked me, but what was funny was, she was trying not to laugh.

"I bet you or Toni put these on her, they ugly as hell." I said and threw the lash at her.

My brothers were falling out laughing; Jurnee had her hand over her eye covering it.

"Move fool!" She said angrily and pushed me.

"Say 'pretty please'." I said to her with a smirk.

Jurnee looked at me like if she had a gun, she'd pull the trigger. "Move Audrey, now."

Why the hell did my dick get hard when she called me by my name? I mean I wasn't about to say shit about it. Instead, I got up and held my hand out to her. She looked at my hand like it was diseased.

"Put'cho damn hand in mine and get up." I wasn't playing and she knew that shit because even though her face was looking evil, she did what the hell I said.

Nobody goes in our house, but I wasn't about to have her go to one of the porter potties mainly because I wanted to keep messing with her.

"Do you and your brothers really live here alone?" Jurnee asked when I closed the screen door and then the big one. She seemed a little apprehensive when she saw me do that.

"Chill girl, I keep the doors closed when we have parties and to answer your question, yes. Me and my brothers live alone in this house." I looked at her look around the living room and kitchen.

"I love open floor plans." Jurnee looked at me and said.

When you first walk into our spot it was a hallway; the stairs that led upstairs were to the left and the kitchen and living room was in the same enormous room. Our black marble kitchen island is the only thing separating the rooms. I dug it to because it had a sexy feel to it. Now, we had a nice crib but the way Jurnee was looking at it was like she was in a mansion.

"Why you look star struck?" I asked chuckling.

She leaned against the back of our dark tan and black plush recliner couch. It curved around half the living room and had a super-size recliner to match.

"Honestly, I assumed the inside of y'all's place would be a mess. Clothes everywhere, pizza boxes for tables and a bunch of naked women all on the walls. The dark tan, black and cream color scheme is a shock. But what's most shocking is the nice ass furniture, clean smell and organization. It's really nice." When she smiled, that's when I noticed it for the first time.

Jurnee's smile was beautiful, her teeth were white, straight and she had the sexiest full lips. They did a pretty spread when she smiled and that full top lip looked even more plump.

"Thanks, yea me and my brothers not no trifling ass niggas. I mean we have our moments when we leave some clothes around or some dishes in the sink but that's about it. Our Mama didn't play that shit when we lived with her. She used to say if me or my brothers talk to a bitch who doesn't know R&B, then that means their Mama's never clean up." We both laughed.

"I agree with that; my Dad plays all kinds of old school music when he cleans up or is in his garage. So, where is the bathroom?"

I showed her and she didn't close the door, so I pressed my weight against the wide counter while she took her other lash off and threw it away. While she grabbed a napkin and wiped her eye, she looked at me.

"Um can you be any creepier?" Her nose was turned up and she rolled her eyes hard again.

"Why the hell you so damn mean, you be havin' a five day period or sum shit?"

On God, she looked like she was about to split the walls of the house in two. However, that shit didn't move me. The difference between me and her was she can look like she was about to flip out. I'd actually behave like she looked.

"You a true jack ass, Audrey. I'm not mean, I'm just not like the rest of the girls. I don't act like I have no sense because a Legend brother is talking to me. You don't mean that much to me. Actually, you don't mean shit to me." Her lip slightly curled up and those eyes rolled hard again.

I said earlier that I don't like being talked to crazy or disrespected. Jurnee went to walk past me but I towered in front of her, looking at her like I looked at Duran's bitch ass earlier.

"Only two other people call me Audrey aside from my brothers. My Mama and Pops. I do like how you sound saying my name. But now that you did it again, it really ain't something I fucks with. You so damn mean and uptight I can hear your pussy screaming loud to be set free. Heed my warning; the next time you talk to me like you crazy, I'ma fold yo' ass in half, place you in front of your Pops and look him in the eye. Get'cho ass outta my face, go get fucked and lighten the hell up."

Jurnee was caught in what I had just said to her; I could tell I was the first person to ever speak to her in that way.

"Didn't I say get outta my face?" I looked even more evil if that was even possible.

Pushing past me, she hurried out the bathroom and I heard the front door slam. I didn't even give a damn, as long as her outta pocket ass was out of my sight. Just mean for no damn reason; a big mean ass virgin. After I turned the light off, I went back outside and surveyed the crowd.

I was expecting her girls to run up on me yelling and cussing, but all they did was party until close to midnight. If I could guess, I would say they all had a curfew. After the DJ was done, I had our boom box speaker playing and the crowd died down. I and my brothers had our bitches picked out. I decided to let Regina stick around and we all brought the party indoor to our basement.

I don't play about my bedroom but the basement and living room was free game. Now it's one in the morning and the red lights were all through the basement, weed flowing. Adrian and Austin went in the back room with four girls. I was on the couch getting some bomb head from Regina. Chill had some bitch bent over on the far end of the couch fucking her.

We got down like this all the time after our parties. While Regina was doing her thang, PenQueen popped in my head. I took a last puff of my blunt and ashed the rest of it. Unlocking my phone, I went to my IMs and was surprised not to see a message from her. We never skipped a night of talking. Sometimes we would send IMs all damn night until morning.

I never told my brothers any of this shit, call me childish or a punk, but they'd clown me. I mean, I'm a Legend, we don't do no damn on-line talking especially without video chatting or picture sharing. Hell, I would clown my brothers if one of them was doing this. Another thing, none of them knew how much I loved to write, read poetry, books and create my own.

I wasn't no deep nigga, but certain things will give me inspiration. It's been like that since I was fourteen. I've always had hidden notebooks and would listen to certain music that matched my mood while I write in my headphone. Like right now the song that was playing always made me think of PenQueen. I don't know how the fuck I ended up behaving like a geek ass nigga who's overweight, lives with his Mama and jackoffs all day.

But here I was, stuck on talking to her and living in a world that was like our own. What I dug was how we both never once brought up pictures or meeting; it's like this was both of our escape. Plus, I'd go to jail if I was talking to a hairy ass man with hairy ass feet this whole time. But something told me that I wasn't. The way PenQueen speaks, the stuff she asks me, and the way we just flow lets me know she's a girl.

I was on some straight corny shit. I thought about someone who has no face, wanted to talk to them and even now. I was bothered because I didn't have a message from her. I sent one and still no response. But at 12:15 am, I saw she commented under a short fiction story from RomanceKing.

She wrote *Gio was amazing to Gisele* and he commented back *Thanks PenQueen, I got inspiration for him from your Leo character.* I don't know why but that shit had me tight; he had pictures up of himself and he looked like he get his beard airbrushed on his face. That's probably who she was talking to right now.

"You ok boo?" Regina asked me with her mouth all wet.

"Worry about that dick, girl." I told her, putting her head back on me.

I don't want nobody but you kissing on my tattoos
I don't want nobody but me talking to you until you fall asleep
We better stop playing before we mess around and someone gets
hurt

I gotta get my shit together and get off this corny make-believe mess I was on. *August Alsina* wasn't helping; I had other stuff I needed to focus on. There were real life women in my face, all that I can have at a snap. This drama with Bishop, his hoe ass cousins and Pops was a thorn sticking out of my people's roses. I even thought I could start something up with Jurnee until she pissed me off with that smart mouth.

But lowkey, I was kind of turned on by her mean ass and that smile was everything. If I was to move something around with that, PenQueen would still be somewhere on my dome. I think I need to finally initiate a meeting between the two of us. I just hope taking this leap wouldn't have me on a murder charge if this wasn't what I assumed it was.

TONI LIZZY SANCHEZ

"Para Papi. (Stop Daddy.)" I giggled and moaned out when he started licking my neck.

"You know when you spit that Spanish shit to me, I go wild." His voice was heavy and intense but what did it for me was his face.

Why God did you make this boy so fine? As sexy as he was, I just couldn't go all the way with him. Even though I lost my virginity on my sixteenth birthday to Wyam McGee at summer camp, I still wasn't about to give this chico any cono (pussy) for a number of reasons, one being who he was.

I had my eyes closed, enjoying him licking and kissing my neck while his hand was inside my pajama shorts and panties. This was the furthest we would go - kissing, fingering and that's about it. Clothes would stay on except our shoes and socks because he was in my bed. As I was about to come, I squeezed his bicep tighter and came all on his fingers.

"Oh Dios, mio Jugar! (Oh my goodness Play)!" My head fell back on my pillow and I felt good as hell.

"Man I can't keep doing this shit Toni, you gone give a nigga blue balls."

I didn't mean to giggle, but he always says this. My eyes opened and he was licking his fingers clean.

"You won't even let me taste her," he said, licking his lips and looking at me with those blue eyes.

It was insane how I had been sneaking around with him for the past month. I stayed next door to Coya and every Saturday morning, she goes to her Mom's house and my Dad goes to work. No one ever sees him come over. Aside from doing what we do, we'd talk and he was actually a cool guy. But outside this room, we didn't have much. For one, he had a chick and I was kind of talking to Miles.

"Play, you know we don't do all of that; you have a girl and I have a dude. Plus, full cheating ain't for me. I'm not sucking two dicks and four balls." I made myself laugh all the time.

"Get that bullshit outta here. I told you Brittany ain't my girl and you ain't with Miles, either. That nigga one of them seasoned Mexican corn on the cob thangs you be eating. He lame as fuck and I swear Toni, if you sucking that nigga's dick I'ma fuck him up. Don't think I didn't peep you calling me Play either, you tryna be funny." He had his long dreads on top of his head. He was brown skin and had a beard that connected to his sideburns. As gorgeous as those blue eyes were against his brown skin, he looked twice as wicked when he was pissed.

"First off, don't threaten me about Miles when Brittany and her big ass forehead is always in your face. I saw her at Chaos' party twerking all on you and you letting her. I also know she stayed after when everybody else left, so fuck you and your threat." I was looking at him the same way he was looking at me. Now I was out my bed with my hands on my hip, my Queen size bed was between us.

Play squinted his eyes looking at me. "You be sucking his dick Toni? Like on some real shit, tell me the truth."

"Did you listen to anything I just said?!" I looked at him shocked as hell because it was like he detached himself from the conversation.

He walked around my bed and got so close to my face that before I knew it, I was pressed against my closed door.

Looking down at me with that vexed expression, he spoke through gritted teeth. "I said do you be sucking Miles' dick? You betta answer."

Folding my arms, I looked at the ceiling then in his eyes. "If you lick Brittany's pussy then I suck Miles' dick." Arching my eyebrow, I refused to give in. The nerve of this fool to be all in my face like he isn't out doing him.

He turned his nose up and made a lemon face. "I don't put my mouth on either set of Brittany's lips."

"Well then I don't suck Miles' dick." I was actually telling the truth.

"Keep fucking with me, Toni and watch I sweep you off yo' feet then drop you on yo' muthafuckin' head all in the same breath."

I smacked my lips. "Whatever Adrian, that attitude you have doesn't move me. You have your bitches and I have my niggas. We keep whatever we have in this room because we both agreed on it."

"I ain't tryna hear all of that; bet no dick go in your mouth. On my Mama, the next time you give me a wishy-washy answer, I'ma wash yo' ass out my damn life."

"Boy bye, if that's how you feel then leave now. You out here having these girls calling each other sis not knowing they calling the same nigga daddy. No me tienes (You don't own me)." This fool did it again.

He completely ignored what I said, bit his lip and gave me that sexy smirk. Pulling the hem of my shorts towards him, he bent down and kissed me.

"You know I go wild when you speak that Spanish shit." We both smiled before kissing deeply again.

"I think you like arguing with me," I said smiling and I looked up at his dreads. I didn't notice earlier because we were making out, but he was freshly twisted.

"Which one if your little bitches twisted your dreads?" My eyeballs went up and I walked from in front of him, sitting on my x-large beanbag.

"Here you go." He chuckled and plopped down on my bed. "My Mama twists my hair like she always does. If you knew how, then I'd let you, Mi Amour."

I always giggled and shook my head when he called me that. It was the only thing he could say in Spanish and every now and then, he'd throw it out at me.

"Tell Chaos me and my girls owe him an ass beating for hurting Jurnee's feelings."

"Yeah he told us about that. Why yo' homegirl so mean, though? She a dyke or something?"

I hated that I laughed, but he was so random. "No crazy, she is not gay nor is she mean. Jurnee is actually really sweet but Chaos just rubs her the wrong way."

"The way they go at it, they need to just rub on each other," he said while picking up my picture on the nightstand of me with a bunch of second graders at the camp I volunteered for last summer.

"Like we do." I said sarcastically and when he looked at me, I gave him a flirty half smile.

Adrian's eyes roamed my legs then he looked at the picture again. "Why you wanna be a teacher so bad? You know they don't get paid shit?"

"Yeah I know, but I love kids and have so much fun when I'm with them. Even when they drive me crazy. They're our future and I want to teach them at that fragile age in their life." I told him honestly.

As much as I loved kids, I never saw myself having any of my own. I just want to be an amazing second-grade teacher, have a fine man in my life and travel with my best friends.

"That's what's up Toni, anytime you have a passion for something it means you'll never work again."

"Thanks, that's why I be on you about basketball." He fell back on my pillow then covered his ears. I picked up my butterfly pillow and threw it at him making both of us laugh.

"Don't ignore me! I'm for real Adrian, you're really good at basketball and that should be your ticket into college."

He was lying on his back and turned his head towards me. "I have no problem using that to get into college. But I don't wanna go pro."

"Yes you do, you just don't wanna leave your brothers," I told him and I knew I was right. We had this conversation last week.

"You don't get it, Toni, I have an obligation to my family's business. I can't just walk away from that."

I propped my head on my hand. "You mean to tell me your family don't want better for you? They wouldn't support you if your path led outside of their plans?" I knew Adrian didn't like talking about this but it was really sad because he was a great basketball player.

"I didn't say all of that, Chaos is going to college for football but he isn't going pro. He's the oldest and Pops wants to groom him. It isn't a big deal; I and my brothers love money and we don't want any outsiders handling what our Pops worked hard for. Can we please get off the subject now?" He grabbed my little ass and placed me on top of him. Even though he had some Puma shorts on, I still felt his hard dick.

"Why you being stingy with the pussy?" He licked his lips when he asked me and his hands was squeezing my hips.

"Because it's only for those worthy." I leaned down and rested my chin on his chest.

"Miles Puckerman is what you call worthy?" He had anger all in them blue eyes.

But, I kept my cool and chuckled. "Who said I've given him some?"

His phone rang and it was Brittany FaceTiming him. I wasn't even tripping because he wasn't my man.

"Go ahead answer it, I gotta get up and clean anyway before my dad comes home." I climbed off him and fixed my shorts.

Adrian put his slides on and then stood up as well. He was 6'0 even and I was 5'5, so I loved how he towered over me.

"I wouldn't disrespect you like that and answer her in your crib." He put his arms around my waist and kissed my lips.

"I'll see you tomorrow, same time?"

I nodded my head, kissed him again and he walked out my room. Once he was gone I sat on my bed and laughed out loud. Me and Adrian aka Play used to exchange smart remarks in art class. One day I was on some stupid mess with Miles and skipped 4th period with him in his class because he had a sub. Well, my teacher came in the classroom, saw me and I got detention.

Adrian did something that gave him detention that day too after school. It was only two of us and Ms. Bells, the teacher who runs it fell asleep, so we roamed the halls talking and just acting silly. I don't even know how I gave him my number, but I did even though I was talking to Miles and I knew about him talking to Brittany.

Still, we texted and kept it at that for about a week, then he came over just like today and the rest, you know. Adrian was perfect physically, but he is a high school guy, he has a big dick, money, own car and place so the hoes stalk him and his brothers.

We could never be together and that was cool with me but it made me hate Brittany even more and you see how he acts when it comes to Miles. He only comes over when Papi is at work and Coya is gone to her Mom's house. It was something about the sneaking around that made what we were doing so hot and sexy.

**

"Hasta luego, Papi. (See you later daddy)." I kissed his jaw and put my purse on my shoulder. It was the day after me and Adrian's little hookup session.

"Have a good time Bean and stay safe." He told me giving me a hug and then finishing cleaning out his cigar pipe.

Chaz Martinez Escudero Villanueva Sanchez. Bet you can't say his long name three times fast, is my entire world and the best Papi any girl could ever be blessed with. He's been in America since he was fourteen and legally since he turned twenty, three months after I was born. Him and Mommy broke up when I was four and she moved back to Mexico.

Papi didn't want me to go with her so she comes here every summer and stays the full three months. Once I turned fourteen, Papi let me decide if I wanted to go to Mexico for the summer. Mommy was amazing; she remarried and now has two daughters. My sisters are really sweet and we have a great relationship, both of them are starting middle school this fall.

Papi works with Jurnee's, Coya's and Brinx's dad. They have their own metal scrap yard. When we were little, we thought it was so cool that our dads had a business together. I was the one who first discovered what they really did when we were all in the sixth grade. I was being bad and doing something I shouldn't have. Papi always told me if the basement door was closed to never come down.

One day I didn't listen because I just had to know

what was down there. Well, when I saw, my little mouth dropped hard on the floor. It was so many guns, bombs, and big crates that I assumed were more weapons. Then there was so much money stacked up, my scary ass ran backwards into one of the tables knocking stuff over. I panicked thinking something was going to explode and Papi came running downstairs.

That's when he decided to sit me down and talk to me. Of course I told my girls and their dads had to talk to them to. So, we learned that they indeed have a scrap metal business, but the real money comes from them selling weapons and explosives. That's all we knew and all we need to know. After that, whatever Papi told me I listened and didn't question anything.

It was just the two of us and even though he dates, it's never been nothing serious. I wouldn't mind having a stepmother as long as he's happy, Papi was handsome. He had a salt and pepper mini s-curl with a long full grey beard that had black highlights going through it.

It fit him perfectly and it was so long that you could see waves in it, he looked older with it, but he was only thirty-seven. We lived in a nice two-story home with four bedrooms, a full basement, nice backyard with a pool and we had a grape tree that me and my friends loved to pick from.

"If we spend the night over Brinx's house is that ok?" I asked him before I left out.

"Mientras consiga el ok. (As long as I get the ok)."

I smiled and closed the front door because I knew that meant yes as long as it was cool with her dads.

"Te ves caliente! (You look hot!)" I said to Coya when she came outside her house the same time I did.

Today everyone was going to the new go kart racing at Belle Isle behind the giant slide. It was crazy because even in the summer if you weren't on the scene or at any of the hangouts then you were considered lame unless you were out of town. Coya came out looking like a real-life chocolate bar. Her long straight bundles stopped above her booty and she a deep side-part.

Her outfit was capri shorts that stopped at just above her knees and they were ripped all in the front. The white t-shirt was cute, but I knew my best friend; as soon as she got in my car and we pulled off she would take it off. Her real shirt was black, stopped above her belly button and it had the word Lounge in cursive white letters. Her black and white New Balance gym-shoes were so cute as well and I loved her black and white nails.

"I know caliente means hot, so thank you boo! You

look gorgeous too. I want that hair." Coya turned her camera towards me and I blew a kiss.

I kept it sporty/sexy today. I wore some grey baggy Nike shorts that was tight around my small waist. My white Nike sports bra was fitted, and I had my over-size chocolate brown and amber color hair out in big curls. I cut a bang in front, wet it and let it curl up as well. My eyebrows were done and I had on some Nike Lebron 17's in grey, white and turquoise.

Pretty, pretty please, don't you ever ever feel
Like you're less than fuckin' perfect

Pink-*F*****g Perfect* ringtone rang from my phone. Only one person had that ringtone and it was Jurnee. Me, Coya and Brinx had that song for her and Brandy-*Best Friend* was all our ringtone for each other. That song fit Jurnee perfectly because she had some body issues with herself. It's been like that since eighth grade. We always told her she was beyond beautiful, so when I heard that Pink song on the tv show *Glee*, I knew it fit Jurnee so we made it her theme song.

"We're on our way boo, about ten minutes," I told her as soon as I answered.

"Ok, I'm ready to kill Brinx; she's tryna put a middle part in my head." Jurnee said and we went crazy.

"Hell naw!" I yelled because Jurnee was on my car Bluetooth.

"Exactly, tell Brinx she knows only them hood rats wear middle parts! Put Brinx on the phone!"

Coya had me and Jurnee cracking up.

"I am not trying to put a middle part in her hair. I just wanted to see what it would look like!" We heard Brinx yelling playfully in the background.

We talked to them on speaker until we pulled up to Jurnee's house. We always did that; before Papi brought my car when he would drive me over here, he would always laugh about us talking like we weren't about to see each other. I stopped the car in front of Brinx's house because that's where they were.

Me and Coya got out but not before she put her other shirt back on. When we got to the door we knocked on it in the beat of a random song.

"I should leave y'all little asses in the heat." Brinx's dad opened the door shaking his head at us.

"Hi Mr. Young!" Me and Coya said, smiling in unison.

Brinx and Jurnee came downstairs and Brinx's

little shadow was right behind her.

"Hola linda. (Hi pretty girl)." I smiled and picked Brooke up; she was Brinx baby sister.

"Hola!" She cheesed so hard at me.

"You got my baby saying that all damn day." Her dad jokingly said as I put Brooke down.

"Give me another week and I'll have her saying more." I told him then hugged Jurnee and Brinx.

"Dad, is it ok if they spend the night once we come back?" Brinx asked him while she squeezed his arm, batting her eyes.

Pleaseeeee." Me, Coya and Jurnee added to the pleading.

He chuckled and kissed Brinx's forehead. "Ok, it's fine with me. You better head out of here before your Daddy pulls up and starts the questioning."

We all hauled out the door. Brinx kissed Brooke on her cheek before closing it.

"The both of you look so good." Coya complimented Brinx and Jurnee as we all got in the car.

I looked at both of them and agreed. "Y'all do look deliciosa!" I said grinning.

Jurnee had on some green capri-leggings and a *Nickelodeon* crop top. It wasn't fitted, it flared out and had

Rugrats and *Hey Arnold* characters on it. Her green and white high-top Converse

Chucks completed her outfit and her hair was curly and down like mine with a side part.

Of course, our best friend had a white hoody around her waist. As much as I wanted to get on her about that, I decided against it because I didn't want to make her feel bad. Brinx had on some jean shorts, a dark yellow and black checker pattern spaghetti-strap shirt.

If her other dad was home, he would have made her put one of Jurnee's hoodies on. A little peek of her stomach was out, and she had some dark yellow and black high-top Airforce 1's on. Her long black hair was straight and in two high ponytails with yellow clips on the side of them.

"Thank you ladies, y'all look good as well." Jurnee said and Brinx agreed.

"So Jurnee, Miles told me his boy Eddie asked about you," I said smiling and looking at her quickly in the rearview mirror.

"Excuse me?" She said sitting up some.

"Ooo girl, Eddie is so fine; he looks like *Romeo Miller* fine ass." Brinx said, and she wasn't lying either.

"Hell yes he is, get on that, pooh." Coya added.

"What exactly did he say?" Jurnee asked me.

I couldn't help but smile because I thought she would shoot the idea down immediately. "I went over Miles' house and we were outside chilling. Eddie came over and asked me about you; he asked were you single and did I think you would be into him. I told him I didn't know; I would let him know once I talked to you." I came off the freeway to downtown and headed towards Belle Isle.

"Wow, he is fine and I do need to mingle a little; he just didn't strike me as the type to like a thick girl." Jurnee said and we all smacked our lips.

"Pooh, even if he didn't you would have had him changing his mind," Coya said turning around facing the back seat.

"I agree Jurnee, thick thighs saves lives." I joked and she laughed.

"Ok, I'll see what's up with him."

All of us started yelling and geeking her up when she agreed.

"Would you let him pop that cherry?" I asked her, laughing because I knew she was about to flip.

"Nooo! Not at all! Eddie is fine but not enough to give him my star."

All three of us always snickered when Jurnee called her virginity her star.

"What about you, Brinx? August been sniffing around you lately. Could he be the lucky one?" Coya asked.

I'd reached the Isle and was driving down the strip to the spot where Miles was parked. Usually all the high schoolers parked in the same spot on the strip - by the bathrooms and giant slide so I knew for sure that's the direction to head in. Meanwhile, I wanted to know what Brinx was about to say. She and Jurnee were the virgins between the four of us; it wasn't a problem for us but sometimes, we'd tease them about waiting.

"Me and August are not even friends; we haven't even exchanged numbers. We chit chat a little when we see each other but that's it. I'm not tryna be a notch on his belt." She answered while messing with the lens on the camera she had around her neck.

"If you don't pop that kat then he is going to slip through your fingers, Brinxy-Brinx." Coya continued to tell her.

Even though we all laughed and snickered, I knew Brinx was about to shut it down.

"Well he was never in my hands to begin with." See

what I mean? Brinx had a classic way she will shut it down and make you laugh.

"How the hell you know it's good if ain't no guy ever sampled it?!" I asked still laughing. I saw where Miles was parked and already it was packed with cars, music and everyone from any high school posted.

"I know it's good *because* it hasn't been touched. It's marinated with lots of sauce. I'll paint my house with nail polish before I ask a nigga why her and not me." Brinx joked and started dancing in the seat. We all laughed and geeked her up.

"Yasssss!"

As I backed my car in the space next to Miles' Charger, I noticed dead smack in front of our cars were four 2020 Suburban trucks. Even though those trucks were common, you can spot these four out always. The trunks of all four were open and them damn Legend brothers were right there. Drinking, talking and looking good as hell. Adrian stuck out to me because of the obvious; he had on some Fendi shorts.

He didn't sag but the shorts still looked good on him, I loved that none of them never wore them tight ass jeans all the Detroit dudes wear. Those long dreads were in four big dookie braids, his short beard was lined up crispy and his yellow and white Fendi shirt looked good against his brown skin. He was just so damn sexy, then my nose slightly went up when I saw Brittany's tranny ass close by.

Ugh, and he claims they are not together. Me and Miles hung out but we were not in each-other's faces all the time and we didn't smash. Still, I played my cool, turned my car off and we all got ready to get out. Coya and Brinx got out first and I notice Jurnee didn't move.

"You ok, mami?" I asked, looking in the back seat at her.

"Um, yeah I uh, I'm fine." Her eyes kept shifting quickly ahead of her and then down in her lap. I looked and saw Chaos in view. I assumed at their party he liked her but when she told us how rude he was, I guess he didn't. My windows were lightly tinted so he couldn't see us unless he got closer.

"What's the matter, Jurnee? Are you uncomfortable because he's here?" I asked her.

She looked at me and bawled her face up. "Absolutely not, I can't stand him. But, I can't get what he said out my head. I feel like I should take this off." We both looked at the sleeves of her hoodie that were tied around her waist.

"Then take it off boo, your body is insanely sexy. Tell him to kiss your ass by showing him your ass." I joked just to make her laugh. "Eres jodidamente perfecta, mami." I smiled wide and so did she.

"Love you, Toni." She responded; we hugged and got out the car.

I cannot tell you how fucking excited I was when Jurnee untied her hoodie before she got out. I know it may seem small, but it was like a head to toe make over to see her without that big, bulky hoodie tied around her waist. It was an everyday thing for her, no matter the weather or occasion. Jurnee was thicker than all of us, but it was sexy.

Coya and Brinx were grinning like me. You could tell they didn't want to make a big deal about it, but they couldn't help it. Jurnee was laughing, you could see she was a tiny bit shy, but I knew within minutes she'd be good.

"Period, Pooh!" Coya yelled and snapped her fingers in a circle.

"You know I want pictures!" Brinx started taking pics of just Jurnee, then some of us. Then she set the camera on the top of my car, cut the timer on and took some with us.

"What up doe, T." Miles and Eddie walked from being over by the giant slide. He looked good, I can't lie. Miles was 5'9, medium build, had a haircut and he stayed fresh. He ran around with some guys from Central and sold lean but that was his business, not mine.

We'd been talking for about two months, but I didn't want to be with him. Miles used to go with Brittany our sophomore year; he went out of town for the summer and cheated. So, they broke up and she slithered to Adrian, but Miles was a hoe and I didn't want no parts of that.

"Hey, you ok?" I asked as I hugged him, like always when we are done hugging he'd keep his arm around my waist for a minute, keeping me close.

"I'm good, just waiting on yo' slow ass." His chocolate face teased.

In case y'all didn't know, I love chocolate and brown skin guys.

"Shut up, you were not waiting long." I flirtishly said.

"Aye, did you talk to yo' girl for me?" Eddie asked me.

"Yup and I'll let her tell you what's up." I turned my head around since Miles still had his hand around my waist.

"Jurnee!" I called her name. They had gone by the gate of the giant slide talking to some girls who we had class with.

She came over to us and I didn't sense her nerves anymore. "Yeah?"

"What up doe Jurnee, can I holla at you for a minute?" Eddie said and when she agreed, I was so happy. They walked towards his ride which was parked next to Miles'.

"Damn, she took her hoodie off." Miles noticed and the fact that he was looking at her ass was exactly why I couldn't be with him.

"Even though I don't care what you do, you still have to respect me when   I'm in your face and not stare at my best friend's butt." I said laughing because he was still looking then he looked at me all shocked.

"Naw, it ain't like that, I was just surprised, that's all. My attention is only on yo' spicy ass." He said, kissing my shoulder.

"Boyeeeee bye!" I pushed him, still laughing.

After messing around with Miles for a minute, me and my girls had a Mike's Hard Lemonade. We were laughing, kicking it and having a good time. Now, it was time for the giant slide and we were acting like some big ass kids.

"He keeps looking at me." Jurnee said, putting her arm through mine.

"Who, Eddie?"

Coya and Brinx were in front of us walking and talking with Miles and Eddie.

"No, Audrey." I looked behind me where their trucks were, and I don't know why I did that because I saw them getting ready to walk towards the slide like we were.

"How do you know he keeps looking at you unless you're looking at him?" I messed with her giggling.

Jurnee squeezed my arm. "I can feel eyes on me so when I look, he'd just stare. He doesn't even hide it."

"Yo Miles, EB?!" Some guy called Miles and Eddie from across the strip.

"We'll be right back y'all." Miles said while him and Romeo headed over to the guy.

"Ignore Chaos, let him drool over you." I said, shrugging my shoulders.

"Who drooling over who?" Brinx asked. She and Coya joined us in conversation.

"Audrey, he's gawking at Jurnee." I answered

putting my arm through Brinx's and she put her arm through Coya's.

"It's because that hoodie is off and he see what'chu working with." Coya stuck her tongue out, cracking up.

"What's funny?" We turned around and these fucking Legend brothers caught up to us quick; Austin was the one who asked the question.

"Why you all in our convo?" Coya responded but not with an attitude; she had that flirtatious look in her eye.

"You got a smart-ass mouth, Barbie." He said to her.

"Barbie? Nigga do I look tall blonde and thin?"

"Not at all but your face and body is perfect like one." All four of us giggled.

"Y'all about to ride the slide?" Adrian asked and y'all knew I was about to be petty.

"Naw, we about to fly jets." I made all of them crack up.

"I swear all females wanna do is lie to niggas, eat seafood and buy bundles." His brothers died laughing.

We reached the gate of the slide and we were in line so we could pay, get a x-large potato sack to sit on and go down the slide and head towards the long stairs.

You had to climb the stairs on the side of the enormous slide. It's wide, steel, and has five steep hills on it that makes it feel like a rollercoaster when you go down it. It's so damn fun and a must do if ever in Detroit.

"Shut up cabrona (fucker)!" I said to him nudging his chest. It was funny what he said so I did laugh but he still was annoying. "I swear I will peel the sticker off your license plate." All that did was make them crack up harder.

"Where are y'all roaches that follow y'all everywhere y'all go?" Brinx asked, squeezing my arm.

"I don't be having shit following me, I be too busy tryna follow yo' Blasian ass." August's bold behind said with so much confidence.

Brinx's exotic, pretty self-turned around and said, "I have no Asian in my blood. I'm mixed with black, Korean, Japanese with pints of anger issues and good kat."

I blew out raspberries so loud, almost fainting. For one, Brinx was fucking with him about the Asian thing. For two, my best friend had a sexiness to her in those eyes that made her look like an Egyptian cat that belongs to royalty.

"Why don't you let yo' homegirl arm go and ride

down the slide with me."

Brinx slid her arm out of mine and went to talk to him.

"Come here, Barbie." Austin said, putting his arm around her neck.

"Jurnee, you gon' ride with me."

As soon as Audrey spoke I promise, Jurnee's arm that was through mine started shaking a little.

"What? No I'm ok." She said in a sweet tone. I couldn't believe how nervous he made her; it was so damn cute.

I guess he wasn't trying to hear it because he wrapped his arm around her waist and pulled her on the side of him. Jurnee's eyes got wide a little; she looked at us like she couldn't believe it.

He must have felt her emotions because he looked down at her and said. "Relax; you good, ok?"

"Ok."

It may seem like that was nothing, but that's because y'all can't see it. Audrey is a 'don't give a damn' type of guy and at that moment, his face was softened, his blue eyes were on her and he said that little bit like he was her protector.

"You think you can stand to ride with me, piñata?"

Adrian's funky big head butt said to me; he had a smirk on his face.

I bit the inside of my jaw to keep from cackling like a five-year-old and to prevent from blushing. "Ugh, I guess I can."

It was our turn to buy our ticket and get the sack. Once we did that all of us headed up the long stairs to the top of the slide. I nudged Adrian in his chest when he kept pressing close to me, squeezing my booty on the low. Thank God my girls and his brothers were in front of us as we went up the stairs. It was hot, sunny and the line was long going up. It moves as people slide down. The slide is so big and wide that five people can go down at once. There can be two to a sack so as the person in front sits down first and the second person sits behind them and has to wrap their arms around their waist.

"Mi amour, sexy ass." His deep voice whispered in my ear and he kissed my neck.

Adrian was making me wet and melt hotter than the sun. I had chills and I was about to slap him because he knows we don't do all of this in public. But I wasn't about to say anything because I was high key loving it.

When the line stopped halfway up, we were close as hell. I purposely pressed my booty against him firmly on his dick.

"You better be taking yo' ass home or with your girls after you leave her." Adrian whispered in my ear again.

I scratched the side of my mouth, turning my head to him and whispered, "I'm doing whatever Brittany is doing." I chuckled lowly because I knew he was about to get mad.

He pinched my booty cheek hard as hell. I wanted to elbow him in the dick. Finally getting to the top, me and my girls laid the sack out. We sat down on top of it and Adrian set behind me; his petty ass yanked me a little when he wrapped his hands around my waist.

"I'ma fuck you up, Toni."

I ignored him and looked down at my girls getting ready. Whatever August was saying to Brinx had her giggling like crazy. Coya and Austin were flirting too and when Audrey sat down behind Jurnee and wrapped his arms around her waist, her cheeks were so flushed. They were right next to me and Adrian. Coya and Austin were next to them and Brinx and August were on the end.

"You ok?" Audrey asked Jurnee and she just nodded her head.

The whistle blew and that meant we could slide

down. Me, Coya, Jurnee and Brinx started laughing and freaking out.

"Go first!" I yelled down to Brinx, cracking up.

"No! You go first!"

I shook my head no and looked at the big hills of the slide. I swear this happened every time we get up her. It's high as hell, intimidating and makes my stomach go in knots but we would ride it multiple times in one day.

"Man if y'all don't come the hell on!" Austin started teasing us and his brothers joined in.

"Ah!" Jurnee screamed when Audrey pushed the both of them down.

From there it was like a domino effect, August pushed him and Brinx, Adrian and Austin pushed me and Coya at the same time.

"My stomach!" I yelled laughing and putting my hand over my mouth. No matter how many times I go down the giant slide, it's the same feeling every time. It's like the big drop on a rollercoaster five times in ten seconds.

Once we were all at the bottom we were like some toddlers on the floor, cracking up and trying to regain ourselves.

"Why would you do that, you could have warned

me." Jurnee actually was laughing and playing with Audrey.

"Y'all were on some bullshit." He was laughing hysterically as he stood both of them up.

Once we were all up and moved from the bottom of the slide, I saw Miles and Eddie walking inside the gate after paying. Miles didn't care for the Legend Brothers, I don't know why, so before anything could pop, I made my way over to him at the bin where the sacks were.

"Damn, ten-minutes and you in the Legend's grill?" He had an attitude looking at me.

"Relax, it's a slide not a marriage." I shot back the same attitude at him.

"It doesn't matter if it was a seesaw, I'm not cool with you in their face."

"You're not my man Miles, I can be friends with whoever I want. You were in Renata's face when I pulled up but I didn't say anything because we are not together. We're friends, that's all, if we are about to argue then I'll hang with my girls and you can do your thing." I cut straight to the point because I wasn't about to argue with him.

"I'm chilling Toni, don't talk to me like I'm a kid. I'm tryna have a good time wit'chu, it's all good." He said with his hand around my waist, but I moved and picked up my own sack because I wasn't going down with him.

I glanced over at Adrian and Regina, Brittany and Nicole were walking towards them. Of course, Brittany was all in his face. It was so embarrassing because he never showed any affection towards her. He doesn't kiss her, hold her hand or anything, she just hangs onto him like an ornament on a tree.

"Y'all going down again?" I asked my friends and they all said hell yes.

Eddie made his way over to Jurnee and asked her to go down with him. Her face was a little flushed but not because she was in lust. I think it was because she had just went down with Audrey and he was a few feet from her and Eddie. When I looked at Audrey's face once Eddie was in Jurnee's face, I got a little nervous. He looked like he was about to not only beat the fuck out of Eddie, but like he was about to rearrange everyone's at Belle Isle limbs. But it got worse when Jurnee and Eddie started going up the stairs of the slide. Audrey's nose went up and his mouth held tension all in it. Regina saw it too; she stepped in front of him swinging that short blunt cut she had with her rat middle part. I wanted to see what she was saying to him but Coya was pulling me towards the stairs. We went on the slide three more times and that made the fun get back in the air. Once we had our fill, it was time to check out the new go kart racing behind the slide.

"Ugh." Coya said when she got in line and she saw Nicole and her sisters in line. I think her face got sour because Nicole had her arm through Austin's, even though he had his face in his phone.

"Girl fuck them." Brinx said, waving them off.

I looked further in front of the line and saw Adrian with his arm around Brittany. Didn't I just fucking say he doesn't show her affection?! Oh he was big slick; I knew he was doing this on purpose. I played my cool and was just ready to get in the kart and drive around the track and have fun. I should snatch the back of his dreads out. Have his ass walking around looking like a damn dalmatian.

"Regina's his girlfriend?" Jurnee said lowly in my ear. She pretended to be messing with my hair when she asked. I knew it was so Eddie wouldn't hear her.

"Not at all, she's a warm mouth and a groupie," I answered, rolling my eyes at them and looking at her. "Let me find out, Jurnee." I said smirking and nudging her in her side.

"Not even on his best day." She said making a nasty face but it was a lie, she was feeling him.

Eddie and Miles paid for me and my friends to ride the go kart. There were big car tires all around creating the maze. I was super excited because the only other go kart place in the city was beat up like it needed to be closed down. This one was new, upgraded, clean and looked hella fun. Once we all got in and put our seatbelts on, we had three times to go around and if we crashed in the tires, then there were workers in the middle of the maze who would help us. On the track was myself, my girls, Eddie, Miles, Regina and her sisters and the Legend's. It was all good. I was about to race with my girls and ignore them.

"Who is riding in the double cars?" The worker asked.

Me and Miles raised our hand; I could feel Adrian giving me the stink eye.

"We are too." He said, him and Brittany walked over to the double car.

"You wanna ride together?" Eddie asked Jurnee.

"Naw, I wanna smoke you on my own." They were laughing together.

"Her big ass booty can barely fit her, let alone

someone else." Regina said. She and her sisters started snickering.

"This big ass booty had yo' nigga's dick hard on the slide." When Jurnee came back with that clapback we showed how hilarious it was.

What was even funnier was the fact that Audrey and his brothers were laughing too.

"Bitch you tryna be funny, watch I slap the smirk off your face." Regina came for Jurnee and that set it off.

"Bring that shit on hoe." Jurnee was about to charge but Eddie blocked her and the workers blocked Regina.

"If y'all are going to do all of this then we will make you leave with no refund!" The worker yelled at us.

Me, Coya and Brinx were quiet because the minute Jurnee swung on Regina, we had her sisters, period. Everything died down and we all got in our kart. When the orange and white barrier went up and the green light flashed, we all took off. It was so damn fun, the karts had speed, the ground was smooth and even the hot wind felt good.

"Whooo!" I yelled when I passed Brinx and Coya.

"Turn left!" Miles yelled over the loud engine.

We both turned and it was so clean, then the back

of our car was hit hard.

I quickly tried to look behind me but all I could see was the back of our kart and Miles face.

"This rat hoe gone make me slap her!" He shouted and I knew it had to be Brittany.

BAM!

Our Kart was hit again, and we almost hit the tires, but we swirled and missed it. Brittany's kart rode fast past us and she stuck her middle finger in the air.

"Let your wheel go!" I told Miles. I wanted to be in control of the kart while I get that stomach full of cum bitch.

I got close to her fast as hell. Jurnee was on the side of me and I wanted her to speed up so I could get all up on Brittany. Out of nowhere, Jurnee's car was bumped so damn hard I felt like it was mine. She lost control and crashed in the tires, then Regina's car was in her place. The way I was about my friends, I said fuck Brittany.

Turning my wheel hard I bumped Regina's ass with all my might that I even grunted loud as hell. I didn't care that her sister slipped way ahead, I had something for her when we were done. Three times around went fast as hell, when we were all done the karts were scattered where everyone stopped.

I got out and Eddie walked over to Jurnee and she unbuckled her seatbelt. When he helped her out, she looked at me the same way I looked at her. We both turned around walking past everyone's kart until we got to Regina and Brittany. It was all the way on; I slapped the fuck out of Brittany the same time Jurnee slapped Regina.

Now, all of us go to the same school even though we can't stand these raggedy ass Talbert sisters, we've still never had confrontation with them. This was some straight jealousy and bitter drama right here. But it was all good because these tricks would know from here on out that we come with all the smoke.

"You dumb ass bitch! Try some slick shit like that again, watch I fuck the other side of your face up!" I yelled at Brittany. Miles had both of his arms around my waist practically pulling me apart from her.

Brittany's weave ponytail was on the floor and the right side of her face had marks from my slap.

"It's on sight every fucking time I see yo' ass!" Regina shouted to Jurnee. Her light face was red as hell from my boo slapping her and her bottom lip was bleeding.

"Then I'll make it my mission to see you every day!"

"Coya and Brinx, you bitches didn't have to put no hands on me! Wack ass hoes!" Nicole screamed with her hair all wild.

"Birds of a feather, dummy ass!" Coya cracked up and so did Brinx.

"You and that big ass you got better stay away from Chaos!" Nicole screamed out while some workers were blocking her.

I hated phones were out recording and the crowd was getting thick.

Jurnee looked at Audrey and pointed at him; she had this sneaky smirk on her face "This nigga right here? He's the reason you so tight and got that ass beat. You think I want him!?" Jurnee was still pointing at him while laughing and now looking at Regina.

Then her eyes went on Audrey and when she kissed him, I think everybody's jaw was on the ground. I mean she didn't give him a peck, my friend tongued him down so tough she had me low key wet. Ha! When she pulled away her facial expression looked like she was thinking.

"Naw, you can have him." When she walked off, all you heard was us snickering and laughing.

Yo' what the fuck." Audrey said and he was

walking towards Jurnee's back, but his brothers were on him like a fly to shit.

Jurnee didn't know because she didn't even look back as she walked to my car, far away from them.

"Bitchhh that was wild as hell!" Coya said, clapping her hands.

"For real mami that was insane, you left him babeando! (drooling!)" It was so many people that we lost Miles and Eddie in the crowd. I didn't care, he'd be texting me later and I knew Adrian would be too.

"Did you get Eddie's number?" Brinx asked Jurnee.

"Yeah we exchanged numbers; I gotta apologize to him. I really don't want Audrey Legend, I was just pissing Regina off."

We got in my car and I started it up.

"That kiss said other things, pooh." Coya said from the back.

This time, Brinx was in the front seat with me.

Jurnee smacked her lips. "That's how it was supposed to look. But no, I don't want that boy."

I pulled out my parking space just chuckling and shaking my head because Jurnee was indeed lying. My phone went off in my lap and I knew it was Miles texting me.

A.L.: **You betta take yo ass home or with your girls**.

I got to a red light so I was able to text back.

Me: **Shut up and ice your bitch lip.**

A.L.: **My bitch didn't get a scratch on her so I don't gotta do shit.**

I blacked my screen out laughing to myself. I wasn't stunting Adrian Legend.

ADRIAN 'PLAY' LEGEND

I looked at my phone and saw that Toni didn't text me back. I wasn't tripping because I bet my life she wasn't about to be in Miles' face. First of all, he was still here at the Isle, all in Renata's face. I knew him and Toni weren't together but me and my brothers didn't fuck with him or Eddie. They sold drugs for Bishop, Duran and Simon, so immediately they became an enemy.

It became personal to me when he got all up in Toni's face. I was feeling her. She was fine, feisty and just the fucking shit. But, I love pussy on my left side, right side, over my head, in front of me and behind me. I didn't wanna get with her and I knew I was a dog. I mean my second language was barking.

But I'm the typical young nigga. I want the girl, don't wanna act right and don't want her sucking no nigga dick. I don't know what it was about picturing Toni with a dick in her mouth that burned my ass crack. I can even get over her fucking, but I don't want to hear about her sucking on somebody. For me, it was too damn intimate. A woman puts her all into sucking off a guy.

Passion be all in you women when giving top, with the low moans y'all do, getting the balls and then when y'all look at us while doing it. Man! That shit is lit and too fucking personal. I'll fuck Toni up and chop the guy's nuts off. I will literally tape his dick to his stomach and cut his balls clean off.

This sneaky thing me and Toni was doing started off fun, hell, it still is. But I ended up feeling her and how we would talk and joke around. I didn't tell my brothers because we didn't have any bitch around us who wasn't giving up pussy or head. Fingering and kissing was elementary shit; they'd clown me if they knew I was not only doing that, but I was enjoying it.

Hell yea, I'd leave Toni's crib with a hard dick, but it didn't beat me loving her company. I wanted to fuck her so bad and I knew the day would come, but I was careful because I knew once I got in Toni, it would be a wrap. I hated that she and her girls got into a fist fight with them dumb ass Talbert sisters because I was enjoying stealing looks at Toni's fine ass.

"You good, bro?" I asked Audrey because he was looking heated.

"Hell naw, I'm annoyed at how stupid Regina is. I Swear if my dick didn't love tickling her tonsils, I would rip them out of her. Then Jurnee got me fucked up, hoeing me like that. She just don't fucking know," he said, shaking his head, looking sinister.

My brother was wild as hell. His nickname Chaos fit him perfectly. As crazy as he was, he wasn't the worst out of all of us, but he hated rejection and takes it the worst all the time.

"Know what? Don't do nothing to shorty, bro," Austin said while giving me the blunt.

We were at our trucks chilling, smoking and watching all the fine ass girls walk around the strip and dance.

"I ain't about to do shit to her; we go together now." He said it with so much certainty.

All three of us looked at that fool like he was crazy.

"Fuck you mean y'all go together?" I asked him.

"You heard me crystal clear. Jurnee shouldn't be walking around kissing people like that. Now we go together." The funny thing was, he wasn't smiling nor did he have humor in his voice.

"You sound like the beginning stages of a stalker, nigga." August laughed and said.

Audrey just shrugged his shoulders and went back to smoking. Some loud music came down the strip and three Chargers parked a few spaces to the left in front of our trucks.

"These roach looking muthafuckas." Austin said about Simon, Bishop and Duran.

"Man fuck them, as long as they—"

Audrey stopped talking and we looked over at them and saw why. Ava got out the front seat of Duran's car. Her shorts were short, and she had that top that had no straps that chicks wear. I mean her cheeks weren't out, but they were still little ass shorts. Audrey was about to go her way, but I stopped him. Even though he will get her in line quicker than any of us, he had a way of doing it that made her cry.

Me and Austin hated to see her cry, so we were softer on her. That's why they called me Kid and him Play, since we were little. Not only is *House Party* our favorite movie and we would try to do the dances, but Moms always claimed me and him were the lighter side of August, Audrey and Pops. Like Kid n Play, we're the lighter side of 90s rap, so the nickname stuck with us from the age of four.

"Let us go holla at her, Chaos. You already on one from Jurnee earlier." I told him, and Austin stood on the side of me and agreed.

"A'ight, swear, I'd rather she hook-up with Chill than that hoe ass pussy." Audrey said and put the blunt in his mouth.

We knew Chill liked Ava. He didn't know we knew and Ava didn't know he liked her. I noticed it first and I of course brought it to my brothers' attention. Chill would look at her on the low when he thought no one was watching. I knew he didn't want to disrespect us and then there was the age thing.

Ava just turned sixteen and Chill will be eighteen in September, so that was a delicate situation, especially for Pops, if he knew. So, Chill never said a word or acted on shit, but we knew he was feeling her. Me and Austin walked over to Ava. She had yet to see us because the way they entered the Isle, they didn't have to pass us.

"Av's." Austin called her little nickname.

When she turned around and saw us, her eyes got wide and she tried to pull her shorts down on the slide.

"Oh damn, what up in-laws." Bishop said with a snake smirk on his face.

"Fuck off man, we wanna holla at our baby sister." I spoke calmly. You'll always get a calm reaction from me in the beginning, Austin as well. Without even letting him say shit, I grabbed Ava's arm and she walked off with us.

"What the fuck Ava, what don't you understand about them fools?" I asked her pointing from her to them.

"Adrian, Duran isn't like his cousins that's what I was trying to tell Audrey and Daddy when he came to see me earlier." She looked at both of us and explained.

Austin grabbed the bridge of his nose. "Av's you're far from stupid, this Romeo and Juliet shit y'all tryna do is going to end badly as fuck. You realize both of them idiots died, right?"

I chuckled and Ava folded her arms, breathing out hard.

"You just said I'm not stupid, so trust me when I say I am not being disrespected. When I hang with Duran we really don't be with his cousins. Oh my gosh, why do I have to explain my social life to everyone!? How many times have y'all had thots over thots around y'all, including Daddy, too. Hell, I don't even like the men my Mama dates but as long as everyone is happy, I don't interfere. Now, it's like all hell is coming down because I'm talking to Duran."

"All hell ain't even close to breaking down on yo' ass. This is just a little light rain." Audrey's ass came from out of nowhere.

Me and Austin weren't even surprised, he was a

hardheaded nigga.

"You want us to sit back and trust your judgement and hope don't shit happen. Cool, we can do that for you."

All three of us looked at him, taken back like a muthafucka. Audrey really wasn't one to reason.

"Really, so it's ok if I date him?" Ava asked him with a small smile.

"Yeah, we'll fall back and not be in yo' grill, however when we leave this Isle you will be leaving here with us. It gets wild the later it gets, and you are still our responsibility."

Ava smiled wider, hugged him and kissed his cheek. Then she did the same to us and skipped off back to Duran.

"What was that? Fuck you up to, bro?" I asked, standing in front of him.

"Pops had a point what he told me earlier; if we keep being on her, it will push her closer to Duran. Let her do her thang, we'll keep eyes on her and make sure she's good. I got a feeling they won't be around long anyway."

It made sense so we walked back over to our trucks and continued having fun. My phone kept getting text messages and I thought it was Toni but it was Brittany. How the hell she mad at me because she got her ass beat? Brittany and Regina were wild and out of pocket as fuck. Regina better be lucky Jurnee got in her before Audrey did because he was mad when she made Jurnee run into those tires.

When they slapped them bitches, me and my brothers were blown back. I knew Toni's ass was a firecracker but Jurnee seemed like a goody-goody, but ma got them hands. I ignored Brittany and put my phone back in my pocket. While laughing with my brothers, I kept my eyes on Ava, making sure she was good, and I knew my brothers did too.

These bad bops came up on us and caught our attention for a minute. We turned our music extra loud when Yo Gotti's *H.O.E. (Heaven On Earth)* came on. The bops started twerking them fat asses and it got a little wild then. I mean Girls Gone Wild off the hook. Pops used to have them on DVD. Me and my brothers used to sneak and watch then when he was gone.

We had our phones out on Instagram Live, showing how much of a ball we were having. One of the chicks had some sexy ass dark nipples so I zoomed in on them and stuck my tongue out like I was about to suck'em. It was a good time and I shifted my attention across from us so I could see Ava. Her back was to us and she was laughing with her little homegirls. The time went on and it got late. The only reason we were about to leave is because Ava was here and we needed to get her home. We normally stayed on at the Isle til midnight but not while baby sister was here. I went and looked for Audrey and saw him in his truck with his head back. At first, I thought his dumb ass fell asleep but when I got closer and saw a head going up and down slowly, I knew he was getting some neck. I wasn't trying to see my brother's dick so I turned my back to his open window.

"Aye Chaos, I'm about to go get Ava."

"I'm going wit'chu, give me one minute." He responded and that's how long it took before he was getting out his ride, zipping up his shorts. "Damn, I needed that shit. My dick been hard since the slide."

I tilted my head back a little with my nose up. "You could have kept that to yourself."

August and Austin followed us to get our sister and when we got over to her, Duran was standing between her legs talking to her. When she saw us though, she slid off his car and pulled her shorts down some.

"We about to leave," Audrey said to her, but his eyes were on Duran.

Ava was nervous because you never knew which

one of us would be with the shits when we are all together. "Ok let me just tell Duran bye." Her face was sweet and she knew who to talk directly to: Audrey.

"I can take her home—"

"But you're not, so." August said before Duran could complete his words.

His cockroach cousins made their way to us and for some reason, I got mad annoyed.

"Everything gravy over here?" Simon asked, running his tongue across his gold grill.

This clown was so damn ugly, nappy ass mini shit locks in his head and the gold in his mouth looked like his teeth were yellow as fuck. I could smell his breath from where I was at so it tipped my patience. But I remembered what Pops always told us about popping off so fast. It showed weakness.

"We good, just collecting our sister," I answered, trying to not look like I felt.

It was hard because Simon kept doing that slime shit with his plaque filled tongue across his teeth. Bishop was smirking looking at Austin.

"I heard my baby mama got jumped over you earlier. Now, I may not do shit for my son, but I can't have his mama out here getting fucked up." His eyes were stuck on Austin.

"Your baby mama got jumped because her sisters were on some dumb shit. And as far as what you can't have, do something about it my nigga." After August said that, he and Bishop were about to literally ram each other.

I was closest to August so I stepped up to stop him and I guess Simon thought I was coming for Bishop. He fucked up big time when he stepped to me and pushed me back by my shoulder. I reacted instantly, grabbed his middle and ring finger and bent them bitches back.

"The fuck you thinkin', spoiled mouth ass!" I yelled when I let his fingers go.

"Ugh fuck!" Simon shouted out in pain.

"That's some hoe ass shit!" Duran came at me and swung, missing me because Austin pulled him backwards on his ass.

"You punk muthafuckas!" Bishop yelled. He went behind his waist. Just like a pussy to pull heat out.

"Think twice because if you take it there, on God, you ain't leaving the Isle alive." Audrey said with his hand behind his back.

Me and my brothers were doing the same thing, ready to blast these fools. Ava was crying but she knew not to help Duran up. Her homegirls were calming her down.

"Y'all think shits smooth, like you run the whole damn city." Bishop spat, his eyes were looking at each of us. He wanted smoke. I could feel it but I think he knew he would die. Whether he took one of us down with him or not.

Me and my brothers didn't fear death, Pops taught us all about it. We were told to embrace it when it comes around, but to always make sure we look it in the eyes and say *Not today.*

"If you feel that way, then you know what to do." Audrey said, looking like a killer.

Duran got up and was itching to pull his heat out. "Out of respect for Ava, it's all good," he said, but Bishop was looking like he didn't want to back down.

His nostrils were flared, mouth tight and hand still on his side. After a few more stares from him, he finally relaxed and moved his hand from his gun.

"One day." He started walking backwards towards his car.

"Get'cho dramatic exiting ass up outta here. Fuck one day; if you want it, bring that shit now." Austin snapped at him, not even reaching for his heat. He had his fist balled up.

"Man let's just roll. Bishop, come on." Duran said to his cousin.

Finally, Bishop turned around and continued walking.

"Ava let's roll." Audrey called her.

"No." She looked at him, wiping her face and then looked at us. "I don't want to be around y'all right now. My friend Amber is going home, she said she will drop me off."

"You being a damn brat but gon' and ride with your girls. We'll follow y'all." We laughed because he was being a dick now on purpose.

Ava started pouting. "No Audrey, I don't need y'all to follow us; we know how to get home. We're not babies."

He laughed and shook his head. "Yet you're standing here having a tantrum like a baby. Like I said, we are following y'all." He turned and walked towards his truck.

Ava stomped off with her girlfriends, mad as hell.

"You know she about to call our Mama on us tomorrow, right?" I told him. Even though Ava had a different Mom than us, she was still close to ours and us to hers.

"It's all good." Audrey responded and we all got in our trucks. The bitch who was sucking his dick got in his ride with him.

I got the one who had them sexy chocolate nipples in my truck. Austin took home two girls and August didn't fuck with none. He was funny acting like that. All these hoes were about to go to our basement, do what was needed, then get stuffed in a Lyft and sent on their merry damn way. Before I was about to pull off, I saw Miles in his caboose ass car pull off. I followed and sent my brothers a group text.

Me: **I'll catch up with y'all in about 10**

My Keepers: **Bet. Bet. Bet.**

"Um, are we following the car in front of us?" The chick asked me.

I was sitting back driving on chill mode just on this bitch ass nigga's tail.

"Just because you got blonde in yo' hair don't mean you gotta ask dumb shit. Yeah, I'm following him. And if you speak on anything you see while riding with me." I glanced at her. "They'll be searching for that sexy ass body of yours." Looking her over really quick and stopping at them big titties, I put my eyes back on Miles' car.

The chick smacked her lips. "I ain't about to fuck with you Legends, I'm not crazy. All I wanna do is get in that famous basement I've heard about." She grabbed my free hand and put it under her shirt.

Her titties were soft as hell, so I fucked with her nipples while still following Miles. I don't give a damn, I was making sure he wasn't going to Toni's house. Only thing to do after 10 at night was suck dick and I be damned. Getting off the freeway, I noticed he was going to Renata's crib. I knew this because I fucked around with her older sister a few times when their peoples weren't home. That was all I needed to confirm about Miles location. I turned down the street to get back on the freeway and head to my spot. I was ready to bust on this bitch tits and stuff her in a Lyft.

**

Mi Amor: I'm not playing I don't wanna see you so don't come over.

I chuckled at Toni's text as I drove to her crib. I haven't talked to her since Belle Isle and that was two days ago. This girl sent me a long ass text cussing me out about my Instagram story when we were at the Isle.

I mean she called me all kinds of nasty, dirty dick,

trifling names that had me reading certain parts twice. I ain't gon' lie, it was sexy knowing I made her that tight but I wasn't about to let her hoe me like that. Nope, that don't sit well with my nut sack at all, so I was heading over her way.

"The hell these niggas flicking me for?" I said to myself when I saw police pull behind me and flash them irking ass lights. I but my turn signal on and pulled over to the left slowly. Even though I had all my papers straight, we all know that don't mean shit. I sat back waiting for them to approach my car. I wasn't moving or getting out shit until I was told to. I wanted them to do what they were going to do and get far away from me.

"Adrian Legend?"

I looked out the window when I heard my name. The face was familiar so I wasn't on edge as much.

"Damn, I thought for a second—"

"Step out of the car." He said stepping back some.

"What?" I looked at him, thrown by his demand.

"I said step out of the fucking car. I won't ask again."

I swear all cops were racist when they put that uniform on. I opened my door and stepped out, before I could close the door, he was slamming me on the hood of my truck, frisking me.

"Man you all up on me like this, can I get some dinner first before you violate me?" I said, being a smart ass.

"Don't talk shit lil nigga, turn around."

I did and folded my arms, waiting to hear why he was being a brand-new bitch.

"So there seems to be a problem that fell into mine and my partner's lap." He said and his partner got out the police car.

These two were on our payroll. They had our back when we were in the streets and kept the heat off us. It wasn't cheap by far, but it was to become invisible for a lack of words.

"What problem could that possibly be? We pay y'all both on time or early and it's never short," I said looking at both of them who were in front of me.

"You see you and your family have made an enemy. Your Pops is being stingy with his connect and you breaking people fingers." The one who walked to my car first name was Joe and his partner is Stan.

Joe continued talking with humor in his face. "We personally don't care what went down but Darius came to us and asked for protection. He is willing to pay more

117

than y'all are paying." He looked at me with that humor grin.

"How the hell is this a problem? Tell Darius to fuck off and y'all keep working for us. That fool is nasty, sloppy and so are his cockroach son and nephews." I was looking at them like the idiots they were.

"See that would be an option, hell we even thought of taking money from both of y'all. But the thing is, we can't have all these drugs in the streets. After all, it is our duty to keep the city safe. So, we figured the highest bidder gets the deal and the loser gets handled by the winner."

Now I understood; greedy rotten fucks. I didn't even say shit, I just nodded my head and sucked on my teeth.

"I get this is a lot so go home, talk to your father and brothers. We're giving all parties time, but not too much time." Joe said and winked at me.

"Oh yeah, one more thing." Stan said and his fruity ass punched me in my stomach, making me cough and bend over in pain.

"We got paid to do that for Darius' nephew Simon. Take care." He walked away laughing.

"Fuck y'all!" I shouted while holding my stomach

and standing up. They flashed their sirens and pulled off. I was so heated as I got in my truck. Taking out my phone, I group texted my brothers and then Pops telling them to meet up with me. We had some serious problems on our hands.

BRINX AOKI YOUNG

"Mmm, I wonder where Brooke is? I have looked everywhere for her and I just cannot find her." I walked around my room acting like I didn't see the moving body in the middle of my bed. Under my comforter all you could hear was giggling and see her little body moving.

Now let's get into me and my story. I'm seventeen-years-old, me and my sister are the product of a blessing. Or so our dads always tell us. I was adopted when I was four-months. Nothing about it was legal; the story is crazy and I can tell it without feeling any way towards my dads. Bryant and Robert Young have been together since they were in middle school.

Although it was like a down low thing but eventually, they came out as gay. Neither of them have kids before me and my sister. My dad Bryant was a stay at home dad. Don't think he's flamboyant because he isn't. However, he is the voice of reason in the house all the time. He dresses all of us because his taste in clothes and shoes is out of this world.

Dad use to be a personal stylist for some

celebrities. I was too young to remember much of that life, but from the pictures and stories, it was amazing, as far as the icons my dad has worked with. It's in his blood to love clothes and know what looks good on a person. His personal style is modern but a touch of prep boy; he wears a lot of loafers, dress boots, men sandals and men boat shoes.

I love how he accessorizes with either a fedora, flat or panama hat and some sunglasses. Dad was brown skin, 6'3, had a thin goatee and he kept a haircut. He was so handsome and loving. He gave up his life of moving around and being at a celebrity's beck and call when I turned three. It was one hundred percent his choice because he wanted to be more hands on with how I was raised instead of being with a nanny.

We moved back home to Michigan from California and have been here ever since. Him and my other dad got married in California in 2008. Robert Young was the complete opposite of Bryant like night was from day. He was all masculine like him but more tough on the outside and in, except to his family. Dad is a street guy, he's had a rough upbringing with him and my late aunt, his sister, Lusia.

He sold drugs from when he was ten with his dad.

Once his dad was gunned down, his mom started doing hard drugs and it was all about survival after that. Dad couldn't save his sister from following behind their mom's footsteps and that's how me and my sister came into play. Lusia had a best friend named Soo-Yun. They met in Las Vegas when Lusia was a prostitute. My dads never lied to me when it came to this story, which is why I love them so much.

Anyway, they both were in that business, on drugs, partying and doing God knows what. Their pimp got a little too crazy for their liking, so my Aunt and Soo-Yun moved back to Michigan. They moved but the lifestyle stayed the same. By then my grandma, Dad and aunt's mom, was deteriorating from her choices. Dad wasn't around Lusia as much except for checking in on her from time to time.

One night she called him screaming and crying from a payphone; she was high and saying something was wrong with Soo-Yun. Both my fathers went to where they were, and she was laying on a pile of newspapers outside in the cold. Dad said when he saw her stomach he yelled, *'she's fucking pregnant!'* Apparently Soo-Yun didn't even know she was.

I was born right there, in the cold, delivered by my

dad Robert and from what he says, I was his at that moment. Apparently, Soo-Yun didn't give a damn because even in the hospital, she wasn't trying to be stuck with a child. God was on her side because my Dads stepped up and had me from the time I left the hospital and made it official when I was four-months.

They were only twenty at the time but ready for the responsibility. The next year, my aunt overdosed a day after my grandma. Dad always says he felt nothing, but I doubt that. Even with hate there is still some love for your family. But he assures me that we are his family. If something happens to us, then he would die instantly.

So, it was the three of us until four years ago. I was fourteen and I knew the story about how I got here by then. I was told that at ten years old when I started having questions about my features. Although, I was given a genetic test and found out I have black in my DNA which explains my juicy lips, strong mind and slim slightly thick frame.

My Dad's asked me always if I wanted to dig more about who and where I come from as far as blood. I told them no, that's just DNA. I was created by sex, but developed from the love of two people who are a product of everything beautiful in this world. Back to what I was saying, four years ago when I was fourteen, I was home alone.

My Dad's were out grocery shopping and I didn't want to go. A knock came to the door and I looked out the peephole to see who it was. All I could see was a woman who had my high cheekbones and slant eyes. Now, if it wasn't my friends or their dads, then I wasn't supposed to open the door. But I couldn't help it. Even though I had never seen one picture of Soo-Yun, I still knew my face.

When I pulled the big door open, she looked at me like she was looking at some bright headlights after being in the dark so long. Her eyes glistened and her lips started trembling. I didn't shed a tear, but I wasn't upset. I honestly was shocked and didn't know what was about to happen. What broke our stare was a small cry. She had a baby with a stretched out dirty sock on her head as a hat.

The baby was wrapped up in a black blanket that looked like it was pulled from the trash. The next thing I knew, she was shoving the baby in my arms. When I held it, Soo-Yun looked at me with tears all down her eyes. Her clothes were all beat up and I could see a grey van behind her with people inside waiting on her. She looked at the baby, at me and then said, *'I'm sorry'* and then took off in the van.

I panicked, called my Dads and they flew back home. Our house was pretty big already for three people. It was in a nice part on Detroit's westside. Six bedrooms, four full bathrooms, a wide fenced backyard and a basement that was off limits to me and my sister. My point is, space and money wasn't even the problem when Soo-Yun showed up and left a baby in my arms.

The problem was the fact that Soo-Yun showed up and left a baby in my damn arms!! It kind of traumatized me in a fearful way. I had a fear that she would show up and this time take me and my sister. Dad, Robert, was so damn pissed he was on a mission to hunt her down. My other Dad however, was soothing me and took the baby out my arms.

When we took all that dirty mess off, we discovered it was a girl. Her head full of black hair was just like all my baby pictures around the house. Her little eyes opened and she had my cat like shape and deep dark pupils. At a snap, me and Dad were attached and when my other Dad came home and saw her, he was too.

Now, four years later my baby sister, Brooke Young, was such a character. Her jet-black curly hair was so full, she had my cheekbones and her smile was so bright. It's crazy because Brooke turned the house upside down but in a good way. I sat down on my bed with the two bag of chips I was holding.

"Well, since I can't find Brooke, I guess I'll have to eat these cheesy puffs by myself." When she laughed harder but didn't move, I sat the chips on my nightstand and leaned back so I could land on top of her body. "I think I'll take a nap—" When I laid on her, she laughed so hard and popped out the covers.

I grabbed her, started tickling her and then kissed her chunky cheeks. Brooke loved being in my bed, probably because it was a King. Her bed was a full-size and her theme was *Word Party,* this *Netflix* show that she was obsessed with.

"I get chips now!" She was breathing hard from laughing.

"*Can I* have chips now." I said, correcting her and giving her the small bag of chips.

Brooke jumped down off my bed and took off running; she was either going to her room or to bother our Dad's.

I kicked my flip-flops off after I closed my door and plopped down on my bed with my head on my pillows. I loved my bedroom; it was spacious with apricot color walls that I painted. My walls were covered in some of my best pictures I have taken. A lot had of course been taken in the city but I had some when I went to Chicago and Ohio.

Taking pictures means everything to me. I took my camera everywhere. Even though this day and age people took their phones out, I preferred the old fashion camera. I had a digital one, the old school disposable camera and my favorite, a film camera.

In fact, I had two closets in my bedroom and my Dad's surprised me for my thirteenth birthday and transformed one into my dark room. The words 'Brinx's Magic Making' was in big orange glitter letters on the door. I practically lived in there and it really was like I was making magic. Photography was my therapy, my tranquility, a way for me to unwind.

Brandy's *Best FRIEND* song started going off from my phone.

"Biha-Biha, what are you doing?" Coya said as soon as I answered our video call.

"Nothing, probably about to wash my hair. What are you doing?" I turned over on my stomach and propped my phone against my padded headboard.

"Bored and wanted to know if you wanted to go to the mall. My Dad said I can drive his car."

"Yeah we can do that, which mall?" I asked, getting up to head to my clothes closet.

"Oakland, I'm not in the mood for Fairlane. I hit up Jurnee and Toni, but they both are busy so it's just us."

"Ok cool, I'm about to put some clothes on. By the time you get to me I'll be ready." I told her and we hung up.

I was already showered I just threw on some lounging clothes. My hair was all over. I didn't wrap it up so it was like a wavy mess. I brushed my baby hairs down and of course put a side part in it. We don't do them middle parts over here. Even though I was trying to see what it looked like in Jurnee's head, I wouldn't let her wear it.

I laid my one-piece jean set on the bed. It went around my neck and had the top part of my back out. It was simple and fitted me nice. I grabbed my orange Coach thong sandals and threw them on the floor next to my bed. I'm glad I vacuumed and did my chores early so I knew my Dad's would let me go. I got dressed, made sure my pink and white toes looked good in my sandals, sprayed some perfume on and put my Coach wristlet around my wrist and was all good.

Opening my door, I went down the hall towards

their room to see if they were in there. Looking in Brooke's room, she was sleep in her bed with her chips next to her. See how quickly she would drop like a fly? They weren't in the room, so I headed downstairs and like I knew, they were in the living room on the couch.

Daddy, Robert, was sitting on the long part of the couch with his legs stretched out and my other Dad's head was laying in his lap. They were watching NFL Network. You're about to see what else make these two so different even though they were happily married.

"Is it ok if I go to the mall with Coya?" I kind of chuckled because daddy looked at my outfit and wrinkles formed across his forehead.

"Bug, where you get that outfit from?" Bug was what they both called me because I used to take pictures of all kinds of bugs.

I looked down at it and then at him. "Me and Dad went shopping and it was in BCBG. He wouldn't let me get the shorts because they were too short but he said the long jeans one was fine."

My other Dad sat up and looked at my outfit from head to toe.

"Robert she looks beautiful, you on some bull right now."

I smiled at him.

"I didn't say she didn't look beautiful, that's always, but the jeans are tight and her back is out. A girl with her back out means she's willing to lay that kat out."

Me and my other Dad laughed so hard, I was holding my stomach.

"You just made that shit up fool, leave my daughter alone." He hit him on the arm.

I knew what I needed to do. "Daddy." I sat between them and put my arm through his.

His hard face with that dark full beard always made him look intimidating but I never once felt afraid of him. "I know my back is out, but that doesn't mean that other thing you said. Now, may I please, please go to the mall with Coya?" I poked my lip out and put my chin in his arm.

"You make Daddy happy all the time, you know that."

I cheesed and kissed his cheek. Anytime he says that, it always meant yes.

"Thank you, oh and Brooke is sleep in her room." I got off the couch and stood up because Coya texted she was pulling up.

"Oh, can I have some money please?" I said with

my hand out and still smiling. I had a credit card but it was for emergencies only and only a three-hundred-dollar limit. I had a job at Life Touch photography studio but the location closed. Dad's wanted me to focus on my senior year and I had no complaints on that.

"You asking for a lot today." He looked at me with a smirk and winked while he pulled out his wallet.

"Let me go check on my other baby." Dad shot up and kissed me on my head. "Have fun Bug, love you."

"Love you too, Dad." I called Bryant Dad and Robert Daddy.

"Here you go, that's enough for you?" Daddy asked when he gave me three-hundred-dollars.

"More than enough. Thank you, Daddy I love you so much." I kissed his jaw and hugged him.

"Mmhm, no more back out outfits. Remember, back out means you'll lay your kat out and that means Daddy putting bullets in some knuckle head's dome."

I just shook my head laughing while I left out the house, he was crazy.

"You look cute, boo." Coya said when I got in her Dad's Cadillac CTS.

"Thank you, I love that cheetah print romper on you." After I put my seatbelt on, we talked and acted silly while she drove. I recorded some videos on my SnapChat and put the caption 'missing two hearts' in reference to Jurnee and Coya.

"Oh yeah, how was your date with Graham last night?" I asked her after we got to the mall. We were in Spencers because they had the best graphic tees.

"Girl, Graham was the night before last. Last night was my date with Lorenzo." She started sticking her tongue out and laughing.

I laughed too; Coya kept dudes at her beck and call. "Oh well excuse me player, how was it?"

"It was cool, we went to Bahama Breeze and then to shoot pool at Main Street Billiards. After, he kept trying to get me to go back to his house because his Mama was working late. But I shut that shit down because I gave Graham some and you know I don't get down like that. Oooh, I love this *Degrassi* crop top." Holding it up she looked at the size.

Every time Coya and Toni talked about their sex life I felt like I was missing out. I loved holding on to it for the right time over the right person. I had already made up in my mind that I wasn't about to be one of those girls who felt who she loses her virginity to be her soulmate. It was all about the timing for me, I wanted to have sex on my time with someone I connected with. Beyond a relationship, I wanted me and the guy to always have a bond even if we aren't together.

"Was he mad?" I asked her as I picked up a *Stranger Things* tee thinking of Jurnee.

"He was but I can't get him to stop texting me so he must not be that mad. I don't care anyway because I don't wanna fuck Lorenzo and I'm not fucking Graham anymore, either. His stroke game was weak as hell." We both laughed because she started imitating in the store what he was doing.

"I promise, you are nuts." We took our shorts to the register to cash out. Both of us brought a tee for Toni and Jurnee as well. That's how we did sometimes for each other.

"Let's head to my favorite store." I said, pointing to Victoria Secret.

"You betta be getting something for my eyes only."

August scared the hell out of me when he came from behind and put his arm around my neck.

"I almost elbowed you right in your stomach," I said with my heart still beating fast from him scaring me. I looked at Coya and Austin was standing on the side of her.

"What the hell are y'all doing here?" She asked laughing and walking up to keep up with me.

I was glad because August was something else and he gave me a set of butterflies that drove me wild. Me and him have never had any form of relationship; he'd give me the eye from time to time and we have spoken in school. But that was all. When we are outside of school and see each other at hangouts, he definitely kept my high cheeks a little rosy and my eyes more slant in a flirty way.

August Legend was just fine; he was 6'0 even and his weight was what I found to be so attractive. Have you ever seen a guy that was thick but not fat? Like, how can a guy be thick and sexy as if I was describing a female? He didn't even look like a normal seventeen-year-old and he didn't carry himself like one; actually, none of the Legend brothers did.

Y'all already know about them piercing blue eyes, but he was a cool honey complexion with a haircut and some thick waves. His chin had a beard hanging from it with thick hair lining his jaw line. It wasn't nappy at all and it had that shine to the black hair. His eyebrows were so bushy; he and his brothers had that and it made the blue pop.

What also made him look more mature was his

tattoos all on his arms, back and chest. This guy was just fucking sexy. I've dreamed and daydreamed about him. Like now, he had a white beater on with his silver chain, a burgundy fitted hat with the 'D' for Detroit on it. His jeans were dark denim and the pocket had burgundy Gucci pockets. The jeans were on him the same way I wanted to be, not sliding down, wrapped around him just right.

"It's a damn mall girl, what'chu think we doing here?" Austin asked her back just as sarcastic.

"Ok smart ass, but I don't see no bags in y'all hands, you must be window shopping." She shot back, making me and her laugh as we got closer to Victoria's Secret.

"Don't try to do me and my brother, we'll buy this mall out if we wanted to." He had humor in his tone so we knew he wasn't bothered for real.

"Bro, I think they tryna play us like we some bums." August's eyes looked at me with a smirk then he bit his bottom lip.

"I think so too. Matter of fact, hold on, stop." Him and August stood in front of us before we walked inside the store. Looking at our bags he said, "How much y'all spend in Spencers?"

"I spent thirty-five and she spent forty." I

answered waiting to see what the point was.

"That's sock money." August said laughing.

"Hell yeah, more like a pair of draws." Austin added and they both took out their wallet.

"We gone give that back to y'all and front the bill for whatever else y'all getting." Him and August held out two twenties for both of us.

Coya grabbed hers but I kept looking at mine.

"So I grab this and what, I'll have a permanent target on my back? I don't think so." I chuckled and told him. I was looking at him now and he was doing the same to me.

Running his tongue across his bottom lip he said, "It's been a target on your back, Brinx, but three things a nigga not about to let you worry about. Bills, bitches and bad dick."

I bit the inside of my jaw to keep from laughing but I felt my lips rise a little in a small smile.

"You want my arm to fall off, Brinx?" His voice was beyond sexy and I wanted to pull on his chin beard.

"Keep your money *Taz,* but since you talk a big game, let's go." I said making sure to put emphasis on his nickname and walked in the store. I laughed when Coya snatched the two twenties out his hand.

I walked straight over to the Victoria's Secret side where the bras, panties, pajamas and lingerie is. August followed me; Coya and Austin went to the Pink side that sold all clothes. As I was looking through the panties and thongs, I could feel eyes on me.

"What?" I asked, looking at him from the underwear.

"You, those eyes and that face; exotic as hell, Brinx." He came over to the side of the display I was on and leaned against it, still looking at me.

"Blue-eyed devil," I said, shaking my head.

"Damnnn it's like that?" When he smiled, I automatically smiled and laughed too.

"Yes, you and your brothers but something about yours says trouble over trouble."

"Out of all my brothers, have you ever heard of me being a problem?"

I looked at him like 'boy bye' and even he had to smirk.

"They don't call you Taz for nothing, aka Tasmanian Devil."

August wasn't even listening to me, he was looking at the panties I was holding up.

"Who you planning on wearing those for?"

Smacking my lips, I put them in the bag that was for the customers at the door and looked at him.

"I have a man I wear these for, thank you very much." We all know I was lying through my teeth.

I had four pair of panties in my bag and two thongs, walking over to where the purses, sprays and lotions were. August startled me when he pressed his body behind me while walking. His hands didn't touch me, but I felt his body and it felt good.

"You and I both know you ain't got no damn man, so quit the lies. Why is that, since we on the subject."

I knew what he was talking about, but I played dumb. "Why is what?"

"Why haven't I seen you with a man at school or even when we are out at swingouts?" He grabbed the bag off my shoulder that held the underwear and held it for me.

"How much can I spend in here since your frontin' the bill?" I asked, trying to be funny and change the subject.

He did a quick laugh then said, "Do yo' thang Brinx. My pockets stacked. Now, answer my question."

"August, I have had a man before and I have one now." My eyes were big because I was getting annoyed as

I put two purses in the bag.

"Now look at me and say that again."

I looked dead in those blue devils he has, and I couldn't even say the words. August stepped closer to me. He smelled so good like expensive cologne. His eyes roamed my face then pierced mine.

"I know you not into bitches cause I can hear that pussy leaking from here. So answer me this, are you a virgin?"

I tried to act shocked. My mouth dropped and my eyes bucked, but I knew he was seeing right through that.

"It's cool, Brinx, that ain't shit to be ashamed of." Even though he looked sincere, I just remembered what my daddy told me.

"Yeah right August, it may not be something I should be ashamed of, but it definitely gives you a reason to stick around." Rolling my eyes hard as hell I was ready to get away from him. I felt embarrassed and kind of exposed.

"Whoa, that ain't the kind of shit I'm on. Believe it or not, I been checking for you and not to be rude, but you reek of a virgin. If that was what I wanted, then I would have been got it. Look, we don't have to put no labels on us, let's hang and see how it goes."

I chuckled and shook my head. "Blue-eyed devil, but you are fine and I guess we can hang. Starting today and with you breaking open your piggy bank because this stuff will be at least two-hundred," I teased, but wasn't expecting him to do what he did next.

That sexy laugh and smile was on his face as we walked to the counter. I got all I came in here for but since he was paying, I got the two purses and body spray as extras. When the cashier rung us up, August pulled out a big knot of money.

Taking the rubber band off it was like a bloom of flowers bursting open. There were all hundreds and fifties. Even with all that money I didn't feel like I was at his feet. I grew up spoiled with nice things, I was just surprised to see a seventeen-year-old with all that money. Coya and Austin came over just as the cashier gave me my bags. She had a few joggers, some shirts and some sports bras and her total came up to one-sixty.

"Ok ladies, where to now?" Austin asked and truthfully, we were here for Victoria's Secret and Akira.

It's funny because me and Coya thought alike without even speaking; we weren't about to burn through these niggas' pockets like some young bitches who never been around money. However, since they were not breaking a sweat, we were indeed about to leave with more bags than we would have if it was just us.

"Coya." Like before, we turned around when we heard her name. "So that's how it is, you play me because—"

"Aye my guy, don't come at her about shit. Whatever you see is obviously what the fuck it is." Austin moved Coya behind him and August did the same to me.

The guy who called her was Lorenzo; he was with his brother. Coya couldn't even defend herself because Austin pretty much spoke for her. I was hoping they weren't about to fight or worse inside this mall.

"Fuck you Kid, I don't even have no beef with you, I was speaking to her. We supposed to be on a level and I see her in your face." Lorenzo said and Austin walked up on him.

"Ok, well now I'm all in your face, now what's up?"

"You betta get the hell off my brother." Lorenzo's brother spoke, but August was on it.

"Stand the fuck down on this, my nigga."

Lorenzo looked at Coya. "You whack as fuck for this shit."

Smacking her lips she said, "I didn't know shopping with my homegirl was whack. You doing all this

141

for no reason, Lorenzo."

He was already waving her off and walking off along with his brother.

"You fuck with some cabbage patch ass looking fools," Austin said laughing and we continued walking like that didn't just happen.

I can't lie, the mall was fun with August and Austin with us, aside from them keeping their word and paying for all our stuff. We just had great mixed energy, laughing and acting silly. There were moments when Coya and Austin went their way for some one on one. I got to know August a little more and I shared a tiny bit too.

"You have this coldness to you, what's that about?" August asked me.

We were sitting on the bench in front of Jimmy Jazz store. The one thing I picked up about August and his brother, they were not big on personal space. It wasn't in an uncomfortable way, more like they were securing me and Coya's confidence of our safety. Like now, August had his arm around the bench and we were sitting so close the sides of our thighs were touching. He didn't make me nervous or anything, but I liked him being so close to me.

"I'm not cold, we've been talking and sharing," I told him while putting my hair on the left side of me.

"That's true but I see you when you're with your homegirls. You talk to them with more light and passion in a way. I get kind of a robotic feel when I see you talk to other people, including me. I'on think I'm trippin' so again I ask, why is that?"

Ok, he had me a little thrown back because I never knew anyone to pick that up about me.

"I trust my family and friends, everyone else is too unpredictable. You don't know whose intentions are good or not, so I shut myself down emotionally when I talk to other people outside of them."

He nodded his head slowly. "That's understandable." Then his eyes went from me to my exposed neck. "I wanna put a nice hickey on that soft neck." He had those blue eyes squinted a little and his fingers were lightly going up and down my shoulder.

He was bold, but just because I was a virgin didn't mean I was scared of him. "Really, well I wanna pull that chin beard and kiss those lips." Pressing my full lips together softly, I crossed my legs.

"Come do that shit then." August dared me.

I could see Coya and Austin walking from the check-out in my peripheral vision. I leaned close to him, grabbing that sexy beard hanging from his face. It hung about three inches off his chin. Our lips were so close that they grazed ever so lightly. Before we kissed I stopped, smiled and looked in his eyes.

"Maybe next time."

When I stood up still smiling, August laughed, sucking his teeth and standing up too.

"I see you like to tease, it's all good. I don't play that blue balls shit though; next time I'ma have you juice them muthafuckas."

We both laughed so hard when he said that just as Coya and Austin finally came out the store. Austin got a pair of shoes and Coya didn't want anything, she just went inside with him. Now, it was time to go and eat because none of us wanted the food court food so we decided to go to Applebee's.

Outside, the heat hit our skin instantly; the guys were about to walk us to Coya's dad's car and then we were going to follow behind them to the restaurant. While we crossed the street into the parking lot, a black Corvette turned and pulled in front of us. Like back in the mall, the guys easily pulled me and Coya behind them.

The car windows were tinted so seeing who was inside was impossible. The driver door opened, and you saw long, black hair flowing in the warm wind. When the woman turned around, those familiar cheek bones made my heart drop. I moved from behind August so I could get a really good look at Soo-Yun. Her eyes went on me and she gave a small smile as she closed the door and walked in front of the car.

She had on some skinny jeans fitting her slim body, some heel sandals and a sleeveless blouse that was tucked in. I never noticed how tall she was, at least 6'0, but it was like a model from a runway. Still, I couldn't believe she was here in my face looking like an older version of me.

"Brinx, hi." Her voice was warm but spoke command and had some excitement in it.

I still hadn't moved or blinked.

"I don't know if you remember me, I mean I looked awful the last time you saw me—"

"Was when you shoved my baby sister in my arms. I remember very clear; I had nightmares for weeks about you coming back and hurting us." Even though I was speaking, I still hadn't moved or blinked. But I was looking at this woman, replaying the last time I saw her until now.

"I'm not here to hurt you, I swear." Her voice cracked and eyes got watery. Clearing her throat she continued. "Can you just take a ride with me and give me ten minutes to talk to you?"

When she stepped closer to me, I finally moved back a little and stepped on August's gym-shoes. He picked up on my hesitation and fear so he put his hand around my waist, pulling me closer to him.

"You need to step the hell back, she doesn't want to talk right now." He spoke up to her.

"Excuse me but this is my daughter, you need to move."

"I don't need to do anything but tell you to get back. She is literally shaking so whatever you have to say to her, you gon' have to save it for another time."

As August talked, I couldn't even look up because she was standing too close to me for comfort. But I refused to let my tears fall in front of her.

"Brinx, I really just want you to hear me out. Please take my card and call me, please."

I lifted my head up and looked at her hold the card out to me. I didn't want to call her, ever. If anything, I just wanted her to go away. I knew this day would come, as crazy as it sounds, I knew she would be back. This woman was the reason I didn't trust anyone outside my family and friends. August took the card from her hand and slipped it in the back pocket of my denim outfit. Soo-Yun wiped her tear and walked back to her car. Once she pulled off down the parking lot, I let a big breath go.

"Are you ok, boo?" Coya asked, hugging me.

"Yeah I'm fine, I just want to leave." I said, blinking my tears away and getting myself together.

"I'll take her." August spoke, holding my bags and pointing to his truck. "Let me take you to yo' crib, Brinx."

I really wanted to ride with Coya because I could let out all my emotions because I was comfortable with her. But, I wanted to be around August some more so I agreed.

"Call me when you get home," Coya said, hugging me again and I hugged her back.

"Ok I promise, love you."

"Love you too." She said back and Austin walked her to her car.

August put all my bags in his backseat, opened the door for me and helped me in. When I was inside, I noticed how clean it was, upgraded and smelled like his cologne he had on. When he got in, he turned the air on because his car was hot from the summer heat. I'd be lying if I said I wasn't glad we rode listening to music.

I'd rap some lyrics and he would be so shocked

that I knew the words. Then he knew some lyrics to Queen Naija-*Karma*, and I teased him about that. It felt good to laugh and for the moment push the fact that Soo-Yun showed up. We stopped at a gas station and I sat in his truck while he ran inside quickly.

Once we headed down my block, I was so happy my daddy's car was not in the parking lot. My dad was home but daddy left and that was nobody but God on my side. I didn't need him all in our faces, especially because I left with Coya and came back with August Legend.

"Thanks for bringing me home and my bad about that drama back at the mall." I apologized once he pulled in front of my house.

"You don't have to thank me nor do you have to apologize for what happened. You and your mom don't get along?"

I took a small breath in when he called her that.

"That's not my mom, I mean she birthed me and my sister, but that's not our mom. My Dad's has had me since birth and she shoved my sister in my arms when I was younger. I just want her to go away; she's a drug addict no matter what car she drives or clothes she has on." I admitted to him which surprised me.

He looked ahead, shaking his head very slowly

then looked at me. "Damn Brinx, I'm sorry that's the hand you were dealt. Whether you believed it or not, you handled yourself good. My bad if you think I overstepped checking her, I just didn't like the look in your eyes or your body language." He had the radio turned down low and his deep voice was really sincere.

"No it's fine you didn't over step, I don't even know how she knew I was there. I don't even know what to do with this. I wanna tell my fathers but then I just don't know."

"Take some time to think about it and then you'll decide. Don't stress to hard. Aye this may be weird as hell but she looks like this chick from this book my mama reads. I think she used to make clothes back in the day—"

"Kimora Lee Simmons." I said with a smirk. "My dad has many pictures with her when we lived in California when I was really little. He used to work for her; Soo-Yun does look like her."

"Soo-Yun, that's her name?"

"Yup." I answered and got quiet.

"Hey, we can get off that subject, just know I'm here if you need me. On another note, I wanna take you out."

That made me give him a flirty look as I put my

hair on the right side of my neck.

"Where is it you wanna take me and don't say your nasty basement." I laughed, joking and he did too.

"Naw, I wouldn't take you to my basement, my bedroom, hell yea. But never the basement." I liked that he was slick and threw that comment in there.

"August, I'll never be in your bedroom, but you can take me out. I'm free Saturday if you are."

"Yeah I'm free, we can do that," he said, taking his iPhone out and giving it to me. "Call your phone so we can have each other's number."

I did what he said and noticed he had him and his brothers as his wallpaper.

"You love your brothers, huh?" I asked, handing him back his phone.

"With my whole heart."

"I like that, that's how I am with my baby sister. Well, I need to get in the house, take a shower and do some thinking."

"You about to do some caking tonight because I will fa sho be calling you." I like how he spoke with confidence, it was a turn on. He got out the truck, opened the back door and grabbed my bags.

I wouldn't have had him walk me to the porch

because of my nosey Daddy, but he wasn't here. Besides, he'd see August when he picked me up for our date. Getting in the house, my smile widened.

"I'm home, Dad!" I yelled when I got upstairs and into my room.

"Ok, Bug, I'm giving Brooke a bath!" He yelled back from the bathroom in him and Daddy's room.

I could hear Brooke laughing so hard and I shook my head laughing too because she loved getting a bath. The minute I closed my door, my smile faded because I pulled out the card from my back pocket. I can't believe she popped up on me and approached me. I don't want that woman in my life. I almost hate her but the reason I don't is because of my Dad's, sister and best friend.

Me and Brooke wouldn't exist and get to be blessed to be in their lives if she didn't have us. However, a mother's love should run deep. We grew in her stomach and she tossed us so easily. The car, the clothes she had on was obvious that she was doing well. I don't give a shit, I didn't want her near me or Brooke.

Why didn't she come here first; how did she know I was at the mall? Was she following me? The way she pulled up didn't seem like a coincidence. All these questions I had made me not tear up her card or tell my

Dad's about today. I was taking August's advice and giving myself a second to think about how to handle this.

AUGUST 'TAZ' LEGEND

"You say you want this dick right?"

Slap! Slap!

"Yes! Oh God yes, I want it!"

"Eat that muthafucka up then." I slapped her fat ass booty hard one more time as she slammed her ass back against me again. I stopped moving and let her throw it back all on her own, that squishy pussy sound was loud as hell.

"Yeah, throw them cheeks back and fuck this dick."

Bitch pussy was so loud all I could do was talk shit and enjoy how I had her. Once she came for the I don't know how many times, I filled up the condom with all my seeds. Pulling out, some sweat from my abs dripped on her booty. I smeared it in and slapped it again before stumbling backwards a little, pulling my dick out of her. I had flipped, dipped and coated this bitch in positions for the past hour.

"Whew, shit, that was everything I needed, bae." She came behind me and kissed my back.

Flushing her toilet, I wiped my dick off with a

towel and went to the sink to wash my hands. "Glad I could help." I kissed the top of her head and went to her room to get dressed. We were strictly physical; she knew it and was cool with it.

When I first started hitting, I wanted more. I was sprung and in love or so I thought. But she hoed me flat, said our age and the fact that she was my teacher, we could never be anything. Man, that shit had me in my fucking feelings so tight, she even went so far and started dating someone else. But that was in my sophomore year, and I got out of my slump and decided to man up.

I realized that she was right. I wasn't trying to settle down. I was young, hung lower than a horse and had a life to still live. Even though she was twenty-seven, she still lived her early years without being tied down, so I wasn't about to do that to myself. Me and Ms. Lane started fucking September 2018. When she came to Cooley, she was just a teacher's aid, but my ass was hooked.

I mean I knew it was my dick doing all the thinking, but she was too bad. From head to toe she looked just like *Tyra Banks*, how I know who she was is because Pops raised me and my brothers off old movies. He claimed we could learn a lot about betrayal, being smart in the streets, being dumb, blind to shit and about our culture.

I've seen *Tyra Banks* fine ass in a few of them flicks, *Higher Learning, Fresh Prince Of Bel-Air,* I even watched *Coyote Ugly* because she was in it. But back to the point, Ms. Lane looked just like her, only she was thicker. I don't have to get in how fine I am, y'all already know that so of course it wasn't much I had to do to fuck. In the beginning, she played it off like it was a harmless crush which I understand because I'm her student.

But I wanted to fuck and that's what I was going to do. So, I got into the main office file while our principal was at an assembly and I got all her info. My bold behind pulled up over her crib one night when I knew she was home. As soon as she opened the door, I was on her like white on rice. No bullshit and she didn't stop me. We fucked long, hard and I was smitten as fuck after.

My feelings came into play around October. I wanted more and was willing to show her. I ain't gon' lie, I was on some girly shit with texting her, thinking about her and even cuddling after sex. When I admitted I wanted more she freaked the hell out and told me how much trouble we both could be in. Why we wouldn't have a future and she didn't want to lose her job. I wasn't trying to hear that though.

I didn't even tell my brothers because I wasn't no child who had to blab about who I was fucking, plus I didn't want to hurt her. You know how someone doesn't get the hint about something until you have to get harsh? Well, that's what she did to me when she called herself getting a boyfriend for Valentine's Day.

I was pissed off but seeing her with him was what I needed to get my head back right. After that, I fell all the way back the remainder of sophomore year. On some real shit, I never knew women want you more when you stop giving a fuck. I started getting notes from her on my assignments, in my locker and even through texts. All shit she got on me for doing when I was sprung, she now did.

So, the end of 10th grade she left another note, this time she slid it in the crack of my window in my old truck I had. It basically said she wanted me to come over and talk to her, we all knew she didn't want to talk. By then my ego was blown even bigger and I didn't meet her for two days. When I got to her house, she had on a sexy see-through lingerie set, some heels and her long sandy brown hair was in a low ponytail.

I paid it no mind on the outside but my insides were about to explode because it was just sexy. I let her tell me how much she missed me, how she used that dude to run me off and she wanted me back. Not only did she want me back, but she actually wanted a relationship. All the stuff she was scared of before didn't matter, she wanted me.

I got real then and told her the time we spent apart let me know I was talking like a child. Only thing that will be between us if we were together was drama and I don't need that. I then told her we could be friends and I would hit her up later. Kissing her on the cheek, I left her standing there hot and bothered. The bitch broke my heart and I wasn't about to just fall in her lap because she missed me.

I dipped out and hit her up a week later, although she was blowing me up every day. I kept our conversation short and sweet. Once I decided to show my face, I put it on her so hard like a slab of concrete. Then I left her alone sleeping and that's how it's been since and she hated it but oh well. I didn't want her like that anymore, but I'd be full of shit if I said her pussy wasn't good.

"Do you have to go?" She asked me while tying her robe around her waist.

I picked my Yeezy's up and put them on my feet. "Yup, I gotta meet with my brothers."

"Can you come back, I can cook and we can watch movies—"

"Nope, can't do that love. You know that ain't what we on Ms. Lane." I got up chuckling because she hated when I called her that. I used to be on first name bases with her, but not anymore.

"Ms. Lane. Really Taz?! You don't hear me calling you August." Her eyebrow raised in a sarcastic way.

I stood up and picked my shirt up off the floor. "That's because you ain't fucking crazy to call me that outside of school."

"But it's ok for you to be funny and call me Ms. Lane? Why are you being so mean towards me bae, what did I do?" She walked in front of me, looking sad.

"You didn't do shit but this." I pointed to her bed. "Is all we have and I made that clear, you even agreed to it when I did." I wasn't playing as I looked down at her because I had her by six inches.

"You're right but—"

"Ain't no buts Ms. Lane, this is what it is and what it will always be."

Her eyes on mine, I felt her untie her robe and open it. Taking my hand she put it on her pussy which was soaked as hell. Once upon a time, I would have stripped and said fuck whatever plans I had. But not right now, I wasn't about to play games about our status.

"Please don't leave, Taz. My pussy isn't the only thing you won on me. Stay, stay and fuck me like you just did." She moved her hand off mine and I continued fingering her.

Picking her thick thigh up with my other hand I gave her a smirk while she shook and came all on my fingers. Her hands were squeezing my arms tightly and she called my name out, then I slid my fingers out slowly.

"I'll text you." Kissing her cheek, I walked out her bedroom leaving her standing there. Before I opened her front door, I went to her kitchen to wash my hands and take one of her bananas from her fruit bowl and I headed out.

I walked down the block where I always parked when I came over here. We didn't want anyone seeing my truck parked outside her house, so it was a precaution. Getting inside I hurried up and turned my air on because it was hot as hell in here. I needed to go home and shower but like I said, I had to meet my brothers at Pops' crib.

Adrian and him had some stuff to talk to us about. I don't know what it was about, but I wasn't in the mood for no bad news. Summer had been pretty good so far and we had our trip to Myrtle Beach coming up. I stopped at the store so I could pick up some Swisher's and some junk food for when my munchies kicked in.

"What up Taz, you been cool?" Ali, the clerk, asked when I got inside. This was one of me and my brother's main stores where we sold from. Arabic's love money and a lot of them believed they were black anyways. Pops has been working with them since before we were able to walk.

"Shit cool this way Ali, how you been? Where that fine ass daughter of yours?" I picked up some three bags of Vitner's hot crunchy chips, two honey buns and three Kit-Kat bars, them were my joints.

"When you are talking about making her a wife then I'll tell you how she's been." He always said that shit.

I put all my stuff on the counter. While he rung it up his son opened the door that led to the back and gave me a Nike bookbag.

"Come on now, I'm only seventeen!" I said laughing while pulling a twenty out to pay for my food.

Ali grabbed three Swisher's and put them in my bag. "Yeah, yeah. In my country you can be thirteen and get married." We both laughed.

I picked up my bag of goodies. "You fucks is wild as

hell, I'll holla later." I left out the store, shaking my head and still laughing.

Little did he know, his daughter has already been in our basement a few times. I've fucked her twice then tossed her to my brothers; her sister was a freak too. Chill has beat her pussy up more times than I can count. The both of them were twenty but y'all know me, my brother's and Chill don't carry ourselves like our ages and we definitely don't sling dick like no kids.

While I drove to Pops' house, I turned the satellite radio on. Before my turn came, I took the left since it wasn't too out my way. Pops house. I haven't been by to see it in a few days and it was time. I slowed down and parked right in front of it then just looked at it. For a year I have rode past this building in Oak Park.

I have been inside a few times because the owner was a one of our custos. It was what I always envisioned for my barber-tattoo shop. One floor, 5000sqft and every time I came here, I had mixed emotions. At first it wasn't a big thing I would think about but with my senior year coming. I found myself thinking a lot about my life once high school was done.

Me and my brothers have a duty, to take over Pops' empire. Nothing was wrong with that, but he had no other passion outside of the streets. Don't get me wrong, he loves the hell out of us but I'm talking about something that was just his own. All he had was the drug game, but I just don't see my life going that way.

I have interests, dreams and plans that doesn't fit into me living and breathing the streets. I haven't told my brothers about this, especially Audrey because I didn't want to let them down. Like I said, I wasn't walking away from our money, I just didn't want that to be the only thing I got going for me. After a few minutes of looking at the building, I pulled off and went straight to Pops' crib.

"What up Pops." I greeted him when I walked in his house.

Pops had a nice six-bedroom crib in Farmington Hills; he wanted our crib to be out there with him but hell no. We didn't want to live that close to our parent, Mama was in Madison Heights so the city was perfect for us. She wasn't down for us getting our spot as teens, but Pops told her we were growing men and needed our space.

It was either live with him or talk her into agreeing to our own house. Another thing I loved about our Pops, he always wanted him and her to be on the same page. He put the crib in his name, and it was up to us to keep up with everything from the taxes, repairs and of course the bills.

"Hi son." After we fist pound, he kissed me on my forehead like he does all of us. "Them knuckle heads in the basement."

I laughed while making my way to his big basement. They were laughing and joking while the TV was on. Pops had six rows of recliners facing a 70-inch TV. On the other side he had an air-hockey table, a Skee Ball machine and a Foosball table.

"Tazmanian, what up bro." Audrey spoke first, getting up and embracing me the same way Pops does.

The rest of my brothers followed after him and then we started talking, laughing and watching TV.

"I'm so ready for Myrtle Beach." I told them while taking my fitted hat off.

"Me too, I'm ready to turn up." Austin agreed.

"You bringing Nicole?" Adrian asked him trying to be funny. We snickered because the answer was clear based off Austin's face.

"Being funny will get'cho ass beat, bro. Hell naw, I'm not taking Nicole, you bringing Brittany?"

Adrian got serious then like he always does when one of us fucks with him. "No I'm not dick head ass boy."

"You bringing somebody?" I asked Audrey.

He was on his phone like always texting.

"Aye." I said out loud and his ass still didn't budge. I looked at my brothers shaking my head with an amused expression. "Audrey!"

"What fool?" He looked up at me with his nose all up like I was bothering him.

"Damn Chaos, yo', no more bullshit. Who have you been talking to? You be zoned out." Austin asked him.

Hell, we all wanted to know, we knew it was a girl. His mean ass ain't about to be texting no guy all day. We were all close to Audrey with us being triplets and him just being the oldest. However, me and him were about an inch closer. I went to him before anybody about anything.

My point is, I knew my big brother better than I know myself. He was into whoever this chick was. I wasn't tripping because we all know the secret I got. But I'm nosey and so are my brothers so we needed this nigga to spill.

"None of y'all are Mama so I don't have to tell y'all nothing." His grumpy ass said, putting his phone in his pocket.

"Got damn bro she got'chu that emotional? Make sure you don't cry while you in the pussy." Austin joked and we all fell out laughing except Audrey.

He got off the recliner and rushed Austin, putting him in a head lock trying to fuck his braids up. "Smart mouth ass nigga, apologize!" He demanded while they were all over the damn basement, literally.

"I'ma fuck y'all up if anything break!" Pops came downstairs and the bass in his voice made them stop.

"Pops he started it." Austin said, pointing at Audrey.

All Pops did was turn the TV off and looked at them like some bad ass little kids.

"Get serious, sons." He demanded with a harsh tone.

We left all jokes and previous conversations alone, sat down in the recliners and got for real. Pops stood in front of us and started talking.

"Adrian got pulled over yesterday by Joe and Stan. I'll let him tell y'all the rest."

Adrian got up and Pops sat where he was; anytime something happened in the streets Pops always told us to spill the news all together. He says when you tell one person it's a domino effect and the story get fucked up as it travels through everyone. Plus, emotions raise and the last thing he wants is for one of us to do something stupid.

"So, basically Darius offered them more money for police protection. I offered for us to match Darius' price, but Joe and Stan want it to be like a bid for their protection. Even though we have other cops on our payroll, y'all know it's best to operate with everyone on the same page."

When he was done it was quiet for a minute. Pops sat back and looked at his Rolex. He was giving us time to process what Adrian just told us. He always did that, I know I'm on 10 right now. Audrey looked like he was ready to blow up and Austin was cracking his knuckles. He did that a lot when he was annoyed or frustrated.

"Pops that Darius, his son and his nephews need to be handled like yesterday. All this is because he wants you to share your connect." Audrey spoke first.

"He does but he'll never get it and he know it, so he is trying this way. Listen, Stan and Joe are pussies and I don't want y'all to get intimidated by them blue uniforms they wear. Move in these streets like I taught you, don't sweat it at all. We'll keep paying them and not a cent more, Darius will get so desperate that him, his son and nephews will move nasty. Then we will strike hard as fuck." He looked at all of us and we agreed without hesitation. He got up and fixed his black jeans.

"August, come upstairs with me so we can chat. Audrey, Austin, I'ma kick y'all asses if anything break."

I got up and followed him upstairs; I could hear the TV being cut back on.

"What's up, Pops?" I asked once we made it to the dining room.

He leaned against the wall with his arms folded looking at me with a smirk. "You know I can smell the pussy on you from here?"

"What?" Wrinkles formed in my forehead and I started smelling my shirt then my arm.

"Still hitting ya damn teacher up huh?"

Pops knew about me and Ms. Lane; him and Mama came to this parent night at school. Man I swear me and Ms. Lane never slipped in public as far as affection goes. Somehow he saw right through it and confronted me the next day. He wasn't confrontational but of course he asked if I knew what I was doing.

How if it got out what would happened and then he gave me some dab, told me if I was Ava he would have been on a killing spree. It got bad when he saw that I was sprung, then he came at me like a hard father. Told me to leave her alone before some pussy have me out here on some dumb shit.

"Yeah but it ain't like that Pops, I swear. I'm just getting my dick wet that's all, and that's not even about to last. I have interest in someone else and she not the type to play with." I told him; it was always comfortable talking to Pops.

"Oh really, who? Please don't tell me I fucked her Mama. You see yo' brothers fucking them Talbert sisters and I've bent they Mama over a few times."

He kept me laughing with his crazy ways, he'll never fuck with any of our bitches but their Mama's was another story. "Pops I swear you wild as hell." I said, finishing up laughing then I got for real. "But the chick I'm into is Brinx."

"Young?" He asked with his arms still folded and leaned on the wall.

"Uh, yeah and I think Austin is into Coya Clark."

When I admitted that, he shook his head and grabbed the bridge of his nose. "I swear out of four of y'all at least two drives my pressure up once a year."

"I know Pops and believe me it wasn't on purpose, hell, I haven't even taken her out yet. At least not till Saturday, and Austin hasn't made a move on Coya either."

"But?" He asked waiting for me to finish.

I pulled on the end of my beard thinking about

Brinx. Even when I bit down on the inside of my jaw my smile still popped on my face. Pops laughed and I rubbed my hand over my face.

"I tried Pops to push it aside but it didn't work, Brinx bad as hell and I just wanna see what's up. Not in that way, I mean if she let me then I'm fa sho—"

"Aight lil nigga, I get the picture." Laughing he breathed out looking at me with his blue eyes like all of ours. "What about Audrey and Adrain, they feelin' Jurnee and Toni?"

"Hell naw, they don't even get along." I knew for a fact Toni and Adrian couldn't stand each other and Jurnee looked at Audrey like he was trash. He can talk shit all he wants, that girl can't stand him.

"You and Austin couldn't find no other girls, it had to be the ones who we get all our weapons from? I went to school with their fathers, they will get just as wild as me if pushed. But, if you and her like each other, then I won't stand in y'all way. Understand, Robert is going to give you a hard time when you show up on his doorstep. He won't hurt you or nothing but he definitely won't be nice." He was laughing after warning me. "Just don't cause no problems, tell Austin too."

"No doubt Pops, love you." I pressed my back off

the wall, gave him some dab and he kissed the top of my head.

"Love you too son, I hope it works out with you and Brinx. Maybe you'll learn something other than your teacher's insides." He jokingly said as I went back in the basement.

**

Let me catch a vibe, let's just take our time
Just relax your mind, and take it easy

DaniLeigh-Easy played in my truck as I pulled up in front of Brinx's crib. I'd be lying if I said I wasn't geeked it was Saturday night. Since the mall me and her have been texting and talking on the phone, she had a good vibe to her. I didn't care that she was a virgin, I figured she was because I never seen her with no nigga at school.

Every now and then I would look at her tropical looks and just want to hump her ass like a rabbit. But now that she basically said she never had sex, I knew I couldn't handle her like I do these other hoes. Brinx wasn't a hoe by far however dates always end in me getting some pussy.

I mean always, and I don't hint it or nothing, I'm a Legend and girls just threw it at me. So, tonight was about to be different because I knew I wasn't getting my dick soaked however, I don't care. I just want to take her out, have a good time and see what it is I want out of me and her. I got out my truck and walked up the walkway of her house.

Tonight, I had on some light grey jeans with a Colin Kaepernick 49ers jersey, with some red and white 13s on my feet. I lined the hair and beard around my mouth up. Brinx always talked about my chin beard so I had that all soft and smelling good with this coco butter hair stuff Mama got for me and my brothers.

The only jewelry I had on was my diamond studs and gold chain. I looked good and smelled good. Ringing her doorbell, I could hear giggling and cartoons playing so I knew it must have been Brinx's little sister.

"What's sup?" Her Pops, Robert, opened the door. He was the one we did business with at their scrap metal place.

"How you doing tonight?" I asked him. We've talked plenty of times, laughed and joked so I thought tonight wouldn't be any different.

Clearly I was wrong because he stood in his door

way with a toothpick in his mouth looking at me like I violated him.

"I'm here to pick up Brinx." I said once again just in case he was confused.

Silence.

"Does she live here?" I tried to joke a little.

Still silence.

"Damn, does she live on this block?" I asked now with an attitude.

"Who you think you talkin' to? You at my door where I pay the mortgage and bills."

I held my hands up, trying not to laugh. "I apologize, I just want to pick up Brinx for our date."

"Where y'all going?"

"To the movies then to eat." I rubbed my beard not stopping my laugh this time.

"You think this shit is funny? Your father is my mans and I been knowing y'all since y'all were little. But you don't get that me tonight, you here to pick up a third of my heart. Don't think I'm tripping because of what you do in these streets. You could be in some slacks and have a paper route, you still have a dick."

"I understand that but it's not like that with Brinx, we are only friends and just trying to get to know each other." I told him on some real shit.

"Get to know each other how?" His nostrils flared.

"Not like that—"

"Robert! Move from the damn door and let the boy in."

Thank God her other father came because he was about to have me out here all night asking me questions.

Still looking at me hard, he moved out the way. As I walked in he spoke in a harsh and serious tone.

"Remember, whatever you do to her I'ma do to you. You break her open and I'ma break you open."

Yo', on God I looked at him like he was crazy as hell. I couldn't believe he said that shit and with an intimidating expression.

"Shut up, you ain't about to do shit. How you been August?" Her other father shook my hand, pushing Robert out the way.

"I've been good just enjoying the summer."

"That's good, did you finish the year strong?" He asked, referring to my grades.

"3.3." I answered. School wasn't hard for me or my brothers, Pops would put his foot in our asses.

While we talked and I messed with Brooke's cute self, Brinx came downstairs. Man she was so damn sexy and I always looked at them cheekbones and eyes. The denim jean skirt she had on stopped above her knees. It had those strings hanging from it that made it look freshly cut. Her beige shirt was long sleeve, she wore all white Nike Vapor Max. Her black hair was straight and she had a Louis Vuitton headband on with a matching purse that was shaped like a can. Them juicy lips were glossy and those long legs looked smooth.

"Hey August." She spoke as soon as she got downstairs to me.

"Sup, you look good—"

Her father cleared his throat before I could finish my sentence. Me and Brinx chuckled.

"Well ok, we are out of here. I know my curfew and I'll meet it, love you both." She said then kissed her sister. "Love you Brooks."

"Aye, hold on—" Robert spoke loud but her other father put his hand over his mouth. "Have fun kids."

I closed the door after Brinx walked outside.

"My dad didn't drill you, did he?"

"A little but wasn't nothing I couldn't handle." I opened the door for her to get in. "Can I have a hug first?" I stood on the side of her holding the door.

"I would but." She tilted her head to her house.

When I looked we both laughed seeing her father in the door. I helped her in, closed the door, walked around to the driver side and got in. It was almost seven which was perfect timing for what I wanted to do.

"So, what are we doing tonight?" Brinx asked me snapping her fingers to the music. As soon as I started my truck the song picked up where it left off.

"Bahama Breeze and then the drive-in. Unless you want to swap, then we can do something until 10 when the drive-in opens."

"No we can eat now, that way we won't mess our appetite up from the movie junk food."

I nodded my head while driving, I would sneak looks at her from the side of my eye. Brinx was bomb as fuck and carried herself with a carefree vibe. Like when I see her laugh and talk to her homegirls it was with confidence. Sounds odd as shit when I explain, but I'm telling y'all this girl was lit.

I drove and we talked about our day, the school year that just ended and about music. When we got to the restaurant, I held the door open for her. Getting inside there was a crowd but that's normal on a Saturday night. I called ahead and had the manager put a table up for me. It was easy because Austin used to fuck on her, and I think he still does.

Either way I pimped him to her so I could get her to hold the spot. Brinx was all sweet while we continued talking. She told me this was her first time eating here. Once we ordered our food I flirted, and she flirted back. Her smile was out of this world, those juicy lips did the cutest curl up all around her mouth when she would laugh hard or grin.

Brinx had me paying attention to her every move which was weird to me because I was used to only paying attention to the obvious on girls. While we were eating my phone vibrated and it was Ms. Lane. I ignored it of course and continued my good time with Brinx. We both decided to order dessert and she got up to use the bathroom.

While she was gone, I pulled my phone out and saw Ms. Lane called me twenty times, sent me six texts messages, three nudes and two voicemails. I didn't think shit about it because it was normal, once I stopped being sprung. Brinx came back just as the waiter brought us our dessert. I ordered the key lime pie and she got the chocolate island cake.

"I knew you two looked familiar."

I almost chocked on my pie when we both looked

up at the person talking to us.

"Hi Ms. Lane," Brinx smiled and spoke.

My face was turned the way it gets before I pop. This shit wasn't no coincidence, I'd be a dummy to believe that. This bitch had to have been following me, probably even when I picked Brinx up. She had on some white leggings, a blue t-shirt and some Gucci slides, the fake smile she was giving Brinx made me want to knock her out.

"I'm fine just decided to get me a bite to eat." Then she looked at me. "Hello August."

I had to get myself together before Brinx noticed. I pasted a fake smile on too.

"Sup Ms. Lane, how are you tonight?"

"I'm good now that I am about to eat."

Ugh, her grin was phony as hell.

"I hope you're taking your food to go, you look drained and tired. I know how women your age need their rest." I grinned back. I could sense Brinx's mouth drop.

Ms. Lane gave me an annoyed look then she flipped her hair. "You're right, I am a little tired, that's why I had my boyfriend drive me here. Well, I'll let you both get back to your dessert. I'm teaching 12th grade

English next year so I'll probably see you both in class." Nodding her head at us she walked off towards the register. Brinx's back was to her, Ms. Lane looked back and gave me the nastiest glare.

"I can't believe you told her she looked tired and drained, August." Brinx laughed while picking up her fork and finishing her dessert.

"Shit I was just being honest, she looks like she might fall asleep at the wheel." Chuckling I took a sip of my water. Honestly, Ms. Lane looked good but I knew how to push her buttons. I did a fake stretch and looked out the window of the restaurant when she walked outside. I saw she got into her car and no one else was in it so that mean she lied about being here with a boyfriend.

Believe me I was checking her about this stunt then the bitch still blew my phone up. I put my phone on silent, paid our bill and we left out. It was a good feeling hanging with Brinx. Her conversation was all that, she responded so well with me as far as my personality.

"The Invisible Man, I wanted to see this movie." She said once we got to the drive in.

I paid our fee, we went and got some junk food, and now we were in my truck setting up and getting comfortable. The weather was on my side tonight; it wasn't humid and there was a good ass breeze so I didn't have to have the air on.

"I wanted to see this too so I knew it would be a perfect pick." I hated to ask her this but it's been on my mind since it happened. "How did everything go with your Dad's and you telling them about Soo-Yon popping up?"

Her body language changed, she crossed those long legs and kind of moved around a little. I wouldn't press so if she didn't want to talk about it then it was cool.

"You ain't gotta answer if you don't want to, I don't wanna mess up your mood."

"It's ok, it's just I'm only used to talking to my friends about her. But I decided to not tell my dad's for a few reasons. But I haven't reached out to her or seen her since that day, I am however deciding if I want to meet with her on my own."

Nodding my head I said, "Wow Brinx, that is a big step. You're mature so you should be proud. Just know both of your fathers love you and will have your back." I put some Goobers in my mouth.

"Yeah I know, I just don't want to drop that on them just yet." She then put some Milk Duds in her mouth.

I couldn't help but look at her lips, Those thangs

were on another level. "Come here real quick." I told her, leaning a little in her direction.

Brinx put her candy down and met me halfway, we were nose to nose. Even her breath smelled as sweet as she looked.

"Can I kiss you?" I asked her with a low tone; this was new. I don't ask to do anything on a girl because they were willing to just let me. Five-minutes into the movie I would have had my dick down a bitch throat. Brinx just required to be treated differently even without telling me. I'd be a no-good nigga to treat her any other way other than someone who had worth.

Her eyes went around my face, lips then they met mine. "Yes you can."

That was all I needed to hear. When our lips touched we both kept it simple and sweet. I tried my luck and let my tongue separate her lips. Brinx fell into it so smoothly and before you knew it, we were in a full-blown tongue tangle. My hand was on the side of her face and then in her soft hair.

She did like she told me and pulled on my beard then her soft hand went on the side of my face. Now, I knew I wasn't about to fuck. To tell you the truth I wouldn't take it if she offered it to me. In my truck is not how I want to get in her insides, especially with it being her first time. But I did go off her vibe and how she was kissing me.

I pulled her from her seat and into my lap. I wanted her to remain comfortable because she had a skirt on. I kept her legs closed, let her cross them and just went back to kissing her. The light weight of her body, the heat she had coming from it and just her in general felt good as hell on my lap. We were still kissing, and I was tearing them lips up. I did what I told her at the mall, and I went in on that soft neck. I nicely moved her long hair, licking and sucking on it.

"Mmm, August."

Fuck! Why did she do that!? Her voice was so sexy and my name coming out if her mouth felt better than pay day. I needed to stop; I had to stop because my dick was about to break off. However, those lips she has, her smooth neck, her timid hands on my face and that voice moaning my name.

It was making it hard for me to stop kissing her, but I knew I needed to slow down. I pulled away slowly and we both were breathing a little more than normal.

"We ain't even paying attention to the movie," she said with pleasantries in her tone.

Laughing I said, "I know right, but we'll get it on DVD."

"Oh really, so you saying there will be a second date?" I never seen a girl smile and bite her lip at the same time. It was like she was being sexy without over doing it like a lot of these thirst rats.

"Hell yeah there will be a second. And a third, fourth and so on. I'm feelin' you tough as hell, Brinx." I admitted with no shame.

"But you really don't know me fully, August."

"True but I want to, I will get to know you in every way." I wrapped my arms around her waist, pulling her into me a little tighter.

Her face had this unsure look. "What if I'm not ready for you to know me in certain ways, would you still be interested?"

"I'm not gon' lie to you, I don't have no women around me who I'm not fucking in either their mouth or pussy."

Her eyes got big from how I was talking, but I continued.

"It's different with you though, and I knew that before tonight. All this date did was make realize what I already knew."

"Which is?" Her curiosity was cute as fuck.

"That I want you to be my girl." I couldn't even believe I just said that but it just came out and I really didn't regret it.

I could feel Brinx breathe in sharply. "Wow August, I wasn't expecting you to say that. The thing is I don't know when I'll be ready, and I know you have needs. I mean you're A Legend, my trust in people...they disappoint, people disappoint , August, and I don't want to be one of them, nor do I want you to do that to me. It may seem all easy now, but all the kissing and touching will get boring. You'll eventually want more, and I don't know when I'll be ready to give you more."

"I get where you're coming from and yeah, you'll send a nigga home with blue balls a lot but it's ok. I'll beat my shit off to your pictures and the thought of your voice."

We both laughed and I liked that she wasn't so uptight that she couldn't take a joke.

"Can we go slow first, continue hanging and see how it goes?"

Part of me wanted to say no because agreeing to this meant she was still single. But I had to be real with myself. I love sex, I love everything about it and being official with her means giving it up until, if ever, she was ready. This way I can still spend time with her and get my dick soaked.

"Ok, we can do that." I said kissing her lips again then we watched what was left of the movie.

**

It was a week after me and Brinx's date and we kept that same vibe. Texting, talking on the phone and hanging. Her dad still gave me some shit whenever I came over, but he knew I wasn't backing down. I was into his daughter tough and there wasn't anything he could do about it. I wanted her to come to Myrtle Beach with us next month.

Even though that meant I wouldn't be getting any pussy for four days. I didn't care, the thought of us not seeing each other for those days bothered me. Now me, Audrey and Chill were at one of our trap houses counting money and talking shit like always. This trap was on the westside Chill sold for us too and he made bank because his Pops stayed in Barton Hills Village.

Wasn't shit but rich people wanting to get high and we were more than willing to take their money. Right now, we were counting money for profit of two weeks. Our sellers, like Chill, sold our small product to custos. Me and my brother sold our product in bulk to the high-end clients. That's where Austin and Adrian were right now, making us an easy thirty G's apiece.

"Sup with you and Brinx?" Chill asked me.

"We good, just kickin' it and seeing what's up. Who was them two bad bitches you had on Live with you last night?"

"His cousin." Audrey joked laughing. Those two would cut up all day if time let them.

"Fuck you fruit loop, them two were twins and they both took turns licking my balls." He cheesed so hard all his teeth practically fell out.

"They were bad as hell, no lie, my nigga." Audrey told him and I agreed.

"So, you still harassing Jurnee?" Chill asked him while putting a rubber band around some money.

"Yeah, shit is actually getting fun."

Like I told y'all, I knew my brother; his answer and laugh was fake. "You feelin' Jurnee?"

"Hell naw, I ain't got time for that girl. I just like fucking with her."

Let me tell y'all something right now, keep this in mind for the rest of this series. Anytime Audrey says 'he ain't got time' in his sentence after you ask him a question, it means he is lying. It's like a nervous habit for him, we laugh every time he says it because we know what it means but he hasn't learned that yet.

"Yo' we got a problem." Adrian said coming into the house with Austin.

All of us jumped up when they said it was a problem.

"What happened?" Audrey asked.

Austin threw the black bag on the couch, it's the same bag of our product he left with.

"The sale fell through, Simon and his cousins got to it."

"Wait a fucking minute! How do these fucks even know who our high custos are?!" Audrey was yelling and it sounded just like our Pops.

"Bro I don't even know, their shit isn't nowhere good like ours but it's cheaper." Austin explained.

"We need to call Pops—"

"No." Audrey shut that down. "He said I'm the oldest and I gotta start handling certain things."

"Well, what do you wanna do?" I asked him, ready for whatever.

He paced the floor a few times slowly then stopped. "They keep striking at us, sending messages and now getting in our money way. Well, it's time we send one back. Nothing too wild just a little whisper in them ear wax filled ears they got. Come on Taz roll out with me."

On impulse I jumped up and we headed out the house. I didn't need to know any details, he'd fill me in once we get to where we were going. All I knew was he grabbed one of the bookbags that had money in it.

"Whose big crib is this?" I asked when we pulled in front of a mini mansion in Bloomfield Hills about 7000sqft.

"Pops tells me shit he doesn't tell y'all because I'm the oldest. Come on."

We both got out and he grabbed the bookbag. The driveway was long and before we could even approach the pavement, we were stopped by three big niggas.

"State your purpose?" The one who was the fattest asked us.

Audrey responded, "Here to see Rock about a sale." He held the bag up and unzipped it.

We were searched and then escorted up the driveway to the front door. They even walked us inside like we were going to see the president or something. The inside was nice, paintings up, art like ceilings and long chocolate brown drapes all over.

It was fully furnished; walking past the kitchen there was a patio door showing the pool. You could see women inside it looking like models, a full bar and some smoke coming from the grill. We got to the back in I guess was a second living room. A guy was shooting pool with three women in a g string and no top was sitting on stools watching him. They were fine as hell, nice full titties and all black which I appreciated.

"Apollo Legend's off-springs in my office. What do I owe the pleasure?" He rubbed chalk on the end of his pool stick. He was the same height as our Pops, dark skin and had a high-top fade with lines on his left side. His three chains and two iced out watches he had on let me know he was flashy.

"My Pops says you got the best under us and we wanna buy it. All."

I kept my poker face when Audrey said that because that's what our father taught us. Never sweat, look nervous or like me and my brothers weren't on the same page. Every decision we make and sentence we speak when handling business is for a reason. The other brothers need to always back the one talking up.

"Now why would you want my product when even

you just said I'm hitting under y'all?" Rock asked, he stood up straight from breaking the balls.

"Do you question all buyers? As long as I got more than enough money, why does it matter?" Audrey was wild, didn't give a damn what he said and was fearless. That's big brother.

"Will y'all excuse us, I need to speak to these Legends alone." Rock commanded from his crew and the ladies, but his eyes were locked on Audrey. Once everyone left the room and it was just us, Rock went to his bar in front of his pool table.

"You two want a drink?" He asked us.

"Naw, we're good." I spoke up while we watched him make himself one.

"I don't ask anyone who wants to buy my product, shit. I sell and we keep it moving but the Legend brothers who I know for a fact have purer powder than Johnson&Johnson. Not only want to buy my stuff but buy all of what I have left. You know what else I find odd, I'm Darius' supplier and I know the history of him and y'all Pops. Those wouldn't have anything to do with each other, would they?"

Audrey gave me the bookbag full of money and spoke. "You seem to already have all the answers but if you need to know, then yes. The two have everything to do with each other, I want all your product and when you get more in, I want that too. I'll pay double both times."

Rock snickered then threw another shot back.

"You know this will cause a war between you and Darius. He'll ask who brought all my goods and I'm not about to lie—"

"I never asked you to, in fact it would be a fucking insult to me if you did. I just said let me buy you up. He'll know what's up and what happens will happen. Is it a yes or no because me and my brother got shit to do." This nigga and his mouth.

But I stood there like his twin, waiting and down for the unknown. Rock held his shot glass in his hand and tossed it back and forth.

"I'm all about money, we have a deal." He made a loud, quick whistle. His guy came in and Rock told him to get the stuff.

"Damn bro, this was smart as hell, but Rock is right. This will definitely cause problem." I told him while he drove us back to the trap house.

"Yeah I know, that's what I want. They keep sending all these messages and expect us to not do shit. No fucking way, I'm ready for what they'll do next."

"No doubt I am too, I just wanna make sure you know. I hate them niggas low key and want to strike hard on them." I took my phone out when it vibrated.

"Hell yeah me too, I wanna kill Joe and Stan too."

I looked at my brother and we both smiled because we were on the same wave. Once I unlocked my phone, I saw it was a text message from Brinx.

One: Can you come with me on Sunday to meet Soo-Yun?

I read it twice, not really believing what she was asking me. Brinx always said she doesn't trust anyone outside her friends and family. It wasn't hard for me to pick up that she had abandonment issues. When we would talk, whether on the phone or face to face, she would make little comments about how people are not permanent. How she feels safe only with her girls and her family. I understood once she told me how her Mom did her so imagine my surprise when I look at this text. But, I was feeling her and without a doubt, I knew my answer.

Me: Of course One, you know I got you.

COYA JOY CLARK

"Yeah I was yo' white woman for 11yrs. Couldn't start that damn company without me, hell I worked my ass off!" I snatched the clothes off the hangers hard and threw them on the floor along with the shoes.

"I got a master's degree in business and there I was his secretary, his office manager and his computer!" I threw the bunch of clothes in my arms all out the closet and on to the floor. My white long robe I had on was open and I had a black gown under it. It was perfectly matching hers and I had my hair down and mildly tamed just like hers as well. I finished mocking my favorite scene she did perfectly.

"732! 732! The number of times we made love! I remember when that bastard told me he lost count, right after 51! I'll show you, fuck me for not leavin' yo' ass then!" I was throwing shoes out the closet as I talked, tears were coming down my face, I swear I was so into the emotion.

"Get'cho shit! Get'cho shit and GET OUT!"

Bang! Bang! "Coya, would you and Angela please shut the hell up!"

I stopped in my tracks and it was like I was brought back down to reality. "Oops." I said to myself looking at the mess all over my room. "Sorry, Daddy!" I yelled back out at him but in a sweet way. Laughing hard I put my movie on pause and fell on my bed. Now I had a big mess to clean up. My clothes were all over the floor, hangers hanging in my closet and my shoes were thrown everywhere.

While I cleaned up I turned some music on 'cause it helps me move faster. Coya Joy Clark is my whole name and aside from being a true daddy's girl and amazing friend, I am an aspiring actress. I've known that since I was five and watched *What's Love Got To Do With It* with my Mama. I fell in love with Angela Bassett and I own every movie she has ever been in.

Every TV show she has either made a cameo in or starred in, I own. That woman is my hero, my inspiration, in my head she is my mother and I mean no disrespect to my own mother, because she is amazing. But Ms. Bassett is just a brown skin Queen. I can act her major roles down to a T, I even can cry on the spot like her.

I have emailed the Academy Award committee many of times about why she hasn't received an award yet. It's way overdue and they will hear from me every year until they come to their senses. All the plays in school since elementary I have made sure I was in, I wasn't a diva if I didn't get the star role it was fine.

I made whatever lines I had shine and I just love anytime I'm on the stage. Now, Detroit has a preforming arts school called Detroit School of Arts High School (DSA) that I could have attended. I have my reasons why, I just did not want to attend so I went to the high school my dad graduated from and where my girls were going to.

But Cooley offers a program called vocational high school (vo-tech) which means students can go to other schools and pick up skills in a special trade or program. It was Monday, Wednesday from noon till the end of the day. I of course took my program at DSA, I can handle the school two days a week for three hours plus Brinx was in vo-tech with me for her photography.

"Hey, Mommy." I hugged her tightly before she even got out the car. Normally I go visit her up in Marquette which is about six hours away.

But she had to come all the way down here to get her high school transcripts. Mommy moved to Marquette when I was eleven. Her and Daddy had a terrible break up and she just needed to get away, but she wasn't about to move out of state because of me. I was fourteen when I learned Mommy cheated and it almost sent Daddy over the edge.

I was literally the only thing that saved him so that's why I live here and not with her. Mommy knew he needed me because of how she broke him. I was angry and spent two-years almost hating Mommy, but my brother helped with that. Yup, Mommy didn't only cheat, she got pregnant and had a little boy.

You want to know what's even sadder?! The guy took off when she was delivering the baby. He actually walked out the hospital while she was pushing and just disappeared. My brother Harrison was seven and I loved him so much. When she was pregnant, I hated him and wanted know parts because he looked like a reminder why my family was apart.

But one day when I was fifteen and he was five we were at Mommy's new house in Marquette and she went to the store. Harrison was born with asthma which must have come from his dad because me nor my parents have it. Anyway, I really didn't bond with him but he was my blood so I would look out for him and that was it. But when he had his attack when it was just us two, everything changed.

I became panicked and watching him gasp for air

made my heart break even with me giving him his inhaler. I end up having to call 911 and he was rushed to the hospital; his body was so little on the gurney. It took the doctors about fifteen minutes to get him stabled and breathing normally. By that time Mommy had showed up, I broke down crying explaining to her what happened.

After that, I became overprotective of Harrison, I realized he isn't the product of anything negative. He doesn't represent my mother's bad decisions, she did that all on her own. Harrison is innocent and caught in the middle, Daddy on the other hand didn't agree. He never spoke on my brother, but he wanted nothing to do with him.

He couldn't come over, come to any event I had. Hell, Mommy and Daddy can't even be in the same room. You see, she actually tried to get Daddy back. I mean she did the whole on bending knees *Boyz II Men* kick Daddy listens to when he cooks. But he wanted no part of her, she wasn't even allowed in the house.

I asked him last night when she said she would be in Detroit, could she stop by. Even though I went to see her a lot I still wanted to get anytime in I could seeing her. Daddy looked at my face and agreed but said she couldn't come inside. It was good enough for me so after I cleaned my room, I showered and threw on a light pink skater dress. Slipping my feet in some pink and white Chuck Converse low tops. My wavy bundles were down with a side part and my baby hair on fleek.

"Hi my Gem!" Mommy hugged me tight when I came outside to her car. Her and Daddy have been calling me Gem since birth. They say I was rare even in her stomach, like a Gem.

"How are you, was it easy for you to get your transcripts?" I asked her after we both stepped under the huge tree in front of the house for some shade from the sun.

"Yup, it took me about twenty-minutes, and I paid for an extra set of copies just in case." As she talked, she would look at me beaming but then her eyes would shift in the driveway.

"Daddy isn't in the house, Mommy." I told her because I knew what she was looking for. He had his Cadillac CTS he kept clean and only drove in the summer. Then a Toyota Tacoma he drove in the winter. The Toyota was in the driveway and she was looking to see if the Cadillac was in front of it.

"No, I know." She gave me a big smile, but I know Mommy; her expressions were just like mine. I had her big eyes, and full lips, I had Daddy's chocolate complexion though. Her eyes were nervous and held a little disappointment. "I just wanted to say hi, that's all." Her voice was kind.

"Mommy." I said giving her another hug. "You know how he is, but he'll come around, I really want us to have Christmas dinner together this year. I'm working on how I'll ask him when the time comes."

"No Coya, I don't want you in that mess. My mess I created, I know you want to see peace between us but you're still a child. Me and your father will work things out and be able to co-exist again."

I breathed out because I just wish I could fix this with a snap of a finger. Not even on the hopes of bringing my parents back together. But I would at least like them to be able to be in the same room. Me and Mommy went to Wendy's to get some frosty's and then sat in her air-conditioned car for about thirty minutes. Talking, laughing and she faced timed Harrison for me while he was at school on the student tablet.

His smile matched ours and he was excited to see me. Once she left, I called Daddy to tell him and let him know I was about to walk to the store. He hated when I walked but I felt safe in our neighborhood. We had nice big homes on the blocks, kids playing but he just hated me walking anywhere. Our house was the fifth from the corner, once you hit it you make a left.

There is another block then a busy street behind it. The store is across the street, the good thing is the traffic light is right here, so I don't have to walk down. I just have to wait till the light turns red and I can cross. Like always, I got horns blown at me and some cat calling. It never bothered me, in fact, I laughed sometimes at it. My phone rung as I opened the door to walk in.

"Hola major abucheo (Hey best boo) what are you doing?" As you can tell from the Spanish, it was Toni.

"Hey pooh, I'm just at the store getting some chips and a vitamin water. What are you doing?" I asked, picking up three bags of my favorite Rap snacks.

"Sitting here with my abuela, greasing her scalp then putting a jumbo braid in her hair. So guess what?"

"Oh goodness, what did you do?" I asked her laughing and already shaking my head.

I loved my friends, they were a part of my life the way acting and my family were. Me and Toni were definitely the spicy ones out of the four of us. Y'all already know we're not virgins but we're not out here spreading our legs for just anyone.

"I'm all done abuela, se ve hermoso (it looks beautiful)."

I could hear them moving around and separating. Toni closed a door then she continued.

"I didn't do anything except decide to give Miles a key to heaven."

I laughed with her when she started rapping Cardi B lyrics in Spanish.

"All that talk you did about he wasn't gettin' it again, what brought this new change on?" I walked to the back of the store to get my vitamin water.

"I just wanted to, but I still didn't give him any head."

Smacking my lips and cackling I said, "He looks like he got turtle head dick so I don't blame you."

"You are awful." She couldn't even talk because she was laughing so hard. "He is circumcised, silly. I just didn't want to go down on him."

"I feel that, niggas don't get that ain't for everybody. I would have gave Lorenzo some if he didn't act a complete fool at the mall. No ma'am, imagine if I would have gave him some how he would have been acting." I told her. Walking past the candy I stopped and decided to pick me out some.

"Ugh, guys get on my nerves with that cry baby ass behavior. This dude DM me on Instagram, so I went to check his profile and didn't like what I saw. He hit me up again like 'damn I said hi ma.' I wrote him back like 'Stop inboxing me, I saw your first message then I checked out your profile. I know what I'm doing in not responding. You know he called me all kinds of bitches." We both were cracking up.

"You're nuts pooh, I promise you are." I got to the counter and let the cashier ring me up. "You ever ran from head and the guy think you're running because they wilding out. But really your running because the head was hurting? That's how it was with Graham, but the dick was decent."

Toni literally was laughing so hard, she snorted.

"It's not funny, I was so scared." I couldn't believe my friend was laughing that hard. As I paid for my stuff, I heard her grandma calling her.

"I'll call you back, Coya, let me see what my abuela wants."

"Ok, bye-bye." I hung up, getting my change from the cashier and putting it in my cross-body purse, saying thank you and walking out.

I got outside as a white Volkswagen Jetta parked.

When the doors opened and I saw the Talbert sisters. I knew instantly that it was about to be some shit.

"Now why the hell are you even outside at two in the afternoon? You gon' crisp that skin even blacker." Nicole was the first to say something which didn't surprise me because she was into Austin.

I chuckled and flashed my smile. "The blacker the berry, the sweeter the pussy for Austin."

"How is it you even can try to be funny and you're alone?" Regina asked me as her and her sisters walked closer to me.

I dropped my bag on the ground, not giving a damn about the stuff I bought. I wasn't stupid by far, my girls weren't with me and these hoes were on one.

"All of this over a nigga I'm not even fucking? If y'all are expecting me to be scared then you failed." I said continuing to laugh.

"Nicole, smack this bitch!" Regina yelled.

All I knew was I was beating the fuck out of one of these sisters. Whoever I grab I'm not letting go no matter what. Regina moved her sister out the way and stepped in my face.

"All I want you to do is stay away from Kid. Tell your little friends to stay away from Chaos and Play. All the beef will stop and—"

I snapped and just swung; you see, I don't like no bitch close in my face. I don't give a damn what you're trying to say. I knew when I saw them that we were about to fight, we don't even have any history. The Talbert sisters are just known for being some loud rats, sucking and fucking whoever they want. Once Austin, Kid, expressed interests in me at Bell Isle, I knew Nicole would be a problem.

I could feel her sisters hitting my back and cussing at me. But I'm telling y'all, them hits felt like cotton balls against my skin. I had Nicole's shirt balled up tight in my hand, she wasn't going anywhere. I was fucking this bitch up; she tried to kick me in the kat like I had balls there, but I blocked her leg with my knee. I knew a small crowd started because I could hear people.

"Come on girl, you done beat her ass enough."

I was lifted in the air and that's when I saw the damage I did. Nicole's face was fucked up, her thirty-inch blonde ponytail was on the floor.

"Stupid ass bitch, look at my sister face!" Brittany kept shouting over and over.

The guy who pulled us apart had his arm out stopping her from getting to me. He was using his other arm to keep me at bay. I had my tongue out laughing and breathing hard from the fight. My head was pounding because them hoes were pulling my hair, but I didn't see any of my tracks on the floor.

I could feel my hair was wild though and my dress was still in-tact which I was proud about. I would bet the fight was recorded by somebody because that's just the world we live in. I just didn't want my titties all over the internet.

"You think this shit is funny!" Now Regina was trying to get to me after she helped Nicole up. "Naw, move let me get at this trick!"

I felt my hair being pulled back, Brittany snuck me from behind. But I caught on quick, twisted my body out her hold and now we were going at it.

"Busted pussy ass hoe tryna sneak me!" I shouted after getting a last hit on her before the owner of the store pulled her back. Suddenly, I felt some arms go around my waist, yanking me backwards. It felt like something from an abduction scene as I was thrown inside a truck. Once I was placed on the seat, Austin stood in front of me.

"Here." He gave me my purse that was broken from the long strap.

I snatched it from him with my eyes still on the

Talbert sisters. They got in their car and pulled off all crazy.

"You out here fighting and wild like that, Coya?" Austin asked once he got in his truck.

"I'm not out here like nothing, I walked to the store and them hoes rolled up on me coming out! All because yo' lil bitch think me and you got something going on!" I was so mad I was shaking, I wanted to continue fighting them one by one.

"Aye, lower your voice ma, for real. Don't direct that anger towards me and we both know Nicole ain't shit of mine. Her tongue plays ping pong with my dick and balls, but that's it."

I was rolling my eyes while he talked. "Can you please just take me home." I calmed down because I just didn't have it in me to yell.

I can count on one hand how many fights I've been in. Aside from a bitch tryna throw shade, it never resulted to blows. This right here was second. My first one was like four years ago. Right now, my temper was at its limit, my head was pounding, and I wanted to cry from all the anger.

Austin pulled off and did what I asked, it took all of three minutes for him to get to my house. Once the truck stopped, I immediately got out and headed inside. I didn't slam his door, but I didn't say goodbye either. I've never been jumped before, all over a nigga that isn't even mine. When I got in the house, I slammed the door and that's when I realized Daddy was home.

"Gem why you are slamming...What the fuck happened?" He ditched the first part of his sentence once he saw my hair and me holding my broken purse.

Isaac Clark was handsome and looking at his eyes always felt like I was looking into mine because they were so identical. He had a black curly mini fro he kept lined up and his thick sideburns connected to his full black beard. The grade of hair he had was so nice that even his beard had waves in them. Daddy was mixed with Indian from his dad's side, he was my complexion and didn't look forty.

"I was jumped coming from the store," I said, throwing my purse down on the couch.

"Jumped!? Hell naw!" He went behind our navy-blue sectional couch and grabbed his shot gun.

"Daddy it's ok, I did what you taught me and messed up one bad. Then her sister tried to sneak me, but she failed. I'm just pissed right now, please don't do anything."

He stood there holding his gun and looking at me. "You know I don't play that shit, Coya. I don't give a damn how many of them it was. A bullet will put all of them down." His face was like a big Pitbull ready to attack.

"I know, but I don't want any of that. I'm not scared and if they want it, it's on. I just wanna go lay down, my head hurts." I hugged his waist and he kissed the top of my head, hugging me back.

"Ok, I'll chill but next time, all I want to hear is names. Did you see your Mama?"

"Yup, she said hi." I said laughing as I headed up to my room.

"Dumb ass bitches." I said lowly after I took my clothes off, put my pajama shirt on and went into my bathroom.

Turning the light on I got to examine my face and body. Aside from my hair being wild I had a long scratch across my neck. It was starting to welp up and it pissed me off even more. My face and body were important to me. No I don't eat all the things I'm supposed to. But I work out, drink my gallon of water a day and keep my skin blemish free.

I want to be an actress and I know that physical appearance is important. After I put some ointment on my neck, I put my bundles in a ponytail and put my scarf on. Before I could make it to my bed, my phone chimed the Facetime ringtone. It was my girls and I knew that meant they knew what went down, it didn't take long for a fight to get posted on social media.

"Coya what the fuck!"

I hated I laughed but it was funny that as soon as I answered they screamed that in unison. Their faces were just like my Daddy's and they were hyped all the way up.

"When I saw the video, it took me a minute to understand what I was seeing!"

"How did that happen, I was just on the phone with you?!"

"Who started it, was it because of Austin!?"

"We saw him put you in his truck, is he at your house!?"

I mean my boos were throwing a million questions at me all at once. They were talking at one time and I didn't know where to start. I wasn't tripping though because this is how we were about each other.

"Ok this is what happened. I went to the store. Toni called me while I was in there and once we hung up, I paid for my stuff. Getting outside, their Volkswagen pulled up and they got out. I don't think they knew I was there because of their reaction when they saw me. Of course, Nicole started talking shit about me and Austin.

Then she gets in my face talem'bout if I and y'all stay out the Legend Brother's face then ain't no beef. So, I snapped because y'all know how I don't like no bitch in my face being disrespectful. The fight that was recorded was exactly how it went down.

Austin came out of nowhere; I don't even know how he got there. All I know was he pulled me back and threw my ass in his truck. I honestly didn't care what he was talking about, I was so heated I told him to just take me home. He did and now we're here." I ran every detail down to them in one breath.

"Damn, well at least you fucked Nicole up and Brittany for trying to sneak you." Brinx said.

I laid across my bed, grabbing my custom pillow Daddy had made for me. It was a collage of pictures of none other than the fabulous *Angela Bassett.*

"Well, all that is nice but it's on sight when we see them again, Coya. At the end of the day they still jumped you and that don't sit well with my spirit." Jurnee spoke with her bonnet and Grandma gown on.

"Pooh it is really hard for me to take you serious looking like Madea," I said laughing and all of us started cracking up.

They calmed me down, I talked to them for about two hours. Daddy made some fried chicken, corn on the cobb and mash potatoes. After I ate, it was seven in the evening and I decided to go to lay down. I scrolled social media and as y'all know, them Talbert sisters were talking all kinds of shit. They were pissed off about how I beat Nicole ass, saying I used a bottle and hit her.

Just all kinds of excuses instead of just saying even with me being jumped, I still fucked one of them up. Before I put my phone down, I saw Nicole had a new IG story. My nosey ass watched it and it was a Boomerang video (meaning it's the same clip on repeat). The video was a truck parked outside her house and the caption said *At the end of the day, he right here.*

See, this that being funny shit I hated bitches to do. I got up, took my pajama shirt off and put on a cute top. I took my bundles down from the scarf and ponytail and took some cute selfies. I was naturally a beauty, so I didn't need any makeup or lashes. Then I put on Kash Doll-*Everybody* and recorded a quick video of me rapping the lyrics.

When I posted it on my IG story, I captioned it *These hoes getting beat up over fun size niggas with fun size dicks.* It was a shot at her and Austin because he did that lame talk about, she ain't his bitch. Yeah right, my eyes don't lie, and he sure is over there aiding her. I was over today. Putting my phone on silent I sat it on the nightstand and got comfortable in bed.

I just wanted to put this whole day behind me. I woke up at midnight and grabbed my phone. When I unlocked it I had so many Instagram and Facebook notifications. But that's not what caught my attention. I had some missed calls from a number I didn't know. It was 313 so I knew it was from Detroit.

Before I called it, I looked at it again because the last three digits looked familiar. Going to Austin's Instagram page, I scrolled down. Some of their wild basement parties they threw he'd post his number telling girls to text if they wanna come. I looked at the number and it was a match; Austin was blowing me up. I laughed hard because I knew it was because of my IG story but the thing is, I'm not entertaining any of it tonight. I went to the bathroom, then got back in bed to watch TV until I fall back to sleep.

AUSTIN 'KID' LEGEND

I'm a ho, I know I'm a ho (I am)
But don't you call me that, lil' nigga, that shit come with the smoke
I'm a ho, got bitches galore
How many Instagram models I done fucked on before?
I lost count, I don't even know

Myself, Adrian, August and the homie Chill were having one of our many turn ups in our basement. I hit up a few of IG models, strippers and money so thick in here that the floor wasn't seen. Summer, winter, spring or fall, we turn up at least two times a month. Pussy Patrol was what Chill always said we were.

I had my phone out on IG live showing off this fat ass dancing on me and the money I was pouring on her. Shit was smooth as fuck tonight and then all of a sudden, Audrey came down here in true Chaos mode. He ripped out our speaker that was built in the wall and he tossed it on the floor like it was light as a feather.

"Bro what's the deal?" August was the first to speak since he was sitting on the end of the couch where the speaker landed.

"Tha deal bro is these hoes need to get the fuck out like ten seconds ago. Come on, out!" Yo this nigga voice was based heavier than the speaker he threw.

We were looking at him like the crazy nigga he was.

"Naw, don't pick shit up, just roll." He said to the dancers when they tried to grab the money. Then this fool went in the room that Chill was in with two girls.

"Aye homie, roll that stomach up, give these bitches a tissue to wipe the cum off their faces. Party is over."

I swear I didn't want to laugh but I couldn't help it. Chill was ass naked and so were the girls. All of them were looking lost as hell; Chill was trying to ask Audrey what the problem was but he wasn't answering. Big brother was on clean up patrol tonight and it was blowing all of us. Once her literally tossed the hoes on they ass, he came back down here.

"Listen, this shit gotta stop until we handle what the fuck is going on with Darius and the rest of them. I explained this shit to y'all the other day and we agreed. I BEEN BUYING ALL THEM NIGGAS DRUGS FROM THEIR SUPPLIER! It's fair game now, we don't know how they about to move. I said NO MORE PARTIES AT OUR FUCKING HOUSE! On God, I'll burn this bitch down with y'all in it if this shit happens again."

Before we could even say anything, he walked out. We could hear him upstairs going to his room.

"My own damn Father doesn't even yell at me like that. He the homie and all but that was straight disrespectful." Chill said breaking the silence.

I looked at him with his boxers hanging off him and his shirt in his hand. "Man put yo' bra on and shut up." Me and my brothers laughed as we started cleaning up.

"The hell you taking all yo' clothes off anyways to fuck some hoes? You act like you're about to make love." Adrian cracked at him also.

"Man, I like to be comfortable when I get a nut in, fuck you. Clothes get in the way." He said, putting the rest of his clothes on. "Chaos interrupted before I could even shoot my load in them bitches' ear."

Now all of us were laughing so hard at his fool ass. All the money on the floor went in three big trash bags. Nobody kept track of who threw what so I hit two of the dancers up. They came back and we just gave it to them once they pulled up. Audrey's a straight goon for real and didn't hear shit when he was pissed.

But the fact is them girls didn't do shit but their job, so it was only right for them to get paid. Plus, we Legends so even when I hit them up and told them to pull through, they did with no hesitation. Chill rolled out shortly after we cleaned the basement up. Immediately after he left me and my brothers went to Audrey's room.

You see, Pops always told us how to respect each other to the point where we don't do the shit we did tonight. Audrey indeed did come to us and said we needed to cease on parties and having everyone over for a while. Bitches can be set up bitches and we don't need none of that with this beef we got going on.

We agreed but then turned around and went back on it, completely wrong on our part and disrespectful. We got to his door, knocked on it and he told us to come in. He had two leather recliners in his room with a black table between them. He was sitting on one of them smoking, looking in his phone. Once we all came inside, he put it down along with the blunt.

"What's up?" He asked looking at us waiting to speak.

August spoke first because that's how it normally was when the three of us were in hot water. "We just wanted to apologize about the party, it was wrong on every level."

"Yeah, our bad bro, that shit was disrespectful towards you and what we all agreed on." I added.

Audrey stood up and showed all of us some love. "I appreciate the apology and I accept, baby brothers. Bad ass niggas since y'all was born." He joked, making us laugh too. "Chill texted me right before y'all came, it's all good and ain't no need to tell Pops."

That was good to hear because he wasn't quick to relax like Audrey. After that we all just chilled at the crib. August and Adrian went to grab us some food from Happy's Pizza, we smoked of course and crashed. Tomorrow was Friday which was when report cards came in the mail for me, Adrian and August. I was just hoping for some good marks because I didn't want shit to get in the way of Myrtle Beach.

**

"The next time Audrey tells me you three acted out again and went against what he said. Not only will I beat y'all ass with a broom, but its two weeks here with me. Understood?" Mama was laying into me and my brothers.

Audrey was behind her sitting at the kitchen table laughing quietly while she chewed our asses all the way out. We were on the couch just letting her go and feeling bad like we always did if we disappointed her. Our Mama was absolutely beautiful, she had long hair that touched her butt.

Her eyes were round, and we used to think she looked like that princess from that movie *Aladdin.* Our grandmother was all black so that's what gave her that full figure with wide hips. We couldn't have been blessed with a better mother and we didn't play about her the same way we didn't play about Ava.

"Yes ma'am." We answered all together.

"Good, now let's get to this report card reading." Mama said then went to the back to get them. Just because we lived alone didn't mean she was about to let us have total freedom. She had our report cards mailed to her house. The only reason Audrey had his was because he was a senior and he got his grades earlier than we did.

"You bold as hell bro, you said you wasn't telling Pops." I spoke out first looking at my brother like I wanted to fight.

He kept laughing. "Does that look like Pops to y'all? No. Mama not telling Pops but I knew she would get on y'all. Better hope them grades make the cut." He went back to cracking up as Mama came from the back.

"Shut the hell up Audrey, leave your brothers alone." Mama came behind him hitting the back of his head.

"Ok, Adrian you're up first." She pulled the chair from the table in front of us then opened the first envelope.

Her eyes read it then she looked at him, when we didn't see a smile, I knew bro was fucked. He did too because he fell back on the couch with his hand on his head then he looked at her. Suddenly a smile went across her face.

"Three B's two A's and a C, I am very happy because the C went up from the D last card marking. Good job baby." She hugged him and gave him a kiss on the cheek.

"Hell yeah!" he yelled geeked up. "My bad Mama, I'm just happy. Ms. Lee be on sum bs with me, but I'll take the C."

August you're up next on the chopping block." Her white teeth were bright as she opened it, her brown complexion matched Adrian's perfectly. The smile got wider when she read his grades off.

"All B's and an A plus in English! I'm so proud of you sweetie."

August was grinning and pulling on his beard when she kissed his cheek. "Thank you, Mama I know I'm your favorite, so I had to deliver."

She smacked her lips, laughing and shaking her head.

"Ms. Lane stays on top of you about your work, congrats on the A plus bro." I threw the whole tree of shade at him because we knew he was fucking Ms. Lane. And if he didn't think we knew, he did now. My brothers were laughing hysterically at my joke, but August gave a fake laugh underlined with anger. Mama didn't pick it up which I knew she wouldn't.

"Let's see how you did Aussie." August said being funny with that name Mama called me sometimes.

I was a little nervous when she opened it because I knew my Biology grade was shaky as fuck. Mr. Slaughter was a hoe ass mean grinch and he gave hard ass quizzes. When Mama read, she breathed out hard and put it down.

"Damn bro." Adrian mumbled lowly so only me and him could hear it.

"Mama, I promise I'll work harder my senior year,

for real." I said trying to soften her and I gave her my sad blue eyes.

"All B's and a D minus, I'm mad but I know you did express problems with Bio. What did you think the problem was, because you only missed two days? So, for me it's like did you turn in any homework, pass the quizzes, do your assignments."

She was quiet and waited for him to answer. That's how Mama was, she wanted to get to the root on anything pertaining to us before she turns up. It was no way we could lie to her, we always said she wore some special invisible glasses that made her really see us.

"I don't know, Mama."

"Yes you do and if you don't give me a better answer there is no Myrtle Beach and you'll be here with me the rest of the summer."

Now, let's get something straight, we loved being with her. We are her boys and she cooks for us, clean up after us and just gives all the love we needed. But, that freedom we had living alone was gone. We couldn't have girls running in, we had a curfew and it was just like how it would be moving back home. Each of us would spend the night or a few days with her but not a whole summer. I breathed out and looked at her because she didn't play that looking everywhere when you spoke to her. "It was a challenging class, I got frustrated a lot and I just stopped trying. I aimed for the D just so I could pass and get out of that class. I apologize Mama, for real and whatever you decide, I'll accept." I was being real because Pops told us as men, we gotta own when we fuck up.

"Well, I have to talk to your father and decide with him what we want to do. Aside from the one mark, I am still proud of all the B's." Smiling she got up, hugged me and gave me a kiss on the cheek.

After the report card reading, we ate the food she threw down on then we were all chilling in the living room.

"Mama where you going?" Adrian asked when she came from her room and stood in one of the three full body mirrors on her dining room wall.

Her jeans she had on were tight as hell, she had a lime green blazer that stopped at her waist on and she wore these loud pink heels. Mama's face was perfect, so she never wore or needed makeup but the top of her breasts was out.

"I have a dinner date, so I need y'all to lock up when you leave."

"Whoa!" We all kind of went crazy when she said

she had a date.

It was definitely a double standard we had for our parents. Pops was a whole thot, fucking somebody's mama or auntie all the time. We praised that shit, he kept a baddie for a week, two weeks max. "That's why you didn't eat dinner with us?" Audrey asked.

He was overprotective a little more about Mama. He wanted her and Pops back together. He'd never admit it because he claimed he didn't have time for that drama which we all knew meant he was lying.

"Yes Audrey that is why I didn't eat with you guys." Mama answered after she fixed her hair. "Don't give me them eyes boy, I am grown and single." She said before going to the back again.

Audrey was mad and he got up going to the kitchen. It was funny but then again it was like looking at a child crushed because his parents were broken up.

"Oh hell no." Mama said that as she walked through the living room to the front door.

We jumped up ready for what she was talking about. We didn't know what got her hype but I low key was hoping we had to show our asses. I was in the mood today but when we got outside and saw what it was, it changed the dynamic.

"Apollo what the hell are you doing here!?"

Pops was leaning against his old school car with his arms folded. Me and my brothers sat in the lawn chairs she had on her long wide porch.

"What'chu mean what I'm doing here, you going on dates and shit. I gotta feel this nigga out." He was calm as she walked off the porch towards him.

"You called Pops, didn't you?" August asked Audrey laughing.

"Hell yeah, he needed to know." He folded his arms, looking like Pops' twin a bit more.

"You don't need to feel nobody out Apollo, do not even start that shit. Get in your car and leave." Mama pointed to his car and tried to open the door he was leaning on.

We were on the porch watching like a hawk and laughing. The two of them were crazy but Pops was further. He still loved Mama and jumps when she says but he cheated, had our sister, and Mama was done. Her and Ava had a relationship because she always felt Ava was helplessly put in the middle.

When Mama and Pops were in the same room, you'd see some flirting a little and could feel the love and respect. But you also knew Pops was crazy over her and would go to war over her.

"Can't do that, Anya." It was so damn funny how nonchalant he was acting.

Mama started massaging her forehead. "Why can't you do it?"

"Because as a concerned father, I gotta make sure this guy is ok with being around my sons. I don't know about you but the kids and their safety come first and people be crazy out here."

Me and my brothers were on the floor laughing but Mama turned up after he said that.

"Are you kidding me, them grown ass boys ain't no babies. You full of shit and this needs to stop! I don't be in none of your business. What kind of example are you setting for the boys since you wanna throw them in the middle!"

"I feel like I'm setting the best example for them. You're our fucking queen and no matter what, I gotta make sure any jokers coming to entertain makes clearance with the king." He put his hand on his chest.

Then a car pulled up behind Pops' ride; he looked at the car and then at Mama. "You fucking with a man who drives a Cooper Clubman, really Anya?"

"I swear I'm about to crack a rib from laughing so

hard." I said to my brothers between my laughter.

"I bet when he get out the car he about to have on some loafers with no socks. Watch, I bet his ankles gon' be ashy too." Pops talked shit loud and with no fucks given.

Mama's date got out the car and we were like some hyenas on the porch. The guy had on exactly what Pops said he would. He looked like this Liberian, bookkeeper type of man with a haircut.

"Gon' and get back in your car, man." Pops said to the guy before his feet could hit the sidewalk.

"Excuse me?" The bookkeeper asked.

You know me and my brothers stood up just in case Poindexter was with the shits.

"Apollo." Mama said and Pops had already grabbed her hand softly and put her behind him.

"Are you hard of hearing? Tap them red slippers you got on together and step the hell on." What he said next took us over the top. "Gon' and get."

"I swear you and your damn boys get on my nerves. Why you worrying about me, you need to be focusing on your son, his all B's and a D minus." Mama stomped off on the porch cussing Pops out as her friend pulled off. Before she walked in the house, she looked at

Audrey and popped his ear hard as hell. "I know you called him, don't touch that banana pudding in the refrigerator."

"Mama come on now, don't do me like that." Audrey followed her in the house, continuing begging.

"Come here, Austin." Pops called me.

Walking off the porch I already knew what this was about.

"The D minus was in biology?" He asked me with the same blue eyes like me. I was only 6'0 like Adrian and August, so he had a few over me.

I was that same light skin complexion as him, with thick wide sideburns that connected to my beard and lip. My hair was long, I kept it in some corn rolls all the time I let Adrian ink my arms, chest and back up. We started when I was fifteen and still add some from time to time.

"Yes sir it was, I just gave up but it won't be like that my senior year, Pops."

He was in thought, I could tell how he was looking at me.

"I'ma give you two choices. You can go to Myrtle Beach and do seven days with your Mama. Or you can skip the trip and do two weeks with your Mama, and you already know that means no going to the house or driving. Y'all know those are the rules, so it's your choice."

This was a no brainer. "Seven days here and Myrtle Beach." I answered quickly and excited because I could still go on the trip.

"Ok. But let me explain something to you; if you get anything below a C your senior year. You will be moving with me the remainder of the school year and I will make you take a summer course."

"Yes sir." I held my hands up in defense. "I promise no giving up, I'm on it, Pops."

He smiled, gave me a hug and kissed the top of my head. "I am proud of them B's though. Go tell yo' brothers to come here and bring their report cards."

I did what he said when I went in the house. I sat down and smashed two bowls of banana pudding then I headed out. I needed to make a stop somewhere.

**

Me: Let me pull up on you real quick

Barbie: I'm busy.

Me: Stop making me chase you around Coya

Barbie: I'm not making you do anything I'm real life busy. I gotta shoot moves all day.

Me: Quit playing.

Barbie: I'm dead ass bro, I got moves to shoot with my homies.

Me: Scary ass.

Barbie: I ain't scared of shit it's money to be made on the floor. If I got time later I'll hit yo' line.

Me: Yo' why tha fuck you talking to me like I'm some bop

Coya had me so fucked up I felt like she violated me on every level. First she put that wack ass IG story up, calling me and my dick fun size. My phone was blowing up about her story and when I saw it, I had to get at her. I got her number from Brinx after I practically begged her.

I didn't give a damn how crazy I came off, I wanted to check her ass. But she never answered my calls, texts or DMs. Today I was getting at her no matter what, but I figured I'd text one more time before I flagged her down and y'all saw how she talked. I can't have that, so sitting in my truck about to locate.

"What can I do for you again, Austin?" Brinx answered when I called her, my brother gave me her number.

"I need another favor." I answered turning my air conditioner up.

"At this point you are about to be forever indebted to me."

I chuckled and said, "I got'chu."

Brinx breathed out hard. "I'm listening."

"Where is Coya at? She being a thumb thug on social media but won't face me. So I need to make her." I wasn't about to lie, Coya was on my list but in a good way.

"Um, are you going to kill her?" Brinx asked me.

"I'ma kill that pussy."

"Oh my goodness Austin!" She yelled and laughed at the same time. "I didn't need to know that!"

"You asks asked and I told you, so where she at?" I could hear her moving around.

"Why are you hounding me, Austin." Coya's voice spoke into the phone.

I always thought her sexy brown skin ass was so fine, like a Barbie. We had two classes together our junior year and I'd talk to her from time to time. Coya was busy with school plays, and her vo-tech stuff. But I love how she still made time to hang and her personality was dope from the little I know.

"Aye where you at man, I'm done with this phone shit." I took my gear out of park and started driving. I bet she tell where she's at.

Giggling she said, "I'm at Brinx house, her dad is home just so you know."

"Man I don't care, I'm not about to bring no heat to the door. I wanna scoop you and holla at you. Send me the addy and I'll be there soon." I hung up and she texted me in less than five minutes. Not to sound cocky, but women always gave in to me and my brothers eventually.

I pulled up to Brinx's crib, got out, walked up her walkway and rang her doorbell.

"What the hell is in the air? I went from only seeing you Legends at the scrap metal to having yo' brother and now you on my porch. Now, I know you're not here to reup on weapons, so what can I do for you?"

I ran my hand over my face laughing because Robert was wild. He didn't play about Brinx so I could imagine how hard of a time he gave August. "I'm here to pick up Coya, she said she was here."

"You know she's like my daughter too, hell I have five of them. So, what are your other two brothers dating Jurnee and Toni—"

"Ooook, Daddy although you are very much appreciated, you're needed elsewhere." Brinx came downstairs pulling his arm and dragging him from the front door.

Coya came outside laughing and shaking her head.

"Have fun boo, call me later." She said to Coya while closing the door.

"Not too much fucking fun!" I heard Robert yell before it closed.

"He crazy as hell." I said, now laughing and shaking my damn head.

"Definitely is, he'll be telling my Dad but I'll handle that later." She got inside my truck after I opened the door for her.

"Ok, gone ahead and cuss me out."

I scrunched my face up looking from the road to her. "What?"

"I know this is about my IG story, your ego was hit, and everybody saw it. So, go ahead." She put her hand on her ear like she was waiting to listen.

Coya was slim in the waist but had a little something to squeeze on. She wore another one of those cute dresses she had on the last time I saw her. This one was green; her feet were in them fur Ugg slides all the girls wore this summer.

Her hair straight and so long that it laid on her pretty brown thighs. Her lips were juicy as hell and she had some shiny stuff on them. I gotta be honest and admit as fine as Coya was, I didn't think about her on any level until recently. Yeah, we flirted and shit in school, but I always left it at that.

"Man ain't nobody about to cuss yo' ass out, if I was I would have did it back at Brinx's crib. I don't give a damn about Robert standing there. I know you got a lot of moves to shoot so I wanna get at'chu before you get too busy." I said sarcastically to her referring to our text conversation.

Coya smacked her lips and chuckled. I pulled into Crazy Crab on Telegraph because I was hungry as hell and every Detroit chick loved to eat them some good ass seafood. We got out and walked inside.

"I love to eat here, you sure you can afford it?" Her voice had humor in it as we looked at the menu.

"You stay with the fresh jokes huh, come give me a hug."

It was cute when she rolled her eyes with a smirk on her face. You know that cute shit you girls did when y'all like a nigga. Blush and get turned on in the same time. Even though she rolled her eyes she still made her way to me. I was looking plain today in some Nike shorts, J's on my feet and a fitted blue t-shirt on.

I went to the shop yesterday; got some fresh

cornrows and I had my diamond studs in my ears. I wrapped my arms around her waist and her sweet scent smelled good. Once we were done, I stayed leaned against the wall and she was on the side of me. Looking down to get a better look at her feet, I noticed her toes were done like always.

"You got some pretty ass feet."

"Thank you, so it is true what's said about you in school. You like feet?" She flipped that long hair behind her back.

I normally didn't like chicks with all that weave but Coya always made it sexy.

"I mean I ain't walking around putting bitches' feet in my mouth unless it's my woman and I haven't had one of those in two years. But yeah, I got a thang for some pretty feet, always have since I was little." I admitted with no shame. I loved some pretty feet; it was something about it.

I think it started with Mama, she would be gone all day when we were little. When she came home her hair would be different, so would her feet and nails. It was something that stood out about her feet, so I started looking at other women's feet first.

If they didn't look nice like my Mama's I swear I

used to think they were so ugly. I don't care if they not painted up, just be clean and not ashy and don't have no corns, bunions or hair on them toes. I'd straight clown you, I swear I would.

"I take it my feet make the cut?" She asked me then me and her ordered our seafood bag. I got the cajun flavor one and she got the lemon pepper flavor.

"Everything about you makes the cut, Barbie." I took it upon myself to pull her closer to me.

"You do know a Barbie is tall, thin and white, yet you call me that."

"And do you know that there are black ones out, too. Perfect waist, sexy legs, nice lips, gorgeous skin and some full titties." When I named all the parts I made sure to lightly squeeze hers, even them titties she got. I squeezed her left one a little and put my hands back on her waist. I did the shit so smoothly she didn't have time to be shocked but them cheeks were flushed.

"You sound like you jacked off to her when you were little." She laughed at her own joke, cute ass. "Why you all on me anyway, don't you have a whole bitch?"

Now I was annoyed. "What bitch I got, Coya?"

"Nicole, I mean you went over her house to check on her after the ass beating I put down on her. I saw her

IG story when she was talking shit, your truck was outside her house." She loved from off me with her arms folded and a slight attitude.

"Yeah I did go over there to check on her but that's all. Look, I can be a good nigga without making a chick mine. Now don't get me wrong, some of these hoes will have me on some disrespectful shit if they pop off first. But all around I try to have some decency when it comes to dealing with females," I told her truthfully.

"Well why you deal with her rat ass?" Coya turned her nose up making a nasty face.

"Because when she sucks my dick she spits my nut out like Triple H."

Not only did she laugh so hard with her hand over her mouth but the two chicks who were in here with us did too. Shit, I was being real as hell.

"I cannot believe you just said that out loud, Austin."

I shrugged my shoulders. "I don't care. So, you still fucking around with that lame Lorenzo?" I had no beef with him, I thought every nigga was lame except for my brothers and Chill.

"I haven't seen him face to face, he's in New York with his family. But we text here and there. Why, you

235

jealous?" She asked in a teasing way.

I waved her off cackling. "Stop it girl, I just asked because after today that's gone have to cease and desist."

"Boy bye! It will take more than some good seafood for me to put all my attention in you."

"You ain't gotta put all of it, just 99%." I gave her a half smile and she did that cute eye roll again.

Once we got our food, I opened the door for her so we could head out. As we were walking in a white woman and her three sons were walking in. They looked like some shit off a SyFy movie. Pale as hell, dark circles and they hair was this weird blonde color. Coya noticed it too. She gave the kids this fake closed mouth smile. Me on the other hand, I couldn't hold that shit in.

"Damn, yo' kids look like they bite."

"Oh my gosh!" Coya yanked my arm hard as hell out the door with her hand over her mouth.

The lady scoffed at me and they went inside.

"Austin!" She hit my arm with tears in her eyes. "I feel so bad for laughing but I couldn't help it. I swear you need a muzzle on your mouth."

After I helped her in my truck I got inside, set our food in the back and pulled off.

"You know I was right, ugly ass kids." I cut my

blinker on so I could make a left.

"Where to now?" Coya asked me.

"My crib." I side-eyed her, waiting to see her reaction.

"I am not stepping foot in that basement, who knows what I'll catch."

I laughed. "Girl for one, we get that shit deep cleaned after every party. Two, nobody said shit about the basement."

"Mmhm, I've seen you and Nicole's Lives and that's always where she's at." This time she rolled her eyes had with an attitude.

"That's because that's where the hoes go. You need to quit arguing and fighting, Barbie's don't do that." I said turning down my block.

"I'll never argue with a bitch who reeks of she doesn't wipe front to back again."

Now I was cracking up at her slick mouth. "Yo' you wild as fuck, let's go in and eat."

As soon as we got inside Audrey was in the living room watching TV and Ava was laying on the recliner. Her big comforter she kept over here was wrapped up all around her because the air was on. Our basement door in the kitchen was open and I could hear August, Adrian and

Chill down there playing the game.

"Ooo I love *JoJo Siwa!*" Coya pointed to the white girl on Ava's comforter.

"Me too, my brothers always tease me about loving her." Ava sat up with a wide smile.

"I swear y'all some Valley girls. This my sister Ava, Av's this is Coya." I introduced them. "Big bro!" I greeted Audrey and gave him a pound.

"Sup bro, what's good Coya." He spoke to us while he continued laying on the couch.

"Hey Audrey, are you done messing with my friend?" She asked him sitting on the stool in front of our wide kitchen counter.

"I ain't got time for that damn girl. Where she at anyways?"

"Didn't you just say you don't have time but then you wanna know where she's at." Coya was laughing like I was.

I sat two Faygo Red pop cans down for us and some napkins.

"Anytime he says he ain't got time for something, it means he full of shit." I told her, cracking open one of my king crab legs.

Coya got a pound of snow crabs with shrimp,

potatoes and corn. I got a pound of king crab with two lobster tails, corn and potatoes.

"Oh shit! You like my pooh Jurnee!?" Coya started teasing him and being girly with it.

"Awwww Audrey you have a crush!" Ava teased as well.

"Man bro shut yo' damn girl and yo' sista up." Audrey's deep voice made us laugh harder.

"I am not his girl, we are bff's and you better make a move on. Jurnee's already into Eddie."

He got up, walked to the kitchen and opened the refrigerator, grabbing a can of pop. "Fuck that nigga, he's only doing what I allow." After he opened his pop, he went back to the living room.

His face made her stop laughing. "Is that why y'all call him Chaos?"

"Don't pay that fool no mind. Let's get back to what you just said, I ain't no damn bff. That shit sound hella off, like we about to go rotate our nipples together over coffee."

"I just don't understand the things that come out your mouth. Who the hell winds their nipples up." Her laughter made her teeth show and they were perfect.

I was being a pervert watching her suck the butter

out her crab legs. I liked that she wasn't trying to eat all pretty. But them big lips and her face made me stare even without trying.

"You so damn fine Barbie, I just wanna put yo' whole body in my mouth, wig and all." Licking my lips, I imagined her tasting way better than this Cajun butter.

Coya almost choked on her shrimp because she was laughing at what I said. "Punk first of all it's not a wig, it's a sew-in." Giggling she put a shrimp in her mouth.

"Coya, you wanna watch the season when *JoJo Siwa* was on *Dance Moms*?" Ava came in the kitchen and asked her.

"Hell yes—"

"Hell no, I brought her over here for me, Ava. You better tell Audrey to get his glitter out and watch it with you." I said the end part loud on purpose so Audrey could hear me.

He put his middle finger in the air making all of us laugh.

Ava smacked her lips. "All my friends are out of town, I like Coya."

"I'll tell you what, let me hang with your brother for a few and I'll come watch it with you." Coya said those words like I really was about to let her dip on me.

Ava got geeked with what she said and went back to sit down on the recliner.

We finished eating, talking and messing with Audrey's bothered ass. Chill, August and Adrian came up and we all kicked with them for a minute. Then me and her went upstairs to my room.

"Now why don't we ever see y'all rooms on any Live videos?" Coya asked when she got inside and took her slides off.

She walked over to the wall looking at my black and white couple I had on my wall. It was a picture I got from Amazon of a black couple. The guy had his arms around the woman's neck, he had a crown on, and he was looking down at her. She was naked with her ass facing us, she had a crown on also and her hair was in an afro.

"Are you ready to see what teachers we have for the fall?" Coya asked me.

I was taking my J's off and putting them on my shoe rack me and Pops built. "Yup, I gotta keep up all good grades too. I got a D minus in bio, my Pops and Mama were digging in me tough. Mr. Slaughter a damn bitch." I turned the light off in my closet and closed the door.

"Yes he is, he gave me a C plus as hard as I worked

241

my ass off. I'm glad to leave him behind, I hope I get Ms. Kern for English 4."

"Damn, I didn't say you could get on my bed." I messed with her while she climbed on my king size bed.

My room had tan carpet, a chocolate brown leather bed frame with matching chocolate brown dressers. I put some tan black out curtains up because I hated that sunlight in my face in the morning. My 50-inch TV was mounted to the wall and under it was my long dresser with my PS4 sitting on top of it.

"I know you didn't think I was about to sit on the floor?" She sat up with her feet under her.

"On the floor, on my bed, on my face, you can sit wherever you want." I answered her, while flipping through Netflix. I decided to put on *Moesha* because I had started watching it yesterday.

"Austin you are a freak." She chuckled and said.

"A big one." I looked at her hands on her thighs. "Why are your nails different colors?" I asked looking at them. She had one of her nails blue, the other green, one orange, her ring finger pink and her pinky finger yellow.

"Because I asked all five of my niggas what color should I get." She wiggled her fingers laughing.

I laughed too. "You talk so much shit Barbie." I

yanked her on top of me and brought her down to my face. Her scent mixed with mine and her body felt good. "You look scared."

"Nothing about you scares me, Mr. Legend, you're not dealing with a virgin. But that doesn't mean you're dealing with someone who will just open her legs because of your last name." Her voice was low, and she slowly started dry humping me.

My hands squeezed her waist then I was sliding her dress up. I made sure to move slow and let my fingertips lightly tickle her skin. "Understandable, but I'm not asking you to open your legs because of my last name."

"Oh really, then for what?" Her lips were so close to mine that they grazed mine.

I could feel her ass exposed and as much as I wanted to squeeze it. I wanted to do it with her dress off first, so I continued moving it up slow.

"Do it because you know you want to." I was hard as a brick and her lips were looking good. I ran my tongue between them and Coya sucked on it.

The next thing I know, we were in a kiss war. Those lips felt as good as they looked, I eased her dress off and my hands went on her smooth back. Her bra was strapless, the same color as her dress and she had a thong on. When her soft hands went under my shirt they landed on my chest. Sitting up with her still on me I took it off and we went back to kissing.

Coya undid my Nike shorts and we both took them off along with my boxers. I sat back and watched her take her bra off. She wasn't top heavy; I'd say a B cup but them nipples were a sexy brown just like her skin. I sat up and sucked on them making her moan out while her hands were in my head, rubbing my braids.

"Damn your dick is huge." She said lowly while looking at me put a Magnum on it.

I looked at her once I had it on and said, "I thought you said it was fun size?"

Her eyebrow arched up. "I'm not ashamed to admit I was wrong."

I laid down flat on my back with my hands behind my head. I arched my right leg up with my foot flat on my bed. Pulling Coya to me, I took her right leg and put it under mine. Then I put her left leg over mine that was lying flat. It's like we were tangled up but in the best way that would give me all pussy and her all dick.

"Put it in." I instructed her.

Grabbing my hard ten-inch, her fingers couldn't

even touch cause I was so thick. She lifted up some and positioned it in her hole and she slid down some.

"Whew, shit." She moaned out while coming down on me slowly.

I just watched while she bit her bottom lip and was letting me stretch her open. Once she was all the way down, Coya froze. I figured I'd help her out, so I grinded my hips a little and she took over soon after.

"Come on, I want that pussy to fuck this fun size dick you claim I got." I talked shit to her.

Coya got the groove and I massaged them titties while her body moved like a deep wave from the ocean. I had her gone; I mean she had her head back and was moaning something crazy. Her hands were behind her flat on her back.

"Uhhh Austin oh my damn, boy. Ssss oooo."

I have never seen a girl moan, shiver and fuck my dick at the same time. As many girl's as I have fucked, this was a first and my ego was growing with what I was doing to her body. Sitting up some, I grabbed her and flipped her on her back with me still inside of her.

Putting her feet on my chest I started tearing that pussy all the way up. I laughed to myself watching her squeeze my arms tight and her eyes rolled to the back of her head. I mean she looked like a possessed sexy demon and with an angelic voice calling my name.

How the hell is that possible? I moved her feet off me, leaned down and tongue kissed her while I slowed my pace down. This time I had to laugh out loud.

"Damn, this fun size got'chu all fucked up." I kissed her lips.

"Shut up Austin, oh my gosh I can't breathe. Feel my heart." She placed my hand on her chest and her heart was beating so fast I could feel it like it was physically in my hand.

I started tongue kissing her neck then I attacked her ear with my tongue. "You want me to stop, huh Barbie? Is the dick too much for you?" I was whispering in her ear.

"Yeah, I think I need to pull out and let you collect yourself for a minute." I took just a half an inch of my dick out and her walls grabbed hold of me, pleading me not to leave it. "Oh shit, she ain't tryna let me go."

I gave her one more kiss then I pulled out because I wanted her back on top again.

When I pulled out, the condom was so wet her juices dripped on my bed. I laid back and watched her get on top. As soon as she opened her legs, more of her juices dripped out all on my dick and stomach.

I swear I wanted to ask her was she a fucking Mermaid, I was two seconds away from singing *Under The Sea* the way Ava does. I had Coya busting back to back so many times. By the time I exploded in the condom, I felt every ounce of my energy fade away and we fell asleep until around seven pm.

JURNEE

"I will have the Tuscan chicken sandwich with extra grilled tomatoes and a bottle of water." I placed my order with the cashier at Panera Bread, my favorite place to eat a good salad and soup. Today, however, I really wanted a sandwich.

"Ok and what can I get you sir?" The cashier asked Eddie.

"I'll have a Ruben full sandwich with a can of Pepsi."

"Alright will that be all to complete your order?" She asked him as he pulled his wallet out.

We'd been talking on the phone and hanging out for the past few days. He's a cool guy who makes me laugh and he's fine as hell. It's been cool hanging out with him except for one problem.

"Damn so you not gon' pay for my food homie? That just hurt my feelings. I mean after all the time we've spent together."

The sound of his voice made my blood pressure

shoot back up along with my annoyance. "Please shut up." I said turning back to look at him.

His tall, cocky ass got on my nerves. I wanted to smack them dreads off his head and snatch those blue eyes out their sockets. So let me tell y'all the shit this nigga has done for the past seven days. He calls me all the time, which I don't know how he even got my number because he won't tell me.

He texts, sends me selfies, tag me on videos he posts on his IG, Facebook and SnapChat. Then he follows me when I got out with Eddie, yup he follows us, but claims he's not. Yesterday he mysteriously popped up when me and Eddie went Go Kart racing. At the movies the day before, someone started throwing popcorn at us from the row behind.

We both looked back and guess who was sitting there with a bucket of popcorn bigger than my head? The first time he popped up was when Eddie took me golfing. Now it's a big golf course so we both didn't think anything of it when we saw him.

But he started setting up next to us then he claimed I was cheating on him. Eddie believed him at first until I explained to him that me and Audrey have not and will never be an item. Now here he is today yet again and it's really pissing me off.

"I am so sorry for all of this, I can't believe you're still even interested in me." I told Eddie giving him a half smile when we sat down with our food.

"I trust you and if you say ain't shit going on between y'all then I believe you. I don't mind him playing his self over something he'll never have."

Audrey snickered loudly while he opened his food; he was sitting at the table next to ours. Me and Eddie were in a two-person booth on purpose.

I ignored him and focused on Eddie. "That's really sweet, next time we should double date with Miles and Toni." I said taking a small bite of my sandwich. I normally do not eat in front of boys but I didn't want to seem rude. That's why I was taking small bites and I'll just eat the rest at home.

"We can do that, my boy digging Toni even though they see other people. Their thang is weird as fuck." We both laughed.

"It is but they are into each other so I think it will be fun." I told him taking a gulp of my bottled water.

"Anything I get to do with you is lit." Eddie flirtatiously said then he winked at me. He was in an Adidas beater with some track pants and Adidas high-top gym-shoes.

I kept it pretty chill to in some burnt orange denim biker shorts with a tie dye light blue crop top that had orange graphic letters on it. I had a hoodie around my waist, even though I took it off that day at Belle Isle, I still wore them. I don't know, I just wasn't comfortable being with Eddie without it. He's never done anything to me, I just didn't feel as confident as I did at Belle Isle.

I blushed and put my hand on top of his; I promise I didn't expect the next thing that happened to happen. A bunch of hard cold pieces came at us like rain. It took a few seconds to realize it was ice.

Looking at Audrey he was leaning back in the chair all unbothered holding his cup of ice. He was pouring some in his hand and just throwing it at us like it was nothing. People were staring and laughing which made it more embarrassing.

"Yo' my nigga how long you about to keep making a fool out yo'self? This shit getting old as hell especially when she keep saying she not fucking with you." Eddie blocked the ice that was coming at him with his hand and arm.

I had enough, got up, marched over to Audrey pulling him out his chair and towards the exit. Once we got outside, I slammed him against the brick wall. Now, this boy was taller and had a stocky build, so I knew I wasn't hurting him.

"What is your problem Audrey, why are you doing this to me when I've done nothing to you!? I'm over this shit with you, we never spoke in school or at any kickbacks so what, are you bored or something? And you better give me a straight answer, or I swear I will slap you." I pushed him again in his chest, this time he didn't move.

"I like this rough side of you, it's hella sexy, Jurnee." His voice was deep, intense but still soft and had you feel the sex in it if that's even possible. He had on this forest green and white v-neck shirt that had the word Gucci across it. The color was a perfect match against his light skin, and those black neck length dreads were half up and half down.

The ponytail was on top of his head making the dreads sprout out. Those thick black eyebrows, black beard and pink medium lips made his blue eyes pop. The tattoos, his arms, height, voice...what the hell was happening? I needed to stop and remember that I do not like him, and he has been fucking up my social life for days.

"Stop playing games and tell me what your problem is and what the hell do you want?" I stopped pushing him and let him speak.

"You, my problem is you and I want you." He looked serious as hell them crystal blue eyes were a hypnotic dream.

But I wasn't buying it. "Audrey, Chaos, whatever your name is. You do not want me, you like to play yoyo with girls and I'm not the one."

"Correction, I play yoyo with hoes, bitches, bops and an occasional rat. But girls who I see potential in, I don't yoyo with. I told yo' ass we go together after you kissed me at the Isle."

I laughed and shook my head, "I was proving a point to your chick Regina."

"Quit calling that damn bitch my chick, all we did was woopty woop'd." He cackled like this was a joke. "Look, stop hanging with Stewie Griffin in there and hang with me."

I covered my mouth because he did not just call Eddie Stewie Griffin. His head was shaped kind of weird which is why he wore a fitted hat all the time.

"I'm not your type and you're not mine so please just leave me and him alone. You're causing unnecessary drama—"

"Did you or did you not kiss me in front of everybody at the Isle? Yes or no." He cut me off.

"Yes but that doesn't mean we go together!" I was getting so frustrated because he was so sexy and his demeanor was as if he didn't care.

"Yeah the fuck it does Jurnee, you the yin to my yang."

I laughed so hard I was holding my stomach; he smiled while just looking at me laugh.

"You sound so crazy, read my lips. We. Are. Not. Together. I'm not the yin to your yang and you do not want me, you will never have—"

He yanked me hard to his chest and before I could react, his lips were on mine. This kiss wasn't like the one I gave him at Belle Isle. It was more tongue, my hands were down by my side and he had his grip around my waist. His lips, oh my God, why did they have to be so soft and why did his breath have to smell good?

More importantly, why am I enjoying this? I'm getting wet and I feel like I want more. His chest against mine felt warm like butter on a hot steak. I had to almost beat my own ass to snap to get back to reality. Once we broke apart, all I could do was push him again.

"The more you fight me Jurnee, the more I won't stop." His face was still desirable because that just wasn't changing. But he looked like in two seconds he would explode.

I still didn't back down and I left him standing outside in the heat while I went back to Eddie. I knew after our date I wasn't going to be able to kiss him, not after I just made out with Audrey. I was so glad he left and didn't pop up anymore while me and Eddie hung out.

**

"Mom, this process takes so long, thanks for coming here to do it."

Mom came over to do this treatment once a month because I had to much hair and not enough patience. I was so proud of her because for the past three years, she had been doing good. Staying at the same job for more than a month, paying her bills and just keeping a good routine. Mom was sort of a hippie and as groovy as that sounds, it's far from it when you're over thirty and with a kid. Lately she has been smiling more, being responsible and sticking to her commitments.

"You are very welcome Fuzzy, anything for you. I

know your dad can't do this and hair salons are not hip to this treatment. Hold your head down, were going to get you under the dryer then washing it out. Those natural curls are going to pop, Fuzzy." We both giggled.

Since I was a little girl, my Mom has done the same hair treatment on both out heads. We had pretty hair, but it was just so big and curly. I'm talking like *Tia* and *Tamera* from *Sister Sister* season 1. So, she made up this treatment, avocado, mayonnaise, raw honey, an egg, half a banana and argan oil in a blender.

She blends it for a few seconds, parts my hair and puts it all over from my root to the end. Then I sit under the dryer for about twenty minutes and we wash it out. My hair feels so soft, smells amazing and gives my curls so much life. I used to do it, or my dad would help but he makes a big mess. It's so funny but it makes the process longer.

"I like how y'all talking about me like I'm not here." He came out the kitchen holding a beer. "My living room looks like a damn hair shop."

"Well you won't let us go in your precious man cave in the basement." I told him as Mom put a cap over my head.

"Hell naw, y'all ain't about to funk up my

basement."

"Blake shut up, it doesn't even smell in here. Don't you have somewhere to be or some game to watch." Her and him played like this all the time, they got along pretty well.

"I do but I want yo' daughter to tell you about this football head shape nigga she is dating." He said, sitting down in the dining room chair in front of me.

"His head is not shaped like a football." I laughed, throwing one of my scrunchies at him.

"Yeah he does, Janeika, don't let her lie to you. I don't even trust his parents because they didn't shape his head when he was a baby. That means they make bad decisions."

Me and Mom were on the floor laughing, I finally got under the dryer while they finished talking and laughing. I was on my phone scrolling Facebook when I saw Regina sharing all these memes. One said *If you sleep with someone's nigga make sure you can fight because bitches dragging bitches these days.*

Then another one was saying *Niggas only cheat with big booty ugly girls because they feel sorry for them.* It was so many and I was reading the comments, some people were asking was she throwing shade. Then her and her sisters went on and on about how they weren't going to say any names. But then they started posting these GIFs of people walking funny with big booties.

They even posted GIFs of *Sister Sister* with their curly hair. People were laughing and saying they know who the jokes were about. It was so many jokes, memes and people laughing. Saying how desperate I was and how all Audrey wanted was his dick sucked. No, they weren't saying my name or his per say but I'm not stupid. I had to blink fast to stop from crying.

"Ok Fuzzy twenty-minutes is all up. You ok?" Mom asked me when she lifted the top of the dryer.

"Yes I'm fine, just sleepy." I lied. For the rest of the time Mom did my hair, I was quiet. I just wanted to go to my room and lay down.

After Mom left, I put my hair in a bonnet, took a shower and laid down. Mom stayed and had dinner with us, we got some KFC. Now I was laying down with Gizmo and Bear laying on both sides of my bed. Anytime I was sad or mad they would only want to be around me. My phone chimed and I saw it was an IM.

SwagWordz: Sup girl, haven't heard from you today.

I smiled when he wrote me, we were sending each

other IMs all the time. Talking about some of everything and of course sharing some writing. I wrote another short story a few days ago and posted it. I was starting to get more people commenting great feedback. I couldn't believe people wanted more of my stories.

I even took it a step further and started posting IG models as visuals for some of my characters. The most honest feedback I got though was from SwagWordz. He encouraged me, gave me great critique and even let me do the same for him. I loved the feeling I get when we IM. It's just sometimes I feel like I'm being a complete fool, like I'm into a robot or something.

Who sits behind a keyboard or phone telling a complete stranger personal things? Talking all night, all day and sharing my writing with him. It's crazy but I can't stop, I feel like I'm talking to a close friend or someone more than a friend. I need help, I know.

PenQueen: Hey you. I was busy all today, I actually was just thinking about you. How was your day?

SwagWordz: I understand how that can be. My day was pretty good, handled some business and got some *Panera Bread.*

I did not have to be grinning so hard, *Panera Bread* is my favorite. Not a lot of guys like that place.

PenQueen: You like Panera Bread?

SwagWordz: It's recently become my favorite place, listen I wanted to talk to you about something.

That's never a good thing. Maybe he's about to tell me he's forty or married with kids. Or I'll probably wind up on a *WETV* special about teens talking to inmates. I was so nervous but then I calmed down because no one knew about SwagWordz. I could just suck the Catfish up and move on.

PenQueen: What's up?

SwagWordz: What do you think about finally meeting?

Oh shit. My stomach dropped and I was just staring at my screen. We never ever talked about meeting and that was one of the things I liked. The image he or she has had of me could be totally blown if I'm revealed. I don't think I'm ugly at all I just know I don't have the shape of a Victoria Secret model.

Not everyone likes thighs, booty and wide hips. I'm the only person in school who is shaped like I am, and it bothered me. I know what's on IG and rappers' videos but that's Hollywood and internet fame. To say I was scared wouldn't even help describe how I was feeling.

SwagWordz: I just think we brush over it and it's

time to see if the vibe is the same if not better in person.

Oh boy, I just need to be honest. I was about to type, my fingers were on the letters. But my nerves got the best of me and I just blocked him. I decided not to get on social media anymore. All I would have did was go to Regina's page and read all the comments again.

Or I was going to hit up the writing board, unblock SwagWordz and open up that door. I already felt weird, hitting that block button was a punch in my stomach. Like I just erased something amazing in my life and now I'm alone. I decided to push it out my mind, watch a movie and go to sleep.

"OH MY GOD!! DADDY!! IS THAT MINE!?" I yelled from the living room then ran outside when I saw it pull up in our driveway with a big white bow on top of it. I didn't even realize I closed the door when I ran outside with him behind it. I didn't even care that I had on my big grandma gown with a bonnet on.

He was laughing and so was the guy who drove the jeep, he gave me the keys.

"I thought you said no jeep?" I asked my dad smiling hard.

"I can never tell my Fuzzy no, but you know there

are some rules." We both looked at the guy who drove get into another call and pull off. He blew the horn and Dad threw the deuce sign in the air.

"Your curfew is still the same on weekdays and weekends. It is up to you to keep up with the maintenance. So, I wouldn't run through my allowance fast if I were you. I got the insurance covered and if you get any tickets I'm taking it for two weeks. I also expect you to keep it clean—"

"Daddy, I promise I will follow each and every one of them. But can I just have a moment to love on my Clifford!?" I was so excited I couldn't stop jumping around in the seat.

"Why the hell did you name it Clifford?" He asked laughing.

"Like the dog, *Clifford The Big Red Dog*. Remember I use to love that cartoon and since my jeep is red, I figured it's perfect."

He just shook his head still laughing and went in the house. Brinx's front door opened and when she saw the jeep, she screamed loud like I did earlier.

"Girlllll it's so damn pretty!" Hopping in the front seat she had her pajamas on too, some shorts and a cami.

"Thank you, I know right! I am beyond hyped."

After playing with the buttons on the radio and navigation system, we both went back home to get dressed. Me and Brinx decided to ride to Coya and Toni's block so we could all hang.

"Jurnee that jeep is fucking perfect!" Toni said as we all got in her room.

"Yes Pooh, congratulations!" Coya added.

"Thank you, best babies, I love it so much." I took my hoodie off from around my waist so I could lay on her XXL bean bag she has. It was my go-to spot anytime we were in her room. Brinx always got on the bed with Toni and Coya loved her plush love seat.

"We gotta hit Belle Isle up so you can stunt on these hoes!" Brinx said, making us fall out laughing.

"Speaking of August, how are thing with you two?" Coya asked and we all were intrigued.

"We're good, he's so damn fine y'all and we can't keep our lips off each other." Brinx's high cheeks were red.

"Whew, shit!" I screamed but only because Toni's dad wasn't home.

"Fuck the lips, have you gave him the cherry yet?" Coya of course had to know.

Honestly, I wanted to know too since we were the

only virgins out the four. I didn't mind talking about sex with Toni and Coya. But all it did was make me want to run from it more because of their horrible experiences. Don't get me wrong, their first times were perfect, but since then, it's been horrible stories. Funny, but horrible as hell especially when they talk about the oral.

"No, nasty bitch." Brinx laughed and answered. "I won't lie though, it's tempting as hell. I've never felt that with any guy. I mean I know we won't be together forever but I still want to at least make sure I don't regret who I lose my virginity to."

"That is so true amiga (friend) I don't regret mine." Toni told us.

"Yup, I don't regret Tarnell for my first. I don't regret Austin from the other day, either."

"WHAT!?" All three of us yelled.

Coya covered her ears, cracking up.

"Y'all...When did that happen?!" I said with my mouth still open.

"How was it!?"

"Ok!! It happened Wednesday—"

"Oh my gosh, when he picked you up from my house!?" Brinx screamed and asked. "I knew it when he said that freaky stuff on the phone."

"At first I kept telling myself that I was not going to have sex with him. But once we got to his room, I knew that was all over. Y'all it was so damn good my body was shaking and trembling all crazy. The positions he had me in blew me away, it's like he's a grown man. I mean I never been with anyone older than nineteen but still. Austin fucks like he's in his thirties, I have to have a repeat."

"Damn, it was that good?" Toni asked what we were all thinking.

"It was so damn good that I wanted to cuss him clean the fuck out and lay on his chest after." This bitch was too funny.

"Was it good enough to make him your boyfriend?" I asked.

"Yeah and no, we're talking so we'll see where it goes."

"Um, if the guy you have sex with isn't necessarily your boyfriend or you don't want him to be your boyfriend. Is that bad?" I can't believe I just asked that question out loud to my friends. I mean yes, I tell these girls everything, but this wasn't something I shared.

"Well the status isn't what's important, pooh. But niggas get bored quick so if you don't give it up, then be prepared to have an open relationship or cheated on."

"Coya that is not true, some guys are understanding." Brinx had wrinkles in her forehead.

"Well it ain't that many and the ones who are understanding are gay."

Even though sometimes Coya says what I don't want to hear, she always has a point and kept me laughing.

"Escuchame mami (Listen to me mommy), it's more about how you feel and if you are ready. You're pretty much the only person that matters when it comes to losing your virginity. Not us, not your age and certainly not the guy's opinion. You just have to ask yourself, is this person worth me giving up something so important. Sin prisa mami (No rush mommy)." What Toni said made so much sense.

I loved when we had our deep conversations.

"So, is this about Eddie?" Brinx asked in a teasing way.

"Hell no, well don't get me wrong he is mad cool, but no. He can't kiss right and his dick is really little." I hated to admit that especially when they got all loud and started cracking up.

"Bitch!" Coya yelled.

"How the hell...Did y'all have sex!?" Brinx sat up on the bed and asked me.

"No! God no! We just kissed a few times and uh, we may have video chatted and I saw something. Well, I didn't see much because it wasn't much to see, but still. Oh my goodness, would y'all stop laughing!" I had to join in because they were holding their stomachs.

"I knew he had a little dick because he was to suave for our age." Coya joked.

"What about Audrey Legend aka Chaos?" Toni asked me, cheesing so hard.

I smacked my lips. "Girl what about him, aside from him harassing me I don't think twice about him." I lied through my teeth, I couldn't get our kiss out my mind. Then I had other things bothering me, SwagWordz. I was missing our conversation and it hadn't even been a full day yet.

"Well he seems to be thinking about you, he's on Live right now." Coya said looking in her phone.

"What, what's he saying?" I asked getting up and sitting next to the love seat she was in.

Toni and Brinx came and crowded around her too. My mouth was on the floor, he had my name Jurnee White pinned to his Live. Pinned is like telling your audience the subject of your Live.

He had on a white and peacock blue Givenchy t-shirt. His gold frame buff glasses looked so good on him and all his dreads were in a very high ponytail. His fade was crispy all around them and his tattoos on his arm were even sexy. Audrey wasn't saying anything, he was smoking weed, sitting in his truck.

He must have had his phone on a tripod or something but that wasn't even all. He had *August Alsina-Kissin' on My Tattoo's* playing so loud and he was nodding his head slowly. Those blue eyes would looked out the window then straight head. It's like he was just kicking it and decided to go Live.

"I'm lost for words right now, I mean this is some cute shit." Brinx said still watching.

"I know right, he's basically dedicating this song to you." Coya said, her eyes not leaving the screen.

Smacking my lips at them, I got up and took my phone out. It was like I couldn't believe he was actually doing this. Seeing it in my phone would confirm it, I guess. Going to IG, his profile was in the corner. It was highlighted and the */word Live was under it. As soon as I clicked it I saw my name, heard the song and saw his flawless face. When he looked at the screen, he must have saw my name. Because he did this smirk that made me wet and my heart skip a beat at the same time. When he licked his lips I almost faded away, then he hit a button that restarted the song. You know what I didn't for the life of me understand? How the hell his eyes were piercing me so hard through a camera. He had two-hundred and twenty -six people watching. Yet when he looked in the screen with smoke coming out his mouth, I felt like it was just me and him. His comments were going crazy, people were asking when did we start talking. Then there were a few that asked what about Regina and they thought he was her man. Audrey must have caught a few because he turned the radio down a little, looking mean as hell then he spoke.

"Aye yo', get the fuck out my comments asking me about Regina. I use that bitch as a cum rag so if y'all dumb asses wanna believe the hype she speak about on her page, then go ahead. But that ain't my bitch, never was my bitch and never will be my bitch. Now shut the fuck up and suck my dick." He turned the music back up like it was nothing.

I couldn't believe he just said that. The comments started going so crazy and his views went up to three hundred. People were laughing, typing the word 'Factz' and of course, the women were saying how fine he was. My loud ass friends were laughing and acting all wild.

"Y'all shut up, he's doing this for a show." I said trying to hide my smile.

"Well if it's a show then take a bow because you the leading lady!" Coya teased.

I was about to say something but Audrey sent a request for me to join him in his Live.

"Oh my gosh! Girl say yes, accept and say yes!" They were yelling like this was a celebrity asking me to go Live.

I looked a mess today, some jeans, a yellow tube top and Brinx's yellow Coach slides on my feet that she let me wear. My hair was the only thing looking good thanks to the treatment Mom gave me. I had it all down with a side part and some heart shape stud earrings. I decided to humor him and accept. Taking a deep breath, I calmed down when I appeared on the split screen.

"What's up wit'chu?" He did not have to bite his bottom lip after he spoke.

"You and your shenanigans, didn't I talk to you about this the other day?" I held my smile in.

"I don't remember much talking, I remember a lot of kissing."

"What!? You didn't tell us about that!" Brinx shouted out first.

I was so embarrassed because I knew Eddie was either watching or someone was going to tell him. But he'll never know it was on our date, I still didn't want to hurt him, though. At least not publicly.

"Can you please stop?" I looked back in the camera after laughing at my girls. "You are making it seem like we have a relationship."

He leaned forward and put out his blunt. "We do, I keep telling you that but you wanna keep fucking with me. I'm being real smooth right now but I ain't about to let you keep cheating on me."

Why was his face looking so serious, even when he licked his lips? He started pushing buttons on his phone and I thought he was about to post in his comments. There were some light wrinkles in his forehead that showed how hard he was concentrating. When he was done he sat back in his seat then focused back on me.

"My bad baby, I had to block these three stalkerish ass females. I hate when bitches try to get too familiar with me on here. They start commenting on everything I post and trying to set up camp in my DM. Shit is mad aggy, anyway, come here real quick or I can swoop you up. We need to have a chat."

I put my head down looking at my pink and white toes. It was a distraction because I couldn't keep looking at him. I was bound to say yes to everything those blue eyes and sexy face asked me.

"Say yes."

"Do it girl."

"Go or I'll kill you." Coya, Brinx and Toni were whispering, egging me to go.

"Yo' girls are some terrible whisperers but you should listen to them. I already told you I'm not stopping till you have a convo with me."

"You promise you'll stop?" I asked him, getting serious now.

"I got'chu, just come through, you got the addy." With that, he ended his Live.

"Well got damn, I guess we are canceling our plans for the day." Brinx said and they all laughed hard.

"I hate every single thing about y'all." I said getting up putting my phone in my wristlet.

"Go see your man!"

I put my middle finger up while I walked out Toni's bedroom door.

**

"It don't take you no hour to get here from Toni's crib." Audrey opened the front door of his house looking like a monster.

"Traffic." I shrugged my shoulders arching my eyebrow. I was late because I drove around and did pointless errands. I had to work up my nerves to come over here.

"Traffic...Man you tryna make me act a fool." He scratched the side of his beard looking to the side then to me.

"Can I come in or not?" I asked getting impatient.

He didn't say anything, just moved out the way. I walked in and down the hall to the kitchen/living room.

"Sup Jurnee." Adrian spoke. He was sitting on the floor getting his dreads tightened by some pretty brown skin girl.

"Hey."

"This is our baby sister, Ava." Audrey introduced us. "This my girl, Jurnee."

I threw my head back then shook it. "The only thing true in that sentence is my name. How you doing, girl?"

Ava laughed then said, "Ohhhh, so this is the one who had you in your feelings the other day? You are gorgeous, I see why he was about to cry."

Adrian was laughing hysterically, and I looked at Audrey smiling.

"Don't listen to that bullshit baby sister talkin'. Let's head up."

I followed him upstairs which I was surprised because I didn't know what he was leading me to. The only time I'd been inside their house was the day of the party.

"This is your room?" I asked him when he opened the door.

"You need a Nobel Peace award." He snickered and sat on the edge of his bed.

His walls were a light grey with white lining and his bedroom set was all black and chrome. He had like a mini living room in the corner with two black leather recliners. A black table and his carpet was grey with a black rug that said Chaos on it.

He had this black, silver and graffiti picture on the left wall and the letters said Chaos as well. Then on his right wall were the same graffiti letters that read Legend with a crown on top. I leaned against his bedroom door after he closed it and looked at him look at me.

I don't know what was happening but we were in an eye lock tough. My heart was beating and my stomach was doing flips. His eyes were kind of squinted and he stretched his long legs out. Finally, I broke the trance and spoke.

"I'm here, are you going to talk?" I asked him clearing my throat.

"Why you been playing me?"

"I haven't been playing you. All of a sudden you started acting crazy. Popping up on me, tagging me in pictures and videos. And giving me and my boyfriend a hard time." Ok, so I threw that last part in there, but so what.

He snickered and folded his arms, leaving them long legs stretched out. "Boyfriend? Eddie is yo' boyfriend?"

I looked left, right and then at him. "Yes he is and—"

"So, if I get up right now, go hunt him down and shoot him in both his arms. Make it so he won't have shit but shoulders. All based off of you telling me the God to honest truth. Is. Eddie. Your. Boyfriend?" His body language was the same but his eyes were studying mine.

I was in shock at what he just said so I stopped playing and told the truth. "N-No, we're just talking, but it's not official."

"That's what I thought, don't lie to me again."

"Ugh! Why does it matter, Audrey? You are not my man, I am not your girl. When I kissed you at Belle Isle it was to piss off Regina. That's all! You are taking it way overboard." I was so mad that I was yelling.

I just knew he was about to snap at the way I was talking to him but he didn't. He just laughed and pointed to my hoodie. "What is that all about, you been wearing them since you were in 9th grade. All year around, no matter what the occasion is, why?"

I looked down at my yellow Champion hoodie. Tightening it up more, I lied and said, "It just goes with my—"

"Bullshit. Didn't I just tell you not to lie to me, again?" He actually looked disappointed and that deep voice didn't help.

I looked down at my feet and then back up at him. "I um, I don't care for my shape."

"Come again." He looked stunned.

"My hips are wide, booty is big and my thighs are...well you know." I admitted and I was so embarrassed. I pulled my hoodie tighter and looked everywhere but at him.

"Come here."

I kept looking down at my feet and shook my head no.

"I said come here Jurnee, please." His tone was demanding and sexy.

My feet moved as I made my way over to him. I stood in front of his stretched-out legs. He opened them wide and pulled me between them by my hoodie. I never thought Audrey was this aggressive but part of me liked it. The other part of me was apprehensive, my arms stayed down on my side and I looked down at him.

Those blue eyes were looking up at me and he slowly untied my hoodie. I have never had a boy this up and close to my space. Yes, I have kissed a guy but his hands were either in my hair or around my waist. They didn't move around my body either. I also swore to smack any guy who tried to touch me in the way that he was. But when he put his hands on my hips and brought me closer...

I didn't know what he was about to do then his soft, pink lips kissed my stomach twice. *Oh my gosh bitch, don't soak through your jeans. Don't soak through your jeans.* I had to repeat that to myself over and over. After he kissed my stomach, he kissed my hips then my thighs through my jeans. He stopped there and looked up at me. I've seen him every day since I was in the 9th grade.

But this is the first time that I am truly seeing him. Push his looks to the side, I felt like I was really seeing him. Like this Chaos shit was just given to him and he lived up to it. But that's not who he truly was. Before I knew it, my hand was on the side of his face, rubbing down his beard. "I never let anyone touch my face unless you're my Mama." He said as my hand repeated what I did earlier.

I chuckled and said, "Well I can always stop."

Audrey shook his head no.

"Now that we've talked, will you keep your promise and stop?"

Once again he shook his head no.

I felt my forehead fold. "But you promised."

His forehead then matched mine. "I didn't promise shit, I said I got'chu. Look Jurnee, I was dead ass when I said you were my girl."

I laughed but not at him, just at the situation. "One kiss did all of that?"

"Yup and I ain't ashamed to admit it. Maybe if your

breath stank that day or if you weren't so fine. Then I wouldn't be this gone but it didn't play out that way. I'on let bitches kiss me. Not saying you're a bitch but you feel what I'm saying. You did and that was the day we became official."

When he smiled wide, I turned into melted snow on a hot day. "Can we get to know each other first?"

"Of course, but we will be getting to know each other as boyfriend and girlfriend." Once again, his face was so serious.

"Audrey let's be for real, I'm a senior in high school. You're on your way to college, y'all have wild basement parties. I'm—" I stopped talking before I slipped up and said I was a virgin.

"Man you basically hoeing me, you think I can't be around pussy and not fuck?"

"I didn't say that, it's just proof in your big thot pudding." We both laughed. "I may look like a *Rasheeda Frost* but cheat on me and I turn to *Left Eye*."

He laughed again and I was able to see his smile and perfect teeth. "Ain't that the crazy chick who burned the basketball player's house down? We watched that movie in Yearbook the day Ms. Ross was absent."

Now I was laughing. "Yes that's her and it was a

football player. But I'm serious Audrey, one fuck up with me and that's it."

"I hear you loud and clear but you ain't the only one crazy. I may look like a dream, but I swear to God. I will be a fucking nightmare if my feelings are fucked with. I got something I want you to read." He said taking out his phone.

I was curious but I assumed it was something on Instagram or Facebook. He turned his phone towards me and told me to take it. When I started reading I got to the third line and my heart jumped up in my throat. Stepping back I looked at him almost ready to cry.

"Where did you get this from?"

"You know where." He still sat there looking at me but not with a mean expression, it was soft.

"But I only sent this to one...I feel like I can't breathe." I put my hand on my chest, looked at his phone again then back at him. "You're SwagWordz?"

He leaned his head back a bit grabbing and rubbing his beard and nodding his head yes.

I scoffed and threw his phone at him and his ugly ass caught it. "So, is this all a joke, laugh on me!? I shared so much intimate things about myself...The person I was talking to wasn't like you! Far from it!" I was yelling now and had tears coming down my eyes.

Audrey was smart but I talked to SwagWordz on another level. We shared views about certain topics, when we talked about sex it was more than a dick and pussy. All I could think about is him and his brothers laughing at me. Or worse, him and Regina talking shit, taking screenshots and sharing them.

He stood up and came towards me. "You need to calm the hell down, it's not even like that."

"Then what was it like, how long have you knows I was PenQueen?" I asked and if he said since the beginning, I promise I was swinging on him.

"I just put the shit together the other day. We were sending each other IMs about me wanting a dog."

As he talked I closed my eyes because I already knew what he was about to say.

"I asked what kind of dogs you had, and you told me. Then you told me their names, you're the only chick I know who has an Instagram page for her dogs. Gizmo and Bear. Trust me Jurnee, I was thrown all the way back when I figured out it was you."

My mouth opened a little and I looked him up and down angrily. "Like I'm ugly or something—"

"Girl shut the hell up, for real you about to piss me

off. For me, it all made sense when I found out it was you. My mama always talks about energy and attraction beyond a physical level. Me and my brothers don't be tryna hear that shit but I think I'm starting to get it." He grabbed my hand and interlocked our fingers.

"SwagWordz is me, it's Audrey aka Chaos. It's more to me then money, bitches and my own crib. I like anime, fantasy drama, writing and corny ass movies. None of what we talked about was fake. I got pissed off when you blocked me after I asked could we meet. I thought you knew who I was and didn't wanna fuck with it.

You right, we didn't talk or anything in high school. But on my Mama, I ain't never looked at you as ugly or unattractive. I always thought you were just mean as fuck and needed some good dick." We both chuckled. "Let's see what's up and where it goes, that's all I want."

I thought about it, looked at his handsome face and I knew what my answer was. "Ok, we can see if it works. But—" He shut me the hell up with his lips. I guess I have a boyfriend.

BISHOP

"How can I get some pussy when that lil nigga keep crying?" I put my now soft dick back in my boxers.

I may have been a shitty dad on an emotional level, but I dropped off money to Regina every week to her. I didn't need my name being on papers. I had enough shit in my name pertaining to the law already. Regina was a bad, big lip redbone that I always go for. My dick hated condoms so I wasn't surprised when she ended up getting pregnant.

We were never together, just fuck buddies and neither one of us wanted that to change. Our son was gorgeous, looked just like me but babies require emotions and shit I don't have to give. When the little nigga gets older than we can link up. But for now, I'll just supply him with the things he needs. Right now, Regina's Auntie was at work so this was the good time to get some pussy.

I gave her five-hundred dollars as soon as I came over. But she was looking good in these little shorts and sports bra, so I had to get in. Our son however had other plans. He was five months, a cute lil nigga, Regina made him a junior and I was proud of that. He would have made daddy even prouder if he would have stayed sleep and let me get in his mama.

"He must sense a nasty vibe because he normally sleeps all night." She picked him up and kissed all on him.

See what I mean, I can't be doing no soft shit like that.

"He ain't sense shit but his Mama funky pussy when she opened her legs." I was full of shit but still, she wasn't about to play me. Talking about nasty vibes.

"Boy bye but you was about to stick that bare dick in me."

I gave her the middle finger after I put my shoes on. "You betta buy my son everything he needs and not spend it going to Burn's." That was a hookah spot club her and her sisters lived at on the weekends.

"Yeah, whateva."

"Peace out lil man." I wiggled his little ass foot and headed out her bedroom.

Regina lived with her auntie, two sisters and two older cousins on the west side. The house was a three floor and always stayed messy with clothes and shoes everywhere. Regina had the biggest room upstairs because of the baby. I took my phone out and was about to call my cousin Simon to swoop me back up. But my dick still needed to be handled so before I left I needed a pit stop.

Passing the front door, I went down the hall to Regina's sister Brittany's room. I fucked on from time to time and we kept it on the low. Normally I wouldn't care but I didn't want to do my baby mama that way. Brittany wasn't as fine as Regina, but her head was good, and pussy popped almost on the same level.

"I already knew you were going to make your way down here. My nephew has been gassy for two days and waking up crying." Her freaky ass pulled her covers back, revealing her naked body.

I took my shoes off and pulled her by the ankles towards me. Flipping her over I undid my jeans, not even dropping them on the floor. My dick was already hard when I seen her hairy pussy. I loved hair on that monkey and Regina always shaved hers off, which annoyed me. Spitting on her ass hole and my dick, I slid in her.

I dug fucking Brittany in the ass while I played with pussy. Naw I ain't no gay nigga, I just admired every hole in a female body. Hell, if I can stick my dick in a bitch ear and nose I would. While I fucked her, I had my fingers inside her pussy, and she was gripping the sheets hard.

Once I got close, I pulled out and made her suck me off the rest. While she did that, I took my phone out and texted my cousin. I had to slip out on the low before Regina came downstairs.

**

"These muthafucking Legend's think they can get over on us. Going to our connect and buying him out. It's all good because I got a new one for us. And since they wanna fuck with our money, I got a way for them to waste theirs. Rock reups soon, we'll get them then." My father Darius was talking to us while we sat in his living room.

Did I mention he was sitting on his couch getting his dick sucked by a white bitch. He was always like this since before I was born. Ma took off and got wrapped up with this pimp. He was dirty as hell, set her up and now she is in jail in Miami. I don't give a damn about that bitch because she walked out on me.

My father doesn't care about her either, let that bitch rot for all that matters. Anyway, he never hid shit form me. When I was little it was always some bitches walking around the house. Naked, in lingerie, panties no top or no panties. Dad always just said I was a boy and it was natural. I lost count of how many times he was called to the school when I was younger.

For me being caught with my hand up a girl skirt or us doing nasty stuff. I never got in trouble by Dad, though. If anything, I was praised and always told boys will be boys.

"I hate them and don't understand why we can't just kill them unk." Simon's wild ass said while opening his beer.

"Because together we can all run this state. Apollo will put me on his connect and we'll be set. Killing them isn't the answer and I ain't gone say it anymore. If they wanna keep playing this game then we'll tire them out. If Apollo or his sons wanted to off us, they would have been did it. He doesn't want bloodshed, it's more like a dick measuring contest."

Speaking of dick, his white chick got on all fours with her ass all in the air.

"I see you looking nephew, she got a sister in the back if you wanna get on." Dad said to my other cousin Duran.

"He not about to do shit, he hooked on Ava Legend." I blasted him.

"Wait a damn minute, you're fucking on Apollo's

only daughter?" Dad looked shocked as hell.

"He ain't fucking on shit, just talking." Simon, his brother, said laughing.

"Damn bitch ass can I speak for myself?" Duran got mad because we clowned him about it all the time.

"Why would you have a bitch around who you not fucking?"

"Come on unk she's not a bitch." His blonde and red dreads hung all over his face.

"Oh shit my bad man, you got feelings for her." Dad tapped the white bitch on the head telling her to stop.

When she sat up her titties and pink nipples bounced everywhere.

"Go get yo' sister, yo' head weak as hell today." He told her in a dismissive way.

Her dumb ass got up and actually did what he said. In a few minutes her sister, who looked like *Iggy Azalea*, came out and continued what her sister started.

"Fuck that, I'll take her sister." Simon got up and went to the back.

"Anyway, answer my question nephew. You got feelings for Ava, explain to me what your aim is."

I sat back with my blunt and waited for Duran to lie.

"It ain't like that, we just kick it from time to time. I don't have any motives or plans. Me and her know what's going on with our families. I don't involve her, and she doesn't involve me."

See what I mean, lie over lie. Duran doesn't talk to us about Ava, that much is true. But he was digging her, and I knew for a fact they have had sex. I get it, Ava will only be seventeen next year, so my cousin doesn't wanna get arrested. Or worst by her Dad and brothers.

"Oh, ok I understand it." Dad said.

When Duran got up and went to the kitchen for another beer, he sat up and leaned forward holding snow bunny's head in place.

"Keep an eye on that, it may come in handy."

I nodded my head and agreed. "Already a step ahead of you, dad."

AVA PRINCESS LEGEND

"Ma, can I spend the night at my brother's house tonight?" I walked in the kitchen at home and asked her.

We were twins, I was 5'4 and she was 5'6 but we were the same brown skin complexion. We were both on the petite side but not straight up and down. We had hips, a C-cup breast and I stood out because I had blue eyes like my Daddy and brothers. Tonight, I wanted to spend the night with my brothers.

Truth is, I lost my virginity the other day to Duran. It had me uncomfortable being around my mother right now. We shared everything; she was my best friend but that was the problem. I needed a mother, not a home girl at the moment. I loved her and she was the best on every level.

But she always kept our relationship so open. I can cuss, smoke, and drink in front of her. Ma always told me she'd rather I do those things with her than without and I get caught up. So open that when I was in the third grade, I got held back. I missed so much school because of Ma's parties that kept me up. Daddy went crazy because he doesn't play about school.

I moved with him until he felt Ma was ready to be a parent again. When I went to junior high, I moved back home and although Ma hasn't changed all the way, she took time to check my homework, help me with class projects and no more parties were thrown at home. All my friends loved Ma and always told me how lucky I am.

They had no idea how she lacked more in the mother department. Every conversation we have had was like I was talking to a friend. Before *Drake*, she was the true definition of YOLO (you only live once) and that's the kind of advice she always gave me.

Like if I told her about having sex with Duran, she would probably start twerking. Never mind the fact that I didn't even want to do it. I felt pressured by my friends and a little by him. Right now, I just wanted to be around my brothers so I can laugh and feel safe.

"You already know I don't mind. I'm spending the weekend with Tina anyways. She won a weekend suite at MGM Casino. We're getting some niggas and it's going to be a real turn up." She said flipping her long blue and black bundles.

"Yuck Ma, please stop talking like that." I rolled my eyes and grabbed a pop out the refrigerator.

"Well I could have said pop my coochie—"

"Ma! Ugh, can you please just drop me off over my brothers' house?"

"No need for that, I'll take you."

We both turned around when we heard Daddy's voice. That was another thing, he had a key to our house. Now, the both of them haven't been together since he cheated and made me. So I never understood why he has the key to our place. He doesn't stay the night or anything but it's still just about boundaries. I love my Daddy and we have a great relationship, but I hated that he could come in whenever he wanted.

"Thanks, but it's ok, Adrian is coming to get me." I didn't want to be around him either.

"No he's not, I told him I would bring you because we need to talk." He leaned against the counter where I was standing. "Gone and pack your bag."

I dragged down the hall to my room and dreaded what he had to speak to me about. I could hear him and Ma talking but it wasn't about nothing. I thought they would have dropped hints, but he didn't say anything. I packed three days-worth of clothes in case I decided to go over my best friend Darcy's house for a night.

"Ok, I'm ready." I said giving my daddy my *JoJo*

Siwa overnight bag.

I went over to Ma who was closing the dishwasher and I kissed her cheek.

"Mama loves you Princess, text me, ok?"

"Ok, love you too Ma."

Me and Daddy walked out the door; it was getting dark outside and it wasn't so hot.

"What did you want to talk to me about?" I asked him when we got in the car and he pulled off. I wanted to get straight to the point so we can get this over with.

"We need to talk about Duran." He looked at me quickly.

I already knew it was coming, I watched the lines in the street go by fast. "Daddy, I know his brother, cousin and uncle do not get along with my brothers. But I promise Duran doesn't put me in the middle of that. I like him a lot and all I'm asking for is trust, from you and my brothers." I kept a soft tone and told the truth.

Duran was an accident, we were all at a Central kickback at the skating ring. Him and his boys were there, and it was some senseless flirting going on. I never knew it would go into me giving him my number. Don't let my age trick you, I'm mature and do not carry myself like a sixteen-year-old girl.

I knew Duran's age and I don't think it's a big deal, it's not like he's over twenty-one. Even though I felt away about my first time, I still liked him. I believe we had a hood *Romeo & Juliet* relationship. Only no one was going to commit suicide.

"I get that and I know you think you're at an age where you know it all." He turned the corner of my brothers' block. Parking in front of the house he put the car in park then turned towards me.

"I need you to understand this, I love you. You're daddy's Ava Princess and I know if I forbid, you'll rebel. If I ship you off, you'll probably run away and cause me and your Mama stress. So, I will let you have you relationship, but know this. I'll mend your broken heart when the time comes for your brothers to put his legs where his arms are.

I know his uncle form back in the day so trust me, Ava. I know how this will end, but since you wanna be grown and stand by your choices. You have to know that there are repercussions to them. So, spend all the time in the world with him. Tell him what I just told you or keep it to yourself. Just remember we are family and that will never change." He leaned over, kissed my forehead and gave me my bag.

"Daddy loves you so much." He was relaxed and even looked at me like I was the apple of his eye like he always did.

I don't think I blinked once since the conversation went left. I couldn't believe what he just said to me. Most importantly, I believed every word he spoke, and it scared me. As soon as I hit my brothers' brick walkway, the censor lights came on. August opened the front door and Daddy pulled off.

"Why you look like your about to cry?" When August asked that after I came inside it was like a batman sky signal. My other brothers came from each part of the house, including Chill from the basement.

"What happened?" Audrey asked, looking my face over.

"Nothing I was just talking to Daddy about Duran. He basically said no matter what, Duran was getting killed by y'all."

All of them smacked their lips and scoffed at the same time.

"I thought some shit went down." August said heading back to his room.

"Hell, I almost broke my neck running up the stairs." Chill also spoke. Him and Adrian went back in the basement, I could hear the game playing loudly.

I dropped my bag, stunned by their reaction.

"I can't believe y'all!" I yelled at the ones who walked away.

Austin was the one of my brothers who was extremely soft on me. Audrey was next but he was closer to our Dad. I hated to disappoint him, it always made me cry. August was my voice of reason for things. But this time, Austin was that one.

"Av's you can have any nigga you want, and you pick Duran. I love you baby sister, but Pops is right."

I shook my head no and fought back my tears. August stared at me kind of funny then he pulled my arm towards the back towards the bathroom.

"Austin what the hell are you doing?" I looked at him like he was crazy.

Closing the door, he faced me folding his arms. "You had sex with Duran?"

I promise I had the best performance lined up for when I was asked the question. Starting with my fake expression of being shocked. To my long speech about how I would never do that until I'm older and ready. But before I could even start, Austin gave me this 'lie if you want to' look. Instead, I felt exposed so I wrapped my arms around my stomach and sat on the closed toilet.

"What the fuck Ava, did he make you or it was something you wanted to do?"

I knew he was mad because he called me Ava. Austin has always called me Av's. My eyes couldn't even go to him.

"He didn't make me, I swear. I-I-I wanted to Austin, just not at that moment." Flashbacks of that night replayed in my mind. My fear, skepticism and even the location was just all wrong.

"Did you say no at all and he not listen? Don't play around with this Ava—"

I looked at him quickly this time. "Austin I'm not lying, I never said no or even gave off a behavior that I didn't want to. He didn't rape me."

His eyes got low and he shook his head. "So basically you did something you really didn't want to do. Why, just to fit in? Because them rat bitches you hang with be having cum dripping out their ears?"

I got so mad. "Including yours? How dare you judge me when you and the rest of our brothers eat, sleep and breateh sex. I hear you guys all the time talk about how if a bitch isn't putting out then she's lame. How y'all have been fucking forever and who holds on to their virginity so tight in 2020. The wild parties in the basement, none of y'all have ever really had a real girlfriend. Tell me Austin, how many of my friends have hooked up with y'all?"

He didn't say anything, just shrugged his shoulders. "Save me the double standard talk Ava, we all know it's just the way it is. I don't want my baby sister out here like that. It's not about the sex, it's you not listening to that voice in your head.

Av's you don't even do something you don't wanna fucking do. We tell you that all the time, Pops tells you that all the time. Losing your virginity isn't why I'm mad. It's because you lost your voice and gave in to peer pressure." Shaking his head again he turned and left out the bathroom.

I felt even more horrible because what he said was true. But, I didn't want to stop talking to Duran. I liked him a lot and I just wanted our families to separate our relationship from their beef. After a minute I left out the bathroom and went to my room down the hall. It's funny because I needed to get away from Ma because of having sex. Only to come here and have it invisibly stamped on my back.

Duran: Damn so you not fucking with me

today?

I read the text Duran sent me. I was so wrapped in my feelings that I didn't realize I hadn't talked to him.

Me: It's not like that I was just busy today. How are you?

I kicked my sandals off, took my shorts and shirt off then put my pajama pants and t-shirt on. My brothers keep the central air on freeze, so I liked to wear pants pajamas. Getting into my queen size bed, I checked my phone.

Duran: I'm chilling, let me come scoop you.

Me: I can't tonight I'm over my brothers' house.

I waited to see if he would text back, but he didn't. I turned on my TV and flipped through the channels. I decided to watch old episodes of Dance Moms when my girl *JoJo Siwa* was on it. Twenty-minutes passed and still no text, so I decided to call him.

You're call has been forward to an automatic voicemail.

"Why would he send me to voicemail?" I spoke out loud to myself.

Me: Why did you forward my call?"

Duran: Busy, I'll hit you up tomorrow.

To say I felt a way wouldn't even come close. I

called my best friend Darcy and Emegin on Instagram video chat. I vented to them about Duran and our texts that just happened.

"Maybe your sex isn't good." Darcy said.

"You think so?" I asked her because maybe that was it. Maybe he's used to experienced girls and I bored him.

"Did you suck his dick?" Emegin asked me.

I was so glad I had my ear buds in my ear. "No but—"

They both laughed then Darcy said. "Oh, well bitch it is your sex!"

These bitches were making me madder, so I hung up and went back to watching TV. About two-hours passed and it was almost midnight. I got up to get a snack and a can of pop so I could start *Gossip Girl* on Netflix.

"Oh my goodness you scared me." I said sitting on the kitchen stool making me an ice cream sundae.

Chill came from the basement and because the carpet on the stairs made it quiet, I didn't hear him.

"My bad, I was just about to get something to drink." He said walking to the refrigerator.

Chill always reminded me of that actor who played *Michael Oher* in the movie *The Blindside*. More so his size and build, Chill had braces and a thin beard around his mouth. I crushed on him hard but of course he doesn't see me as shit but my brothers' little sister. He was so fine though, and I have had dreams of his big ass being my first. But that will never happen, one because of my brothers and two because of my age.

"It's ok, I didn't know you were still here. How have you been, are you excited about college in the fall?" I asked him putting some cherries on my ice cream.

"Yeah I'm ready, Wayne State is close to home but still gives me that college experience. You ready for your junior year?" When he grabbed his pop, he sat on the stool next to me. He had on some basketball shorts and a black t-shirt.

"I am more than ready, I'm talking to my Mama about letting me go to Cooley." I put some ice cream in my mouth.

"Oh word, bout time you left them whack ass Trail Blazers and became a Cardinal." He teased.

Laughing I said, "Shut up, don't be talking about my school."

When he laughed his braces showed. "If that's your school then why are you leaving?" When he put his can of pop to his lips and licked the residue off, I got excited. He was just hot as hell.

I didn't want to tell him the truth about why I wanted to leave Central. I knew August didn't tell our brothers about me sleeping with Duran. For one, Audrey would have come and talked to me then went straight to beat Duran's ass.

"I just want a new atmosphere." I lied, eating some more ice cream. A little of it fell on my chin. My breathing changed when he wiped it off with his finger.

"Ain't nobody fuckin' wit'chu are they?"

Oh my gosh, he licked it off his finger like it was nothing to it. Then he waited for me to answer, looking serious.

I was in a small trance as I blinked slowly. "Um no. No one is bothering me I'm just over Central. Plus, my brothers are at Cooley, I know they will pick me up for school every morning." I needed to stop looking at his lips. I needed to act like I have a boyfriend.

"A'ight, as long as you good then bring that fine ass to the red and black side." He smiled talking about Cooley's school colors.

But I only heard one thing. "So, is it the colors you think I'll look fine in or just me in general?" I smirked while eating some more ice cream.

"I was referring to the colors."

It was like a record scratch, a loud audience shouting oh shit and a pie in the face all wrapped up in one. My flirtatious smirk went away quick.

When he laughed I almost dropped the ice cream in his lap. "I'm fucking with you Ava, you know you got all the sauce."

Whew chile, I felt so much better when he said that. "Yeah whatever, you basically called me ugly." I said messing with him.

"Man I'll never in a million years think of you as ugly. If we being real, I used to only think of you as a kid."

I looked at him when he said, that. "And now?"

He turned his body towards me and the way he surveyed me. Then he pulled the stool I was on closer to him and we were nose to nose. No words were spoken, just our lips touching then a whole make out session. I melted into this kiss; it was everything I wish my kiss during my first time was.

When his big hand went on my waist and brought me closer, my imagination took off. I replayed my first time but with Chill instead. I let his hand go under my sports bra. My body burned up when he cupped my breast. The kissing got more intense sitting on stools. He did this small grunt that turned me on more.

But we both stopped when we heard the door close from upstairs. It was like we were brought back to reality and what we did was out there in the air. Chill licked his lips standing up and grabbing his pop. I thought he was about to take off running but he gave me a half smile and kissed my cheek.

"Goodnight Ava."

"Good night Chill." I bit my lip blushing.

"Da'Vante." He said before heading back to the basement.

I giggled and put some of my now melted ice cream in my mouth.

"What'chu doing up so late, still thinking about what Pops said?" Audrey asked me when he came downstairs into the kitchen.

Duran came to my mind when he said that, and I felt so bad. I practically cheated even though I didn't have sex. I still did something that if he did, I would have dumped him, for sure. But the guilt wouldn't last long because of me and Chill, excuse me, Da'Vante's, kiss.

"No, just needed a tasty snack." I said putting the bowl in the sink. "Oh yeah, I'll be going to Cooley next year."

Audrey seemed surprised. "I'm here for it, I hate Central anyway. That way I don't have to go back and forth. I can see you and my girl all in one place."

I turned around with a wide smile when he said that. "Girl? Are we talking about Jurnee?" I asked him while he made a sandwich like it was in the afternoon.

"I wouldn't lie. That's my new baby."

"New baby, you make her sound like a car or piece of jewelry."

"Naw it ain't like that, I'd beat a nigga's ass about my ride or jewelry. What I'd do to a nigga over Jurnee." He cut his big club sandwich in half like it was a work of art. "Well, that's a different story."

My big brother was insane, I just laughed, shook my head and told him good night. When I got back to my room getting in bed, I unlocked my phone. I saw it was a text from Duran.

Duran: Let's hang tomorrow.

At first, I started not to text back because I was mad about him taking so long hitting me up. Then he sent me to voicemail like I was random. I blacked my phone out and decided to let him dangle like he did me.

"Damn, I forgot what you look like." Duran said sarcastically when I got in his Charger.

I got a weird feeling when I got in here. I hadn't been in his car since that night I lost my virginity. Before any of you judge, just think back to how you lost your virginity and then see if you can throw a stone. Also, I'm already feeling like crap over how I let things go too far. Austin was right, our Dad always taught us about peer pressure. Always making decisions based on how it made you feel, no one else.

"Stop being like that, I was just busy." I halfway told the truth. I spent three days at my brothers' house instead of two.

Like always, I had so much fun, those four boys were my heart and I loved being around them. We went to Belle Isle with Jurnee, Coya, Brinx and their friend Toni. I thought because they were all paired off that Adrian would try to get with Toni. But once I saw how they argue and insult each other, I knew that would never happen. Plus, some dude named Miles was there and she went to chill with him for a while.

It was real fun and then we went to the beach and

acted like big kids. D'Vante was there too and I was low-key excited, but girls swarmed him and Adrian. I couldn't show my feelings, so I played it off like it didn't even matter. I ignored him and did me. I even got this hottie's number when we all went to ride the giant slide. I couldn't help but notice how bothered Chill was.

Yeah, I decided to go back to calling him his nickname since he wants to be an ass. Anyway, he gave me the stink eye and kept saying little slick shit on the low. I didn't care but it made me have a better time knowing he was bothered. Now I was over Darcy's house and Duran asked if he could see me. I knew I couldn't avoid him forever, so I agreed.

"Man don't play me with that busy shit. Tell me the real, did you just wanna fuck and be done?"

I was offended as hell. "Duran, you knew I was a virgin! Why would you think I only want sex!?"

He took the blunt that was behind his ear and lit it. Duran was fine, that skinny boy type that all the rappers look like today. He was slim so he could get away with his skinny jeans. His light skin and freckles made his blonde and red dreads stand out.

Duran was a smoker, a party head. Him, Simon and Bishop flashed everything they owned from money to all the stuff they buy. It didn't bother me especially when Duran would be affectionate with me in public. I soaked it up and would be lying if I said I didn't.

"Well that's what it looks like. We were cool as hell until that night and now you are acting all off. Like you used me, or a nigga raped you or something. Look at how you sittin', you ain't gave me a hug or kiss. I'm not for this after school special drama. I dig you Ava but not the games, that's something I'm not with. Now, you can tell me what's up or we can end it here."

I didn't know if it was him or the weed that made him talk so dry. I did know that I didn't want us to be over so I told him the truth.

"That night...I just never imagined my first time being that way. I mean come on Duran, we were in y'all garage at the house party. I'm not saying you made me because you didn't. I just feel weird, like—"

"Like you regret it." He finished my sentence and I nodded my head yes. "Nobody has a good TV show the first time. At the end of the day, it was yo' nigga. The way it's supposed to be, we used a condom and it was good. When we have sex again it will for sure be in a bed." He put his blunt out then looked at me.

I blushed because his hands rubbed lightly up and

down my thigh. "Ok."

"I know how to make you feel better, but if you don't want to then I'll stop." Taking his seat belt off her leaned over to my side. When he kissed my lips a few times his other hand went under my skirt and pulled my panties down.

"Duran I told you—"

"I'm not about to fuck you, I'm about to taste you."

I moaned out when his head got between my legs. I've had my kat eaten before but that was when I was fourteen. It was bomb then like it was bomb now, Duran was throwing down. I put my hand on top of his head. My body was grinding and I put my hand on the window.

"I'm cumming! Oh my gosh. Oh my gosh. Oh my gosh!" I came all in his mouth and it felt amazing as hell.

When he was done he grabbed some napkins out his glove compartment and wiped his face. "Feel better?"

I laughed and fixed my skirt. "So much better, thank you." I leaned over and kissed his lips.

"When your brothers go to Myrtle Beach, you need to hang with me. I got some parties on the floor we can go to. You need to get lit too, not just them."

I was going to decline and just hang with my girls. However, he was right about my brothers going to Myrtle

Beach and live it up. Chill too and he'll forget all about our kiss and the fact that I'm sixteen. I didn't want my feelings hurt, so I pushed the kiss out my head and focused on my boyfriend.

"That sounds perfect."

AUDREY

"How do you expect me to explain to my father about Myrtle Beach? He's not about to let me go on a four-day trip with you."

"My dad isn't about to have that either," Brinx added.

Coya and Toni raised their hand and said the same thing. All of us were spread out in our living room chilling in the central air. Today was so damn hot outside it was like Michigan turned into Arizona. This was new for me and my brothers, we normally would fill our pool up and have a party. Or one of our basement summer foam parties but we were on a different vibe lately.

All of us except Adrian had a chick we were really into. Aside for the other reason of us not having a party. We would have rented a suite and had a private turn up. Jurnee, Coya and Brinx grabbed our attention. Toni and Adrian could hit it off but y'all know how them muthafuckas are. They can't stomach each other. Jurnee on the other hand had this Detroit goon on a different wave.

I still can't believe it was her for months that I had been talking to on that writer's board. I had a feeling I was talking to a girl because of how easily of a groove I fell into when we IM each other. My mind stayed on someone I had never met or even seen a picture of. I was comfortable talking to her, sharing my writing and just vibing.

We had a different subject every damn day. Now I don't know about y'all, but usually there are limited of things to talk about. But not with PenQueen, we chatted about everything under the sun. When I talked about my writing, love for anime, and corny movies. When I got used to talking to PenQueen every day, I knew I had to meet her. It was either going to end well or in a body bag if someone was playing with me.

To my surprise, Jurnee slipped up and named her dogs. Man my fucking stomach dropped a little and I was shocked as hell. Low-key, I had a little thang for Jurnee since my party. But on my Mama, I would have pushed that quick feeling out if PenQueen was legit. Actually, the dog in me would have had both until I was able to choose. But when it came out to be her, it was like solving a hard ass math problem.

No question, I was making her my girl. When she

blocked me after I asked her to meet, I flipped out. I thought she knew it was me as SwagWordz and was being funny. But her reaction when I told her confirmed she really didn't know. Jurnee was bad as fuck, thick as hell, gorgeous, perfect face. Her body wasn't like no other chick in school.

That's why I was shocked to learn about her minor lack in confidence. The hoodie thing, her not liking that her thighs touch and her take on being built like a model. Don't know real man want to lay up with a bag of bones, at least not this man. My bad for any of you reading this that are on the slim side but I gotta keep shit a buck. Thick is what gets the dick, bottom line.

Jurnee kept saying I was her man but then she would say we are just getting to know each other. But naw, fuck that, she was mine. My woman, my girl, my bitch, whatever way she wants to call it. Jurnee Ariel White was my girl and right now we were trying to get the girls to come to Myrtle Beach with us for my birthday. It wasn't much of summer left and I wanted a trip to close it.

"Tell him it's an end of the summer kickback. All of Cooley will be going, y'all went to the senior ski weekend up north. Just tell him it's that same type of trip." I was sitting on our X-Large plus recliner that was in the corner of the living room.

I loved either sitting on it or the long couch. I had it reclined back and Jurnee was laying back with me. Her soft booty felt good on my lap. I just wish she would take this hoodie off and keep it off. As soon as she was in my presence, I would ease it off her eventually. Like right now, I untied it as I talked, and she didn't stop me.

"Eso no va a funcionar (That won't work.)" Toni said some shit looking at Jurnee.

"Yeah it will, we'll all ask each other's dad's together." Jurnee told her and Toni said ok.

"You speak Spanish?" I asked her, grabbing the blanket behind me because her arms were cold as hell.

"Yeah and no, Toni speaks it so much all of us have picked it up some. Thank you." Thanking me for the blanket, she put the whole thing over both of us.

"You're welcome baby." Kissing her neck, I chuckled to myself because anytime I called her baby she would bite the corner of her lip.

It was cool being with her the past couple of days. The way we kicked it was the same as when we used to IM each other. Jurnee had me on a whole other mood. From falling asleep on the phone. Texting each other even if we are in the same room to having to see her every day. I just felt good as hell when I was around her.

"So y'all are willing to give up thots and dirty pussies for this trip?" Coya's wild ass looked around and asked us. She was laying on the floor with Austin. This foot loving nigga had her feet in his lap and was rubbing them.

I love a bitch with pretty feet as well, but our brother had a thang for them. I bet his phone is filled with foot pornos.

"Don't nobody be messing with no dirty pussies." Austin said laughing and Adrian added his two cents.

"Fuck that y'all the ones boo'd up so I'll have all the thots."

Toni laughed sarcastically. "And dirty pussies to go with that dirty dick."

We all laughed because these two were non-stop.

"Why don't you come wash my dick off with that kat." Adrian was nuts as hell and that shit was so funny when he said that.

"Man I wish y'all would just sixty-nine and quit all this bickering." I finally said after I laughed.

Toni turned her face upside down. "Ugh, he is not my type."

"Then what the hell is your type, and don't say Miles." Brinx asked her; she and August were stretched out on the couch.

"Street niggas mixed with a sweetheart." Jurnee answered for her laughing.

"Exactamente! See, my girls know what I like."

Adrian looked heated as hell. "Females swear they want a street guy and expect him to take her on picnics and sunsets. Naw muthafucka, ain't none of that but you can roll wit' me to this shoot out and trap house."

Me and my brothers laughed hard as hell, this nigga was a straight fool. Toni and the girls didn't think that was so funny.

"You're a 'street nigga', yet me and you do all kinds of things together and talk deep. So why can't she have both?" Jurnee asked me trying to look mad but she was just too fine.

"You right but the rode isn't always that easy messing with a goon like myself. I told you earlier, I'm a nightmare dressed like a dream." I told her honestly again.

"Ok that can mean a bunch of stuff. Are you a cheater, abusive, a serial liar, what does that mean?" Coya asked me and everyone including Jurnee looked intrigued.

"I don't cheat, when I make a girl mine that's what it is. That's why I don't make every chick my woman. You see my girl gotta rock with me when I'm Audrey and when I'm that crazy goon Chaos. Ain't no talking me down when I'm in that mode and I need my girl to still be like 'fuck what anybody gotta say, that's still my nigga.' That's what I mean by nightmare, dream."

"Hell yeah bro-bro that's what I'm talking about!" Austin held Coya's feet in place while he leaned over and gave me a pound.

"All of that is fine but the minute I feel unappreciated or you cheat on me. All you'll see is my back as I walk away." Her and her girls started going crazy after she said that.

It reminded me of that *Wendy Williams* talk show, every time she says some shit the women like. Her audience goes crazy, it was annoying because it was always a diss towards men.

"The only time I'll see your back is when I'm jay walkin' in that pussy." I don't know why I got so mad when she talked about walking away. I get it, if I break her heart she got the right to dip. But something bothered me when I thought about not having Jurnee.

"Then don't mess up." She looked at me with a sweet face that also looked like a warning.

I heard her loud and clear but right now, I was looking at her lips. "Gimmie a kiss."

Jurnee pecked my lips twice and on the last one I sucked on her bottom lip lightly. "Sexy ass. But you can kill that walking away talk. I won't fuck up and you damn sure not walking away."

"Well if you do my pooh wrong I'm beating yo' ass!" Coya yelled breaking me and Jurnee out our trance.

"Hell yes!" Brinx added and Toni said some shit in Spanish.

Y'all act like girls don't fuck up. Bitches will thumbs up a picture with three niggas in it she fucked on the low." August said and all us guys agreed.

"Facts. When men cheat, it's with a random baddie. Nothing special because we be thinking with our dicks. You women cheat with a whole damn upgrade." Austin preached real shit.

"Yup, and that shit hurts us like a muthafucka. Like bitch, when I'm done crying I'ma kill yo' ass." August set the room a blaze when he said that.

"That nigga wild!" I yelled laughing my ass off at him. Even the girls were holding their stomachs.

"Well I'm a whole other type of petty. If three dudes I fucked take a picture together I would comment. Look at my boys!"

Man these girls were cut throat, just like me and my brothers. They cussed, didn't act like some groupies like most bitches we hang with. It's never been this type of vibe chilling with the opposite sex. First thing first, we weren't in the basement and none of our dicks were out. After, we got some Chinese food and ate together. I wanted some alone time with Jurnee, so we went to my room.

"I noticed every time we are together my hoodie magically disappears." Her thick body climbed in my bed and she laid on top of my covers.

Jurnee has chilled in my room all day until her curfew. But we have never been under my covers and she makes sure she's fully clothed. When we kiss, the minute it gets heated she'll but a halt to it. I ain't the kind of nigga who rushes his woman for some pussy. But the heat was so high between us it was off the meter.

The way Jurnee stops me is like she doesn't trust me with her. Whatever it was believe me I was going to get at her about it. I took my shirt off and got on my bed next to her. I still had my grey sweatpants on, but I saw

Jurnee take a deep breath. Grabbing my remote I turned the TV on.

"You don't need to have no hoodie tied around your waist."

"So just show all my body off, booty shorts and see through tops?"

I looked at her like she was crazy. "Be dumb if you want to. It's a difference between curves showing and actual body parts. Gon' and play peek a boo wit'cha goods and watch what I do." I was serious as a cancer cell.

Jurnee laughed and said, "Is there any way you can talk without making threats." She crossed her sexy legs. Jurnee had some shorts on and another tube top I like to see her in.

"Oh!" She screeched when I yanked her on top of me.

"I can serenade you true goon style." I told her moving her long, big curly hair out or faces.

"Really?" Her voice was so sweet.

My eyes looked her face over, them lips, skin and I took her glasses off so I could see her hazel eyes better. I wasn't laying flat on my back, I was more rested on my headboard. Putting my hand around her neck I had a little pressure to it but still gentle. I brought her to me so I could kiss her cheek, the corner of her neck and then her ear.

I could feel her goosebumps and tiny shivers. Keeping my hand around her neck I moved my fingers down a little so I could lick on it. My tongue trailed to her ear and Jurnee practically came. Keeping my lips there, I spoke in her ear.

"I'm into you so heavy it's wild. When we get married my wedding vows will be the most beautiful five words you'll ever hear." I was whispering then I licked her lips again.

Jurnee was squeezing my arm and did that tiny shiver again. "Can I hear them?" Her sweet voice asked

I told her yeah. "Bitch I'll kill us both."

Before she could get mad and be all surprised like I know she was, I had my tongue down her throat kissing her. I didn't even let her get a word in or even breathe her own air. I dug making out with Jurnee, it was sexy as fuck. Our tongues were wet and lips worked over time. My hands always roamed her back and squeezed that big booty she has. It was getting hotter by the second until she jumped back with her eyes big.

"What's wrong?" I asked her.

"Something...what was." Her eyes looked around

my body all frantic then she looked down.

I was so damn confused.

"Is that your, um." Her finger pointed and I followed, looking down too.

"My dick?"

"Your dick? T-The whole thing?"

I laughed because when she asked that her eyes were glued to my print. "Why are you acting like you never had a dick in your face before?"

"No, it's not that. I mean I totally have had dicks...In my face...Not in my face but you know." She did this nervous laugh.

I looked at her body language, the way she played with her fingers. Her broken sentences and the way she stuttered.

"Jurnee, are you a virgin?"

That nervous/fake laugh happened again, and she waved me off. "Hell no, I'm just as experienced as you are."

I got mad as hell and I felt my nostrils flare. For one, she was lying, and I told her about that shit. Two, I've been with a shit load of girls. So, the thought of that much dick in her was about to set me off. Jurnee saw it too because she stopped with that fake laugh and got real.

Clearing her throat she answered, "Yes, I am a virgin."

We were silent for a few minutes. I knew why I was, because Jurnee was beyond beautiful. Her shape, personality and all made me think someone broke them skins in. I just assumed she hadn't had any good dick.

"Well, I take it from your silence everything you said about us goes out the window."

At that moment I saw her attitude and fear mixed in one. Baby was about to pop, I folded my arms. Rested my back on the headboard and just let her blow.

"I'm not surprised, you're a whole whore house. It's all good Audrey, I won't stop you from going back to doing you. But I swear when it's my turn, yo' ass is going to need a brick of cocaine to ease the pain."

I stayed the same, expression calm, eyes on her and arms still folded. "I hope you're done talking all that bullshit. Wasting all that good ass breath and lung power over nothing. So fucking what, you're a virgin. You act like it's the end of the world. In two-seconds you ended our relationship. Called me a hoe and basically said you about to be hoeing as well."

Now she looked like a stubborn kid. "You were quiet so I thought you were about to play me. I'm sorry."

"It's cool, you'll learn really quick how serious I am about us and this relationship. All this walking away and quick to break up talk. It's gon' be a wrap for that. Anyway, I don't care about you being a virgin. I like that no other dick has been in you."

Jurnee laughed.

"Speaking of dick, reach in my sweatpants and grab mine."

Yoooo! Her eyes almost fell in her lap, I didn't want to laugh.

"Huh? Wh-Why would you want me to do that?"

"Have you ever touched one before? Be honest. Matter of fact, tell me what all you've done." I wanted to know how far she has been.

Most girls save the pussy and let niggas fuck in the ass. Some give oral, others only liked to get fingered. I wanted to see what all Jurnee has done.

"Nothing, well aside from kissing. I haven't done anything, I've seen it on pornos but I haven't acted out anything. I've never even masturbated."

"Now that is shocking as hell. Even I've beat my dick before but I like that you've never done shit." The proof was in the way my dick started jumping. "That means I'll be your first for everything. Like right now, I want you to reach in my pants and grab my dick."

This time she laughed. "Audrey I can't just grab it."

"Yeah you can," I opened my legs wider, so they were around her. "Go ahead, grab it and pull it out."

Her hesitation was cute; she did that hair flip and cleared her throat. Then she scooted closer to me and went for it. Her little hands trembled a little when she opened my sweats and saw the little trail of hair on my pelvis. But she swallowed her nerve and grabbed it. Them eyes bugged when she realized she needed two hands. I didn't move, I just bit my bottom lip and watched her pull it out. Jurnee looked so damn good handling my pipe. Once it was out, balls included, her face was red.

"Um, Audrey that's way too much dick. You're a freak and I don't mean sexual. How long has it been this big?"

I laughed. "That I am, but not in the way you're thinking. Not every man is the same size, but that's not the point. I need you to get familiar with this big muthafucka, it's all yours, baby. Ain't no rush or pressure. Stop focusing on all the parties and bitches you used to see me with. I was single at the time, so I was doing it all. I kept a condom on and have never had an STD."

"That's good to know Audrey, because I really like

you."

Wanna know some funny shit? Jurnee was literally talking to me while playing with my dick. I don't even think she knew she was doing it. Her soft hands touched all around it, the tip and even the balls. I wasn't minding because I wanted her to know my shit in and out. Know how to make it jump, get hard and spit up.

"I really like you to, Yin."

Her giggle was cute. "I'm really the yin to your yang?"

"Yup, I told you that already, come here."

She leaned in my face and we kissed.

"You must like my dick because you haven't let it go." I teased her then licked her bottom lip, we were still nose to nose.

"I do, it's huge but soft and kind of pretty."

That made me snicker. "Yeah, he a bad bitch."

Her laugh was sexy and it made my pipe grow in her hands.

"You gon' have to chill on the strokes unless you wanna be covered in me." I was dead ass. Her hands were making pre-cum appear, she was fine as hell and I was just all around attracted to her.

"Um, can we try something. I-It's—"

I cut her off when she started that stuttering again. "Jurnee you don't have to be nervous or scared to ask me shit. Just ask, I'll never tell you no unless you ask some off stuff."

Instead of her speaking she took her tube top of. Her titties were hot, full and her caramel nipples made my mouth wet.

"I watched this porno the other night. This girl stroked her boyfriend until he came all on her breast. It looked fun and I wanna try it. I mean, only if you want to."

"Man Jurnee have you seen you, I'll do anything that requires intimacy with you. Only don't ever touch my ass and none of that open relationship shit." I leaned over my bed and picked up my shit. It wasn't shit but a plain navy-blue shirt, so I didn't care about using it.

"Do yo' thang." I told her.

Jurnee got between my legs on her knees. She was about to put my dick in her hands again, but I stopped her.

"Wait, do you have the video saved to your phone?"

"Yes." She answered.

"Go to it, let it play." I watched her do it.

The video started and Jurnee sat the phone on my

bed. Putting my dick back in her hands she went back to that stroke. My dick never went back down, when she touched it all it did was grow more. I've done a lot of shit to bitches, but this is a first. Letting a girl jack me off to a porno, I've fucked while one was playing. But this was different, it was hella hot and Jurnee's fine ass was looking so good.

"Is the clear stuff coming out normal?" She asked, looking scared like she did something wrong.

"Yeah that's normal, it's just pre-cum. Just gon' and smear that in and keep going."

She looked at the video as if to check and see if she was doing it right. It was feeling good as hell and the view in front of me was everything. I couldn't wait to get in that new pussy. Untouched, not broken in, inexperienced.

"Jurnee when you give me that pussy, I'ma treat that muthafucka right." I told her as my breathing changed. "Look at me."

When she did and licked her lips, I felt my body heat up.

"I'ma lick it, suck it, stroke and make you feel so good. Come kiss yo' nigga."

She straddled my lap while still stroking me. Our kiss was wet, sloppy and nasty. Jurnee moaned in my mouth. The way she was kissing me, stroking me and moaning let me know she was mine. Before I even put my dick inside of her, she was already giving me her. Something about knowing that made me feel on top of the world. I felt like I didn't want to part from this feeling. Like I'd do anything to make sure I wouldn't.

"Stroke that shit baby, make it spit up." I told her then she took one of my moves and licked my bottom lip before she sucked on it.

"I can't wait till I feel you inside of me. Fucking me better than any of those pornos I watch. Being my first everything."

When she moaned those words it was a wrap, my heartbeat sped up.

"Tell me when you're about to cum, just like in the video. Tell me baby, ssss tell me."

"Oh shit girl, I'm 'bout to cum. Ugh."

Her aim was on point, I swear when I saw the first shot of nut hit her titties. It made more come out, it was freaky as hell. Her face was looking like she just came, Jurnee was a big ol' freak. I was finally catching my breath and about to say something, but Jurnee took off running to my bathroom quick as hell. Thank God I had one in my room because she had nut all on her.

"Yo' you good?" I asked when I came in the bathroom and sat on the closed toilet.

Jurnee was cleaning herself up which was what I wanted to do but she rushed away so fast.

"Can you please bring me my top?" She asked but making sure her back was to me. Her position was making it so I couldn't see her in the mirror.

"Aye," I grabbed her hand and pulled her to me, making her straddle my lap. I wasn't even focusing on her perfect titties bouncing. Right now, I was concerned about her. "What's wrong?"

"Nothing, I just feel kind of dirty and like you look at me different now. I just let you...Well, you know." Her face was looking all shameful.

Lifting her head up so she could look at me I kissed her lips.

"You don't need to feel shameful, perverted or anything because of what we just did. That was fun, sexy, spontaneous and clearly one of your fantasies. I dug that I got to fulfill that with you." I kissed her collar bone then her cheek. "Next time let me do the clean-up. I wanted to jiggle them titties with my nut on'em."

We both laughed hard as hell.

"You the damn pervert!" She teased and I kissed

her again.

"My Yin?" I asked her, biting my lip.

Jurnee playfully rolled her eyes like she didn't want to answer. Then she pushed herself closer to me. "My Yang."

**

Myrtle Beach

"Hi daddy, we made it to Myrtle Beach and we are arriving at the hotel now."

"Ok Fuzzy, have a good time. You know I'm just a phone call away."

"And you'll fuck this world up, I know daddy. Love you." Jurnee hung up with her dad and put her phone in her purse.

We had just arrived at the hotel and I was happy as hell Jurnee was here. All the girls were, their dads brought the school kickback story. Me and my brothers posted about this trip for weeks, we did a countdown. Anywhere the Legends go people wanted to tag along. So, we weren't surprised when it actually turned into a school kickback.

People from my senior class and the upcoming seniors caught their own flight and some are driving. It didn't matter to me, the theme was still #Chaos18thbirthday. I was still having my party only now I decided to rent a beach house for the night so it would be enough room. Ava called me last night begging me if she could come.

At first, I was going to tell her no and leave it at that. But something was off in her voice not to mention she has been wanting to be at our house a lot. We were close to our baby sister and didn't mind her being over. But she's never wanted to be over that much. Pops thought maybe her Moms had a new boyfriend and he was on some bullshit.

Ava's Moms shut that down though and told him she never had no guy at the house. Maybe she was having one of her female moods and just wanted to be around us. Either way, I talked to Pops and told him let her have her own turn up with her girlfriends. So, he got them a suite at Kalahari in Ohio. With him chaperoning in his own room of course, but it was some fun she needed.

"How are we doing this room situation?" Austin asked before we all got on the elevator.

I don't think any of us thought about it. I knew the only ones who were officially a couple were me and Jurnee.

"If y'all wanna room together take my suite and I can get another room." I told them because I know how girls can be. I don't need nobody feeling pressured, arguing or being uncomfortable. If one chick isn't comfortable in a group, then it will throw the whole vibe off.

"Yeah it's up to you ladies how y'all wanna do this." August had my back with this.

"Well I don't have these kinds of problems, so I'll see y'all on the top floor." Chill fat ass laughed and got on the elevator.

"Can we have a minute?" Jurnee asked me and my brothers so they could talk.

It was cool with us, we stepped to the display counter in the lobby while they talked.

"I low-key want to room with Brinx." August said.

"Hell yeah I feel the same way about Coya." Austin added.

I wanted Jurnee in my room but my Yin was a virgin. I didn't want her feeling any kind of way.

"They won't go that route because of Toni. Her and

this nigga fight like cats and dogs." I joked pointing to Adrian.

"What!?"

Me and my brothers looked over at the girls when they yelled loud. Then they were all in Coya's face laughing and ding that girly shit girls do.

"The hell wrong with them?" Austin asked.

"Me and Toni been hooking up." Adrian said all nonchalant.

We looked at him all bizarre.

"Fuck outta here, y'all can't stand each other." I laughed.

"We can't but my lips and tongue love's her body."

"How long?" August asked what we all wanted to know.

"A few months wasn't shit heavy just something we like to do. But I caught feelings and she did too. We still go at it just after we hook-up." He rubbed his hands together laughing.

"I should have known, the way y'all argued you had to be hittin'nat."

"Naw no sex, just other shit."

We still high-fived him and the girls came over.

"Ok, so we talked and if it's ok with y'all each girl

would like to room with her honey. Or in Toni's case, her dirty secret." Brinx joked around.

We were cool with it and I know I was geeked about Jurnee being in my suite for four days.

"You sure you cool with this?" I asked her putting my arms around her waist while we all got off the elevator.

Jurnee was looking good in these black stretch shorts. I dug that my girl was a gym-shoe head. I've seen her in slides and sandals but she kept some fresh kicks on. While my arms were around her waist. I removed her yellow hoodie and she smiled at it.

"Yes, I'm fine with being in your room. I was the first one to vote yes on it." She turned her head to the side and looked at me smiling.

We got inside our room with me sitting our bags down. It was early and after we settled, then we were going to hit the beach. My party wasn't until the day after tomorrow. So, we were going to have some old fashion fun.

"Do you mind if I just hang back while you all go to the beach." Jurnee asked when I came out the bathroom.

We've been here for about two-hours and everyone was ready to head out. I took my chain off just in case I decide to get in the water. I had on my Jordan swim trunks with matching slides and Jurnee re-twisted my dreads yesterday.

"You ok, why you don't wanna go?" I asked her tossing my shirt on the king size bed.

Our suite was nice as hell, a sitting room with a TV in it. Full kitchen, dining room table and the bedroom was my favorite. A king size bed, big window facing the beach and the bathroom was on next level luxury.

"Cause I'm just tired."

"You looked up, I notice you look up when you lie." I sat down next to her on the bed. "You gotta stop this lying shit Jurnee, it pisses me off. What's the real reason, yo' coochie running red or something?"

"Oh my gosh, Audrey!" She laughed and hit my arm. "No, I am not on my period. I just don't care for me in a swimsuit."

Every time she said something about her body it just blew me back. I took my phone out and went to my Instagram account.

"You see this, it's my senior class. Well, every girl in my senior class. Look how these bitches are posing. Trying to stick what little ass they have out, turning weird ways to make them have hips." I stopped scrolling after we laughed and I put my phone down.

"Jurnee, your shape is out of this world. This ain't back in the day when having meat on your bones was shamed on. I'm not a girl but I been around them long enough to understand one thing. When bitches talk about the same flaw on another girl it's because they jealous of that flaw. Think about it, you're not mean or stuck up. But how many chicks have you ran across that just flat out don't like you?"

The face she made let me know it was a lot.

"Exactly, don't be ashamed of nothing pertaining to you. Physically, emotionally or any level. Soak that shit up because every bitch should have a reason to hate on you. You so damn bomb you got this nigga to fall for you through a keyboard." I preached some real facts to her now.

Jurnee's eyes were glued on mine and I could tell she was fighting back tears. Smiling she said. "Did you just say you fell for me?"

Damn, did I say that shit? I didn't even realize I was being that real. Playing it off I waved my hand at her and stood up. "Get'cho fine ass up, put on yo' swimsuit and come hang with'cho nigga." I kissed her shoulder and picked up her little bag she had next to the bed. It had her swim stuff and sandals in it.

"No hoodie either." I joked laying back on the bed when she went in the bathroom. I scrolled social media while she changed.

"Damn." I said when Jurnee came out the bathroom.

Looking down at her body her eyes got big. "What, it's ugly?"

I stood up and pointed to my dick. "Does it look like that swimsuit ugly?" Licking my lips I admired her physique.

Her swimsuit was a two-piece. The top was long sleeve and stopped right under her titties. The bottoms were like these high waist panties girls wear that gives them shape. Only Jurnee had it naturally so it accentuated her curves even more. Man I wanted to say fuck the beach, get her in the bed so she could jack me off again. This time, I wanted to cum on them thick thighs.

"I'm glad you like it and look." She did a cute ass turn in a circle. "No hoodie, I'm not even wearing the skirt that goes with it."

Her smile turned me on even more.

"You're a virgin so I'll keep all my thoughts to myself. But I will say this much, you look good as hell.

Come on let's roll." My dick was about to break off, I had to squeeze it real quick to calm down. I picked up her beach bag so I could carry it. It had our towels, my jacket, our phones and wallet in it.

"Damn y'all stay hugged up."

"Damn you stay sucking on Coya toes." I talked shit back to Austin when he hated on me and Jurnee.

The beach was nice, and I like that it wasn't as packed. I couldn't wait till tomorrow, the lady at the front desk of our hotel helped. She gave me these brochures about all the stuff to do at Myrtle Beach.

"Fuck you nigga I ain't even gotten around to putting her toes in my mouth yet." My damn baby brother was a whole mess, but we all thought it was funny as hell.

"And my feet are very pretty." Coya added laughing too.

"Has your brother always loved feet?" Jurnee asked me.

"Hell yeah, since that fool was about five." August answered her.

"Don't try to play me like it's just any ol'feet I'll fuck with. I'on do men, old people or fucked up looking ones. But I'm not no weirdo, I just appreciate a woman with a pretty pair." This boy smiled hard then kissed

Coya's feet.

We were sitting on beach chairs with the girls just taking the beach in before we get in the water. Chill was in this baddie's face he picked out when we first got here.

"I ain't the only one with an obsession." Austin said, opening up a box these girls were not about to let close.

"Oh really, let's hear it. August you first." Brinx said sitting back down between his legs. She was putting sunscreen on.

"You already know I love lips and now you got me loving cheekbones."

"Well I'ma leg nigga myself. All kinds as long as they ain't hairy." Adrian said and August high-fived him.

"What about you baby, don't be shy." Jurnee's cute self held her head back, looking at me.

"Ass!" My brothers answered loud as hell all together.

I couldn't do shit but laugh and so did Jurnee. We all got up and went in the water like some big kids. Chill even came over with the chick he was talking to. She was cool, chocolate and had two long braids in her head.

"Yo' hair long as hell and pretty." I told Jurnee when she came from under the water.

"Thank you, in the morning it will be all over my head."

I couldn't help sometimes just looking at her. I never would have guessed the way she always was in school that she was this cool. Like her personality was fye (means perfect) and her looks just topped her off.

"Gimmie kiss." I told her while we stood up and a wave brushed against our legs. Our tongues played tag and her wet lips felt good.

"You gotta excuse my hands baby, you just so thick and it sets me off." I told her honestly, kissing her neck. I knew she wasn't used to no man being all on her. But she gotta learn fast because I was an affectionate nigga with my girl. I loved to squeeze, grab, touch, kiss and lick all the time.

"It's ok, I actually like it. You don't act ashamed to be physical because we're in public." Her hand rubbed down my beard.

"Never that." I told her as we walked back to our beach chair. After I dried her and myself off, I sat down pulling her down with me.

Jurnee was between my legs getting mine and her phone out her bag. I saw my sister tagged me and our brothers in a post. It was long as hell and all mushy thanking us for having her back and being there for her. That's my spoiled little Ava. I looked down at Jurnee on her phone because I'd be dumb not to. I saw she was tagged in a post and it was that punk ass Eddie. She must had sensed me peeping because she hurried up and backed out of it.

"Naw, go back to that shit, let me see what he tagged you in." I told her.

"I knew you were watching nosey." She laughed but I was so for real.

"Mmhm, click on it." I read it and it was a status he made saying he touched down at Myrtle Beach. I wasn't stupid, he had to be tagging her tryna be funny. Me and Jurnee have put each other on our social pages. It wasn't no secret we were together, homie was feeling a way. But he got the wrong one, on everything I will destroy that clown.

"Y'all still talk?" I asked her after I read the status.

"Not at all, I kind of didn't end it. I just stopped talking to him so maybe he needs some closure." Her voice was all sweet and she sound like she meant what she said.

But I wasn't having that. "He don't need shit from you. Everybody that follow me and you know we together. He tryna be slick tagging you, but I'ma slick my fist down his throat if he don't chill." I was heated and didn't care, I hated a slick ass nigga. Like take the loss my guy and move on.

Jurnee looked up pushing herself up towards my lips. Kissing me a few times she said, "No need for all of that. I'm with you and I don't cheat so let him tag away. I'll just remove him." She kissed my lips again.

I didn't like that I got all soft when she did that.

"I'on even know why you messed with him anyway. He what, about 5'7, 5'8, that's around your height. You weren't even talking to a man, you had a lil mama."

She put her hands on her face laughing so hard. I wasn't even trying to be funny but he was short as hell. Don't let that height fool you, short guys are sneaky Stuart Little bitches.

"Did you just call that man a little mama?" Jurnee was laughing so hard she had to wipe her eyes.

"Plus listen to you sounding all jealous, you acting like we're a forever thing." Her thick ass stayed between my legs and sat up on her knees facing me. Damn she was so fine.

My eyes looked her up and down. "I'll have my

mind made up if we forever tomorrow."

Her eyebrow arched up. "Really, why tomorrow?"

"Because it will be our first night together. If I wake up to you and feel a certain way then it's a wrap. You my baby for life, no nigga will come after me, you'll foreva be the Yin to my Yang." I yanked her to me and kissed her.

See, Pops told me he knew he wanted Mama as the one. When he woke up to her their first night, he said he knew then. He said he felt like he wanted to wake up to that forever. Pops also told us he was the one who fucked it up. I've woken up to a few bitches, but it be in hotels or our basement.

That shit doesn't count, Jurnee got me in my feelings and I dug our story. Tomorrow will let me know what's up. After me and Jurnee caked up for a few more minutes we got back in the water with everyone the beach was fun as hell. When we were all done everyone went back to their suite. We all got dressed and headed out to dinner, it was a strong vibe when we all hung out.

"I had so much fun tonight and I'm stuffed." Jurnee spoke from the bathroom. It was around two in the morning. We hung out in August's suite for a while.

Me, my brothers and Chill were smoking and the

girls were drinking some wine coolers. It was easy to get some alcohol underage when you had enough money. I was laying in the soft bed under the covers going through Netflix on the TV. I took a shower first because Jurnee was still with her girls. I would have loved for her to take a shower with me. But I didn't want to do all of that our first night. I had on my boxers and that was it, I hope Jurnee don't trip about that. I either sleep in boxers or nothing and I didn't want to scare her.

"Don't you dare pick a movie, you picked one before we went to the beach. It's my turn and we are watching *Dirty Dancing.* I still don't get how you've never seen that."

"Fuck." I said under my breath when she came out the bathroom.

Her back was to me and she had some boy shorts on and a sports bra. Them cheeks were swallowing the lace. That dip in her back that separates it from her booty was even sexy. I was definitely going to have a hard dick all night. She was putting her stuff in her suitcase and she finally walked towards the bed. The lights were off, and the curtains were closed.

The only light was from the TV. I could see her clear though and as she got closer, she looked scared.

Giving me a close mouth smile she nervously pulled the covers back. I tried to just look at the TV, but I couldn't keep my eyes off her. When she got in the bed, I wanted to laugh so hard the way she made sure she was far from me. Like I was going to just start pouncing on her the minute she touched the bed.

I let her start the movie and get comfortable. Once she did, I turned my head to her. "Can I scoot you over here some?"

"U-Um yeah that's fine."

Fuck why does she turn me on so bad. I put my arms around her waist and pulled her to me. Her body was warm and soft as hell plus she smelled sweet.

"I can hear your heart beating over the movie." I had her close as hell to me, so I was able to just look down at her.

"My bad, this is a first for me."

"I know and I need you to know you're not obligated to do anything. Tonight or the entire time we are here. You got it baby?" I had my hand on the back of her neck messing with her curls. See it's the shit like that she had me on, caking and being all mushy.

"I know and I appreciate that." As she talked her smooth leg was going up and down mine. "I still can't believe you turned out to be SwagWordz. I told you so much personal and intimate stuff. A total stranger who I had never even seen a picture of had me opening up. Audrey Legend is my boyfriend, sounds so weird." She giggled and continued rubbing her leg on mine.

"Well make that shit sound like new life because I don't see me wanting it any other way." I stopped her leg midway and started rubbing her thigh up and down.

"Why you be looking at me like that?" I asked her not with an attitude but out of curiosity.

Jurnee shrugged her shoulders. "I just like looking at you. Aside from you being extremely fine and the blue eyes. You just have these little things you do that I like looking at. Like when you're watching TV, you crack your knuckles. When you eat your jawline gets intense and you lick your lips.

Or my favorite, anytime you say my name no matter the reason you always bite your bottom lip. I don't think you even know you do it, but you do."

As she talked, I was listening, not saying nothing.

"Oh my goodness you probably think I'm weird as hell now." She put her hand over her face and she would have rolled off me, but I had her thigh.

"Relax woman, I don't think that at all. I just never

had anyone pay that much attention to me. I mean I've had girls on my dick but you talking with admiration. Making a nigga get chills and shit." I did a pretend shake making us both laugh. "I dig that though, but you know what I dig more?"

Jurnee shook her head no.

"Kissing you." I kept hold of that thick thigh while we kissed. I think us being in the bed half naked made it more intense quicker.

I was losing control, I mean I wasn't about to rape her or nothing. But I was getting lost in just making out. All this shit me and Jurnee do was like making love but without penetration. That was new for me, everything I did with a female ended in sex. Hell, some begin with it. I don't know anything else beyond it. It sounds crazy but the writing chat room board we met on was necessary.

I know me and I would have pushed away from Jurnee the first moment she told me she was a virgin. Putting in work, being all sensitive to her needs and shit would have turned me off. I never have to lift a finger when it came to women. The only time I put their needs first is in the bedroom. Even then I'm not licking no pussy or kissing on the mouth. But I wanted to do it all with Jurnee.

Even though I have brothers, Pops and my Mama around. I don't share everything with them. Writing, getting into what inspires me, favorite authors and just a whole other side they know nothing about. All while still being me, being Chaos, looking after my brothers and running these streets like a true goon.

Pops never believed all of that can be done and I never argued him about it. PenQueen became that person and knowing it was Jurnee all along is everything. It came together and played out for the best. Now, I was on top of her sucking on her neck then making my way back to her lips.

"I need you to trust me, ok. We're not about to have sex." I told her while unzipping her sports bra.

Jurnee nodded her head yes. "Ok Audrey, I trust you."

I smirked and kissed her again. Then I put a nice hickey on her neck, worked my way to them titties. The fact that I was the first to do all of this to her made me show out. I licked on her tits and let my tongue play with her nipples. Her body jerked a little when I bit down lightly on her nipples.

"Ahhh, can you do that again?" She moaned out looking down at me.

I didn't even say anything, I just did what she asked. I could suck on her titties all day but I wanted to taste more. Going down I pulled her boy shorts down and was surprised to see her pussy shaved. I assumed since no one was gettin' it that it would be hairy. But that fucker was fat, hairless and before I even touched it, I just knew it was smooth. I kissed and licked all on her thick thighs first.

"Whatever you feel just let that shit happen. Let your body do its thang all in my mouth. I want you to cry out, pull my hair, cuss, do whatever you feel. A'ight?"

Her head nodded fast as hell; she was clueless, but I love how she trusted me. Opening her legs I was able to see that kat up close. It was soaked, I was turning her on before I even started. When I licked on them thighs again, I saw them juices slide out. My stomach growled from being hungry for it. I held her thigh in each of my hands tight, spread them wide and went it.

Jurnee tasted like warm water. No smell, lips soft and that clit was like a pearl in a clam. Once I put it in my mouth, I sucked lightly on it. My tongue did circles on it, I repeated that over and over. Jurnee was so wet I felt her juices over my lips. My beard, and even my nose was wet because I had my face so far in that kat. I made sure to not put any fingers inside of her, I wanted all tongue and lips. When I tell y'all this girl was going crazy, she let loose and I don't mean only in my mouth.

"Audreyyyy oh my gosh. Sssss baby." Her moans were making me go crazy on feasting her. "Uhh, uhh you...I...O-O-Ohhh my gosh."

Her body shook and she arched all the way up. Her thick thighs were trying to close but I wasn't having it.

"Mmhhm." I made noises while I drank her up like a cold pop. Her thighs were shaking so bad in my hand but they weren't slipping out of them; I eased up off her clit after she was done cumming. Any juice that even tried to slide out of her I grabbed it with my tongue.

"Not done baby, I wanna do it again." This time I pushed her legs so far back that her eyes got big. "I bet you didn't think they could go back that far huh. Jurnee when I really get a hold of you, I swear I'm going to have your body do the fucking impossible. But right now I just wanna fuck you with my tongue. I want you to hold them legs back for me. Cum all in ya man's mouth, spoon feed me that pussy, my pussy." I didn't give her a chance to say anything, I just went back in.

I tongue kissed that muthafucka, swirled my tongue all around the inside of her lips. I was licking that pussy like a cat licks milk. Only my tongue was wide so I could lay it in on her pussy like a soft blanket. I could feel her legs getting weak but Jurnee did what I said and held them back. Once she exposed that pussy some more, I used my tongue, folded it and put it inside of her. My whole mouth covered her whole and I literally was fucking her. Her walls make my mouth so wet. While I was doing that, I used my thumb and massaged her clit.

"Audrey, baby oh my God I just can't! I'm 'bout to fucking...Ugh! Ugh! My God, what the fuck!"

Man she called out some of everything, my name, God, she cussed and body shook again. I didn't miss a drip, it all went in my mouth like I wanted it to. This time she couldn't hold her legs and I didn't mind. I pulled my tongue out of her and made a loud slurping sound so I could get the last drops. Kissing and sucking on her thighs again I played with them titties and then kissed her. I couldn't believe she let me, I was a nasty nigga but I didn't know what would be too nasty for her.

"Oh my goodness that was so good. You had me use the Lord name in vain, I have to repent later." That made me and her laugh so hard. Her chest going rapid and she was out of breath.

I rubbed my beard, smearing her juices in and I

licked my lips looking at her. "You so damn sexy it's crazy and that was so lit." I said pulling her on top of me. My dick was so hard but I didn't even need the pussy right now. I just loved seeing her satisfied.

"Did I have an orgasm?" Her look was funny as hell.

"I'm pretty sure you did. Believe it or not it will be way more intense when I penetrate you." I told her for real while rubbing on her thighs. Her wet pussy was on my bare chest and I swear I felt that clit acting like a pulse. I looked down at it wet my chest and then back at her gorgeous face. "This is my pussy now Jurnee, don't make me act chaotic over it."

Putting her hand in her hair, she flipped it to the right and bent down to kiss my lips. "Coya and Toni say guys say that *after* they have sex. Not before." She had humor in her tone.

I put my hand around her neck biting my bottom lip. "I don't give a damn what they said, I'm telling you now. As a matter of fact just so we have an understanding. I want you to tell me, tell me you're mine and that that's my pussy." I was so serious and she better say them words.

Even though she was looking all shy, she spoke.

"I'm yours and this is your pussy, Audrey Legend."

Mm! Damn that turned me on to the capacity. "Sit on my face, I wanna make you cum again." I told her licking my lips and getting ready to taste her again.

Yeah, none of you guys get fly as me, whoa
Matter of fact, none of you guys get high as me, whoa
Post my drip up daily just so they can see, whoa
Turn me up some more so my haters can hear it, whoa (yeah)

Lil Baby- *Whoa* was setting the vibe. It was the day of my party and this vacation has been all the way up. Yesterday me, my brothers and the girls did so much fun stuff. Parasailing, jet skiing, and the girls talked all of us fellas to a damn spa day. Even Chill was dragged into it, I ain't gone lie. The pedicure and massage felt good, way better than the Chinese people back home.

We paid the girls back though when we made them come to Wheels of Yesterday. It was a museum of all these sweet ass vintage cars. I could live in that muthafucka if given the keys to it. We ended the night at this nice hookah lounge. Now, it was my 18th birthday party and the turnout was crazy. Before we got to Myrtle Beach I had some invites made. So, yesterday we were passing them out to people.

Also, we had people from home here too. Couldn't believe they actually followed us here just to turn up wit'cha boy. I had really been enjoying myself with Jurnee. This was a first for me and my brothers. We were out of town and didn't have different bitches follow us. I wasn't getting head in a rental or fucking one chick while she ate another's pussy.

Now I was all caked up and didn't even mind it. Hell, I didn't even miss the random women. We did go Live a few times; I had some dancers here. Everyone was dressed in street clothes, the women had on some sexy dresses or tight shorts. I wanted me and my brothers to drip in Fendi from head to toe. My actual birthday wasn't until Monday, the day we go home.

But I wanted my party here and on Monday I just wanna get a room with my girl. Speaking of her fine ass, she was in these sexy high waist jeans. Her top had thin straps and had her titties sitting up nice. That big curly hair was down with her side part she always wore. But what really made her look extra good was the yellow and white Jordans she had on.

And the fact that she didn't have a hoodie tied around her waist. I got a little annoyed with the way men were looking at her, but it was all good. I gave them a window to look for two seconds. Anything over that and I was running through them. My mind went to the fact that when school started, I'll be downtown at Wayne State and she'll be at Cooley.

Even though it was only a fifteen-minute drive. I knew high school niggas, hell I'm kind of still one. I've always heard what they thought about Jurnee. Her body, ass, her smile, that hair and the fact that she didn't fuck with any guy. It made her become a quest to conquer. Who would be the one to break her down, get between her legs and make her theirs?

When no one would succeed she became that to every guy as the stuck-up bitch. The one who was mean and invisible, all a while I was talking to her. SwagWordz and PenQueen were a match made and didn't even know it. When school start, the true test will kick in for both of us. Believe it or not it would be harder for me.

It's not Jurnee that I don't trust, it was niggas. The fact that I was getting mad right now just thinking of a clown tryna get mine was pissing me off. It was making Chaos come out and school hadn't even started.

"You ok baby?" Jurnee asked me putting her hand in my dreads then rubbing on my beard.

I looked at her pretty ass standing in front of me. I

had a gazebo in the backyard set up for only me, my brothers, Chill and the girls. This beach house rental was a present from Mama and it was fire. Jurnee and her girls were dancing and having fun, all of them looked better than any bitch here. Chill and Adrian were talking to some random bitches.

Toni didn't seem to mind, and I assumed that's just how they thang worked. But he seemed bothered as hell when she was dancing with a guy. I could tell they were complicated but he better figure some shit out soon. Because Toni had a no fucks given attitude like him and that's a crazy mix. Austin was always more calm, but people underestimated that a lot. Anyway, I grabbed Jurnee's arm and pulled her on my lap.

"I ain't gone have no problems from you when school start, right?" I asked her with my hand squeezing her thigh.

"Not at all, I'm not a cheater, Audrey. You're the one who will be at a university and you're a Legend. I should be asking you that."

"You don't have to even focus on that. I may smile at a bitch or two but nothing past that. I'm just genuinely a happy guy." I flashed my award-winning smile at her.

Jurnee rolled her eyes playfully and nodded her

head. "Fair enough, well I may flirt with a nigga or two but nothing past that. I'm just naturally a flirtatious girl." Her pretty white teeth flashed at me. Her attempt to get up was stopped by my arms stopping her.

"Jurnee on my Mama I will split Cooley in four parts if I find out your flirting with anybody." I was looking at her with no smile or humor.

Scratching the back of her neck she said, "See what we are not about to do is this right here. You can't tell me you'll smile in girls' faces then get mad when I say I'll flirt. I was taught to do what's done to you. Treat people the way you want to be treated. With that being said, what you do I'll do. If you sneak and do something with a girl then imagine me sneaking and doing the same thing with a guy." She shrugged her shoulders like what she was saying wasn't a big deal.

I had my eyes squinted still looking at he. "You really pissing me off."

"I don't care, let me up." Her thick ass tried to move.

"Hell naw, I bet you don't go nowhere." I picked up my cup and took a sip. My other arm was holding her in place.

"Audrey stop playing." She wiggled some more

getting madder. "So you'll just sit like this for your whole party?"

"Yup, I don't give a fuck. I got'cho soft booty sitting on my dick so it ain't no thang to me. But if you make it a thang I'll shut this whole bitch down, put everybody out. It will then just be me and you, still sitting here in the same position. Do you really wanna do that to your friends? Look at them, having a good time, laughing and shit. You gone fuck all that up." I was calm as I kissed her shoulder a few times.

Jurnee was looking at me with her mouth slightly open. "Audrey it's too soon for me to see this Chaos side."

"Jurnee it's too soon for you to make him come out. You lucky I didn't flip when I saw Miles here with his boy Eddie. But did I trip, no I didn't. I want him to stay and see you all on my dick and me all up yo' ass. Now, I apologize for my comment about smiling in bitches faces. I was dead ass wrong." I told her honestly, I'm man enough to admit that.

She gave me a cute half smile. "I accept, I apologize for my flirt comment."

"I accept as well, but I don't like you talking about that tit for tat shit." I told her trying not to get mad all over again. I couldn't stop squeezing her juicy thigh, it was my thing.

"I can't apologize for that but I meant it. If you don't plan on doing anything then you shouldn't let it bother you."

I felt like she was fucking with my head, so I let her up. It was best of she get away from me before I flip out. All I know is, Jurnee was my girl. Her untouched body wasn't about to be touched by anyone else. I don't wanna hear about it, see it, think it or imagine it. I watched her with her girls having a good time.

"You look heated bro." August said to me giving me a fat blunt.

"Jurnee gon' make me fuck her up." I told him lighting it.

Chill and our other brothers came over from the buffet table sitting down.

"What she do?"

I put the blunt down and picked up my cup, dropping a half pill in the bottom of it. Sometimes we'd pop a pill just to get that extra faded. But we knew how to handle it as far as never over doing it for our bodies. I get real chilled, eyes low and dick is ready to do even more of a performance.

"Something that's gonna have me on tip if she

pushes. When school starts keep an eye on her for me. Let me know any and everything when it comes to any funny shit. I'm telling you bro I'ma leave a nigga head on top of the flagpole."

August laughed and dropped a half pill in his cup too. "You wild as fuck bro but you know I got'chu." He pounded my fist as the girls came back over to us.

Jurnee sat next to me and I couldn't even stay mad. Her energy and presence had such an effect on me it was nuts.

"Can I get a kiss or you still mad at me?" Her pretty face got in mine and asked.

I was good and high now but not enough to not let her soften me. "You can get whatever you want from me." I spoke in her ear because the music was loud. Before I moved I kissed her ear because I knew she liked that.

Smiling she gave me an intense nasty kiss and said, "Can I get a repeat of last night?"

Man, I bit my bottom lip just thinking about how good her pretty pussy tasted. "Hell yeah, if you want you can get that now."

"No nasty, it's a lot of people here." She giggled.

"And it's nine bedrooms, we'll have privacy." I put my cup to my lips and she watched.

"Can I have some?"

My low eyes slowly went to hers. "Naw baby, this ain't the cup for you. I got some extra fizz at the bottom of it. But we got all flavors of wine coolers over by the food." I kissed her cheek.

"No, I want some of yours. I know what fizz means. I 'm with you and I know you're not about to let anything happen to me. I just want to try a little."

I thought about it for a second and then gave her my cup. "Don't make no habit of this shit. I don't want my girl on this level, leave that to the rats and hoes." I told her watching her drink from my cup.

Her face was like she tasted a sour lemon. "It's so strong." She laughed and then drunk some more.

I chuckled and took it from her. "First and last time you'll drink that."

"Who the hell let these basset hounds in South Carolina!?" Toni yelled out making us look at who she was talking about.

"Aw shit." I said lowly because them damn Talbert sisters were here.

You know how you go over a friend house who has roaches. When you get home ya' Mama shake all yo' shit out before you come inside thinking that's gon' help. But one sneaks in the crib anyway. That's how I felt, even though Regina was looking good. I just wasn't interested in fucking anymore. The hoe act like she was my girl or something.

Never been in my room, never kissed her on that mouth. My tongue never been on that kat nor have I ever been in her raw. I treated her like the hoe she was only with me she knew she was always good. Me paying for Lyft rides, VIP sections, supplying weed and drinks.

That don't make me yo' nigga, it just makes me a gentleman. Regina took that and ran with it, she treated me like I was her man. Running off females and fighting over me. I would never care because I never found myself making anyone my bitch. But now that I had Jurnee, I wasn't about to have that shit going down.

"Looks like your girl didn't want to miss her man party." Jurnee's smart ass mouth said.

Looking at her, she was definitely a light weight. Her eyes were low and she looked tipsy as hell. Plus she kept giggling and couldn't keep her hands off me. But when she saw them Talbert sisters, her face changed.

"I don't want you in no shit baby, what I tell you the day we went to the beach. Every woman gon' always hate on you. Fuck'em." I kissed her neck.

"I know but them hoes jumped Coya."

Shit. I didn't know that. Before I could even say anything the girls were on the Talbert sisters' asses. I mean they turned into some fucking boxers in a ring. Wasn't no punk ass or that loud scream that girls do when they fight. All you heard was the word bitch, hits thrown and that was over the music. Good thing they were away from the food and we were outside. Still, we didn't want the girls fighting. We each grabbed a girl and pulled them off separating the madness.

"Damn girl, I never knew you had them hands." I laughed calming Jurnee down.

The Talbert sisters were taken to the front of the house. I don't care if they left or not. But if they come near Jurnee again, I was shooting everybody, I don't care.

"I been waiting on that, stupid hoes wanna jump my girl." Jurnee was fixing her hair.

"Bitch! That was so bomb! It was like we all were thinking the same thing." Toni said after she fixed her long skirt.

"All I kept saying was please don't let my booty show." Brinx added, she had on a dress that wasn't long enough to keep her cheeks from falling out.

"Wouldn't nobody had left until I checked

everybody phone." August said pulling Brinx's dress down some more.

Once everybody got back in a party vibe, it turned up to the max harder. Drinks, weed and the effect from the pill made the night become hypnotic. The D.J. I had was setting every mood just right. Jurnee was dancing on me and I kept sticking my tongue down her throat every chance I got. Loud laughter, dancing and just a good ass time.

I don't remember when, but I knew I put the other half of the pill in my cup. I was fucking faded and so were all of us. I knew we weren't making it back to our hotel, but I knew one of the bed's had me and Jurnee's name on it when it was time to sleep.

The sunlight from the exposed sky facing the house was all in my eyes. It almost burned when I opened them. Looking at the walls of the room I had no idea where I was. Like I do when I get drunk I laid still. Closing my eyes I thought to the last thing I remembered. My party, music, and the beach house. That's where I was, at the beach house Mama rented for my birthday. Opening my eyes again I did the next thing I do. Looked on the nightstand, I saw my wallet, a stack of money and my gun sitting on it. I felt good as I laid back and wiped my eyes.

Some smooth legs went up and down mine and I smiled turning over.

"What the fuck." I almost fell out the bed when I saw Coya sound asleep.

Not only was she sleep but she was naked. As a matter of fact, so was I. My heart was beating so fast I had to make sure it didn't fall out. What the fuck! How the hell did I end up in bed with her!? We weren't even near each other, I was near August and Brinx more than the others. Naked! Fucking naked and in bed!

"Yo, wake up." I shook her shoulder.

Moving around a little she wiped her eyes and opened them. Her eyes had the same reaction as I did from the sun light. When she opened them all the way and saw me, they opened so big and she jumped up.

"Chaos what the hell?!" Grabbing the sheet she looked at me like I violated her.

"Shhh. Be quiet before someone comes in here." I told her and she listened.

Coya's reaction was identical to mine, she looked at herself under the sheet. Her mouth opened then she looked at her clothes on the floor.

"Oh my God. Oh my God. Oh my God. No. No. No. Please God no." Looking at me I could tell she was about to cry.

I was already getting dressed.

"Did we…I… please tell me we didn't—"

"No. I know we didn't, I may be fucked up but I don't have that feeling of having sex. I've popped before and partied, when I wake up my dick feels drained and I always have a condom on." I opened my wallet and had the same two Magnums in there. "Push everything to the side and tell me how you feel. Like down there." I pointed down to her private part. My dick was big and thick as hell, a girl can feel if we have had sex.

Coya stopped breathing hard, turned around and opened the sheet. I assumed she was checking herself.

"I know my body too, I didn't have sex." We both breathed out hard in relief. But it didn't explain how we got like this.

"This all just looks foul, I mean why would we get into bed together. Get naked and go to sleep. No one noticed we were missing?! It was a bunch of people here." She said picking up her clothes.

"Man I don't even know but as long as we didn't have sex then I can forget about it if you can. Jurnee and my brother will hit the damn roof if they see this."

"I agree, I would never do that to my girl or to

Austin. I swear I wouldn't." She wiped her face.

"I know Coya, you don't even strike me as that type. This is all fucked up, but no one is up yet. You stay here, I'll ease out. Find my girl and we put this behind us. Deal?" After I was fully dressed, I checked and made sure I didn't leave shit in the room. I stood in front of her with my hand out.

Coya looked scared and like she wanted to cry again. "Please don't play me Chaos, this will destroy everything if it got out. With your brother and most importantly with my girls."

I felt so bad because she was terrified. I'm telling y'all right now, me and her didn't have sex. I would bet my life on it, like I'd literally take a bullet to the dome right now. But she was right, we wouldn't be able to explain ourselves. But I wanted her to believe that I wouldn't play her.

"Coya I swear I ain't that kind of nigga. I practically am in love with your best friend and I wouldn't dare hurt my baby bro like that. You got my word."

She calmed down and looked relieved then she shook my hand. I walked out easing the door open. It was people sleep on the floor, couch, chairs. The dining room table had two fine girls sleep with no top on. Usually I'd stare at some titties, but I needed to find my girl. Chill was on another couch sleep with two girls on the side of him. The house wasn't trashed, just people sleep. Bikini tops were hanging and red cups were everywhere.

We had a speaker here so the music could continue when the D.J. left. *Mario's* voice was playing but not loud. I got past the living room and down the hallway. Every door closed I opened to see if Jurnee was in there. The first two rooms had naked girls in the beds. Damn we partied hard. I went upstairs and I swear if Jurnee was in bed like I was. I don't even know what I was going to do.

I don't know if I would be understanding because of my situation. Or would I kill who she was laying next to, unless it's one of my brothers. I looked in the bathroom that was on the left. Adrian and Toni were sound asleep in the jacuzzi tub with a damn blanket. I just chuckled and kept it moving. Where the fuck was my woman at?

I opened the next door and it was August and Brinx knocked out. My stomach dropped because I didn't see Austin and I didn't see Jurnee. Now, me and my brothers have swapped bitches before. But never a main one, never our girl. Opening the door before the last I was glad as hell when I saw Adrian on top of the covers fully clothed and sleep. I was glad because she wasn't with him.

But now that Chill and my brothers were accounted for, a nasty taste went through my mouth. Pulling my gun out my mind was now made up. I was killing whoever was in the bed with her. Girl, boy, two and a half men, three men and a baby. I didn't give a damn, I don't want to listen to reason. I was killing whoever it was then taking my girl back to our room. I opened the door and Jurnee was sleep under the covers.

Curly hair everywhere and I didn't see her clothes off. Just her shoes and socks on the floor, I was glad that I didn't have to spill no blood. I went to the bathroom to take a piss, splash some water on my face. There were clean towels and toiletries. After I handled my face I brushed my teeth and breathed out. Last night was a ball but this morning.

Whew! My blood pressure had gone up and down, heart fell to my feet and a little bit of fear. Fear from the thought of losing my girl and I ain't scared of a damn thing. The possibility of killing someone was the icing on me and Jurnee's beautiful wedding cake. That was the least of my concern, it was her deciding not to fuck with me. As long as Coya kept that shit quiet then we were good.

I thought back to what Pops said about knowing the first overnight stay together that Mama was forever. Taking my shoes off I got in bed and wrapped my arms around her. Even with her outfit still on she felt good. I kissed her jaw a few times and moved her hair over so I can kiss her neck.

"We forever baby." I whispered in her ear then went back to sleep with her for about thirty-minutes.

**

"Y'all have become my new favorite custos. Pay on time and over asking price but you definitely have developed some enemies." Rock told us while we loaded my trunk.

Myrtle Beach was fun as hell and a good way to end summer vacation. But it was back to reality now. School was starting soon, I was now and officially a Wayne State Warrior football player and college student. Things were good with me and Jurnee, now me and my brothers were back at Rock's spot buying drugs.

We didn't sell the shit because it was a lower grade than ours. But, we weren't letting Bishop and his raggedy cousins have product. I don't give a damn who else buys from Rock. We didn't do shit with these drugs but trash them. We damn sho' wasn't about to hit the streets and put our name on this wack shit.

"You say that all the time like we supposed to care. All you doing is getting paid and supplying." I told him not caring that he got his boys standing around us holding big guns.

"Ok youngin' you right."

"Daddy can I...Oh I'm sorry I'll come back."

I along with my brothers turned around when we heard someone call him daddy. I would have thought it was one of his bitches. But the voice sounded too sweet, like when Ava calls Pops. When we looked at the girl it was Darcy, Ava's best friend.

"It's ok daddy's baby, I'll be done in a minute." Rock said to her. When he saw the way she looked at us he got all bent.

"Aye! Why the hell y'all eyeing my daughter?!" He grabbed the gun from his boy hand and pointed it at us.

Pops didn't raise no hoe ass boys so we didn't even flinch or look scared.

"You need to relax, she's our sister best friend. We never knew she lived here, when our sister goes over her house its always on the westside." I told him since he had the gun more aimed at me.

"It's true Daddy, them nor Ava knows about you." Darcy spoke up, which I didn't need her to.

All I was going to do was break his arm towards his boy. The reflexes would have made Rock shoot him in the head. My brothers would have attacked his other two boys and it would have been bodies all on the floor. Darcy's too.

"Oh shit, my bad youngin'. I just don't play about my daughter, she lives with her Mother full time and with me all summer, her mother gets her on the weekends. Just in case you thought she was on some funny shit. Naw, nothing like that, she doesn't like what I do." He smiled taking the gun out my face.

"But now I know we all connected, y'all can be my extra eyes for me. Make sure my little girl stays out of trouble and trouble stays out of her." He continued.

Shit that nigga far too late, Austin been had his dick all down her throat. August done fucked her twice too at a party.

"We ain't no damn babysitters, she hangs with Ava so anytime she with her then she's good. That's the best we can do." Adrian spoke up and told him. Facts baby bro.

Rock looked like he couldn't believe the way we

responded to him.

"I don't get in any trouble anyway Daddy, me or my two best friends don't." Darcy said and you could tell she was trying to ease the tension.

"It's all good, I understand. Just thought y'all could do me that solid but it's all good."

I laughed as I got in my car because he low key looked hurt. Fuck you and yo' daughter homie, this is all business.

"Y'all buy that shit what he said about Darcy and her not telling Ava about him?" I asked as we got on the freeway. I was driving us to our warehouse where Pops was waiting for us.

"In a way yeah because she doesn't try to be in our faces." August answered, he was in the front seat.

"Yeah she doesn't, if she was watching us then Ava and her would have been around us more than normal." Austin added.

"Yeah but she ain't even told Ava, that's right there is kind of tart." Adrian put in his thoughts.

I was about to say something but flashing lights then a quick siren went off behind us. I breathed out because I hated dealing with 5. Then we had a trunk full of drugs. Pulling over, I wasn't scared and neither were my brothers. We had a way out of this but it was about to cost us and Pops wasn't going to be happy.

"These two fucks." I said to my brothers when we saw Joe and Stan coming towards us.

Stan had that usual blank look on his fat ass no neck face. Joe came to my window with that cocky smile and chip tooth showing.

"Top of the morning Legends. We got a call that some illegal activity has taken place."

"What?" I turned my nose all the way up when he said that.

"We need you to pop the trunk." Joe said and Stan went to the back of my truck.

"I swear to God this is straight bullshit." August said shaking his head.

I already knew what was up and it was fair game to Bishop, his cousins and his grimy looking ass Father. Chuckling, I popped opened the trunk. Joe went to the back with Stan and we heard them going through stuff. I could hear him rip the plastic that held the coke. He took a big sniff then laughed loud as hell. While he walked back to my window, Stan was taking the bags out the trunk.

"Well we have two options. I can say you're clear and take the problem off your hands. Or, me and my partner followed a lead and we struck a gold mine. But then I'll have a lot of paperwork to do." He looked up in the sky tryna look tired. "I just don't wanna do that. I'm tryna see my girlfriend today and then go home to my wife and kids. So, what's it gonna be?"

I looked at him like the lowlife fag in blue he was. This had Darius' name all on it, I can't even say his son because he wouldn't make a move like this. They are about to get their drugs back and it's like we paid for it. Bishop not smart enough or have the braincells to think of this.

"Do what you gotta do." I spoke with so much anger, but I was calm.

Joe saw how I was looking at him, my eyes were doing all the snarling and everything my face wouldn't do. When I get to a certain level of anger it's always in my eyes.

"I don't know what those blue evils are thinking, but I suggest you don't be stupid." Joe said to me then he smiled. "Enjoy the rest of your day, Legends."

I squeezed my steering wheel hard as hell as they rode past me. Man I wanted to kick my front window in. I closed my eyes and took a deep breath in and slowly out. My mind raced and I went into thinking. Thinking of our next move, thinking of a way to get Stan and Joe, a way that will make us come out on top. No jail time, all alive and still running these streets. Bishop, his cousins and his Father needed to be put down like rabid dogs.

JURNEE

"Boo I don't know if I like that skirt, it makes you look like you're straight up and down." I told Brinx.

Me and my girls were at Southland mall school shopping. Since we started high school, our Dads have let us shop by ourselves. When Toni got her car she became transportation. Before, one of our Dad's would take us and pick us back up. Today we were in my Jeep and having a great time. The first day of school was in two days and we were all excited. Senior year was about to start and it was going to be a great year.

"Ew, you're right." She agreed and went back into the dressing room. She gave me the skirt and I gave her the pants in exchange so she could try them on.

We were in Charlotte Russe which I hated but Brinx and Toni loved this store. No reason, I just didn't like the style of clothing for my body. They stick with the same kind of bubble gum pop style. But for some reason my two girls find the right pieces and make it work. The skirt Brinx had on though made her look like she had no hips whatsoever.

"American Eagle is after this." Coya said from behind me. She was laying upside down on the couch in the fitting room being silly.

"Yes, y'all know I love that store, then we need to go to Champs so I can get two pair of gym-shoes." I added.

"I swear if we don't have at least three classes together I'm going to the counseling office and cussing Ms. Smith out." Toni said from behind the dressing room.

"I know right, Mrs. Allen teaches writers comp this year and I want in on that class as an elective." I told them putting some earrings next to my ear. Charlotte Russe has nice jewelry that I don't mind buying.

"Are we doing vo-tech this year?" I don't need to but I can always use the extra hours for college apps." Brinx asked as she came out the dressing room. All the clothes she wanted she gave to me. The clothes she didn't want she hung them on the rack.

"I could use the extra hours also." I agreed taking my phone out because it vibrated. I smiled when it was Audrey.

Yang: I miss you baby, you coming to my crib after your done shopping?"

Me: I miss you more and only if you want me too.

I knew he was about to say something smart. I liked being with Audrey and every day I woke up, I still couldn't believe it. I was actually in a committed relationship with someone I would have never trusted. I had fun with him in Myrtle Beach and he showed me every day that this was real. I wanted to show him too, actually I had something to ask him when I see him later.

Yang: Just for you saying that I'ma blow in yo' pussy hard as hell when I see you.

I laughed out loud because he was a mess. But I tingled a little thinking of him even touching between my legs. Audrey was addicted to being down there since Myrtle Beach. He ate me out so good that first night that I thought I would die from cumming so good. Then he kept telling me *just wait till I give you this dick.* Oh my gosh, I have a feeling that I might cry when we first have sex.

"Jurnee snap out of it and tell Audrey you'll talk to him later." Brinx teased me.

We walked up to the front so her and Toni could pay for their stuff.

"How are things with you two?" Toni asked me.

"We're good. I like him so much that I feel like I love him."

All three of them looked at me fast.

"Damn, that's kind of fast." Toni commented first.

"Not really, I slept with Austin pretty quick. If you feel it then you feel it."

I put my arm through Coya's when she said that. "Thank you pooh, besides me and Audrey have been talking for months only we didn't know." I finally admitted to them. I told them the day I found out Audrey was SwagWordz.

"Wow Jurnee, that's like something you see on TV." Brinx said smiling hard.

"It's so romantic and I love it. Who would have guessed he writes and is into the same stuff you are." Coya also said.

"I can definitely see how y'all progressed now. Four months of talking to someone every day for hours. That's a whole other level of bonding." Toni told me while she paid for her stuff after Brinx.

"I know, it's so crazy because I thought he was full of it or playing with me. But he had journals, books of all genres and so many Japanese anime DVDs. But what I love the most is how he treats me the same in public and when we're alone. I thought he would want to keep us a secret or something. But he is on me tough and I like it."

"Girl bye. I could have told you he wouldn't want

to keep y'all no secret. You're gorgeous best friend." Brinx said as we all walked out the store.

"And don't think we didn't notice you're not wearing a hoodie." Coya started hitting my booty.

I laughed and covered my face. "I got tired of Audrey stealing them. I want him to meet my Dad. What do y'all think?" We were on our way to American Eagle.

The mall had a lot of people in here shopping for school.

"I think it's a good idea because you two are official. August came to pick me up for a date so he had to reveal himself. But, we still are not official and I still haven't had sex with him." Brinx told us.

"I think it's a good idea too. Plus our Dad's know them already, so it won't be too awkward. Me and Austin aren't official either, but I think my Dad will be ok with it." Coya said.

We got inside of American Eagle, checked our bags in from the other store and started looking around.

"My Dad will flip out, he always said he didn't want me with a street guy. He sees me meeting a college clean-cut guy. That's part of the reason why I kept Adrian a secret. Mi papa nunca lo aceptara (My Dad will never accept him.) will hit the ceiling. Me and Adrian can never have a relationship." Toni looked kind of sad.

I walked over to her and hugged her. "You never know until you try. If you like him Toni and want to be with him. Your Dad has to listen and understand, he should trust you and you decision making."

"He can be so stubborn." She confessed.

"What if we have our Dad's talk to him? It might make things easier." Coya suggested.

Brinx agreed. "Yeah I think it will, whenever you're ready just tell us and we can set it up." Toni smiled and felt better. "Thanks boos, I think that would be best."

We were happy she was good and went back to looking through clothes. American Eagle was my go to for the fall. I loved their jeans, flannel button-up tops and their hoodies. Only this time I'll be actually wearing them like they should be worn.

"Are you ready to meet up with Soo-Yun?" I asked Brinx.

When she told me and Toni about what happened at the mall we were so surprised. That was a sensitive subject for her. But she told us that she decided to meet up with Soo-Yun to hear what she has to say. We of course asked if she wanted us to go with her. But she told us she was having August go instead.

We knew Brinx, she didn't like to show any kind of feelings when it came to her birth mother. I believe she just didn't want us to see her true feelings about it. Rather it went good or not, Brinx wasn't comfortable with us seeing her emotions pertaining to that.

"I'm ready to get it over with. I don't want her to show up on my doorstep and disrupt my Dads or Brooke."

The cashier gave me my three bags and we walked out American Eagle.

"I understand that, I like that August is going to support you. I think that's so dope." Toni told her.

"Yeah he is really sweet to do this. I just want Soo-Yun to go away, like you made the decision to not be a mother. You cannot just pop back up and play the role." Brinx said putting her wallet in her purse.

"Would you want a relationship if she asked for one?" Coya asked and we were hoping Brinx wouldn't get mad.

"No, never." Her face looked unsure, but angry too.

We picked it up and quickly changed the subject talking about anything else. I had a good time school shopping with them. We got a lot of clothes, shoes, accessories, and some purses. Then we went to Target and got school supplies out the way. Once I dropped Coya and Toni off, I went home to drop my stuff off. Brinx decided to stay with me so she could go to the Legends' house with me.

Eddie had been texting me today and I wasn't going to respond. But, I felt the need to at least apologize to him about the way I ended things. It was cordial and he accepted which made me glad because I didn't want drama. After I put my clothes and stuff up, Brinx went to her house to do the same. We headed back out to Audrey's house. I loved having my own car.

"Hey Taz." I greeted August by his nickname when I came through the front door. Austin let me in, and I already spoke to him.

"Sup Jurnee, what up my one." He kissed Brinx on the lips.

Usually all of them would be in the basement. But today they were sitting at the dining room table playing cards. Brinx sat in the chair next to him.

"Let me finish this one hand then we can head to my room." He told her.

Adrian came from the back, spoke to us and sat down to play cards with him.

"Where's y'all brother?" I asked them putting my

purse on my right shoulder.

"That fool upstairs, being all anti cause, he misses you." Austin said and they all started laughing.

I was laughing to as I headed on up. I could hear *That 70s Show* theme song coming from his room. He loved that show and had me even watching it for the first time. It was actually funny as hell and I was on season 2. Getting to his door I knocked and he told me to come in. Gosh it was like anytime I saw him. Rather in person or in FaceTime, he just got finer. Audrey was laying on his back on his bed.

Those hairy legs were long and crossed. He had on Nike fleece shorts and no shirt. I never noticed how detailed sexy he was until we got together. Him and his brothers were fine. Even a toddler can comprehend that but being close to him let me see just how perfect he was. I've seen him naked more than twice and same for him. We even showered together and what I love was how he didn't try to have sex with me.

Like not even once, no pressure, he didn't ask if I was ready. It was like it wasn't a monkey in the room. It made me want him even more. But I just want to be sure, I have a feeling when I lose my virginity. I'll become clingy, a hopeless romantic. Whether we stay together or become friends. I want to always have the person I choose to have sex within my life forever.

"And just like that, my attitude gone." He looked at me licking his lips and those blue eyes were beaming at me.

I took my Ugg slides off and got in his bed. I had on a floral strapless romper and my hair was in a ponytail in the middle of my head. I laid on the side of him on my stomach with my right hand on his soft beard. All the hair on Audrey's body was so soft and smooth. He smelled so good and I loved sniffing him. Looking in his face I asked.

"Why did you have an attitude?"

"I can't even hear anything until you give me a kiss." His voice was always deep and intense but in a lustful way.

I kissed him and his right hand went on my back then down to my booty. When he squeezed it I got more into the kiss. I pecked his lips one last time then we calmed down.

"I was missing you so I just came up here so wouldn't nobody piss me off." He answered my earlier question.

I chuckled and shook my head. "What are you gonna do when school starts for both of us?"

Shrugging his shoulders, he started messing with my hair. "Did you get all your stuff for school?"

"Yup, supplies and all. I burned through my Dad card." I joked.

"You know I would have brought your stuff for school, all of it." He pulled me on top of him.

"I wouldn't let you do that, we haven't been dating that long." My hands were on top of his chest.

His hands were rubbing up and down my back. "I don't give a damn about any of that Jurnee. I'm telling you I would have, I got enough money to cash out on that."

I knew he was for real, I can look in his eyes and tell.

"I want to ask you something." I said to him a little nervous to what he would say. "What's up?"

"Will you meet my Dad? I mean I know you already know him. But I mean meet him as my boyfriend." I really hope he agrees.

"Of course baby, just tell me when and I'm there." His smile was everything to me.

"Is tomorrow ok? I want to do it before school starts. That way you can start coming over to my house." I took my dress off after I asked. I had on a nude seamless strapless bra with a matching thong.

Audrey looked at me hungrily then his big hand grabbed me by the front of my bra. Still holding it, he made my breasts pop out. He yanked me down to him and kissed me so aggressively.

"I'll never tell you no, Jurnee." He said against my lips then we went back to making out.

"Why are you so nervous, Fuzzy?" My Dad asked me as I looked out the window for the 100th time.

Today was the day that Audrey was being introduced as my boyfriend. To say I was jittery and scared would be an understatement. I wanted and prayed for today to go well. Tomorrow was the first day of school and I wanted a clear mind. I didn't want my man and my Dad not getting along. I love my Dad, respect him and always want to make him proud. But I can't leave Audrey because he doesn't like him. Nor can I have my Dad disappointed in me, I'd be stuck and that's not cool.

"I am very nervous." I admitted looking at him.

It was a regular day, Dad was in a good mood. I wanted to get it out the way so me and Audrey can go to the movies and out to eat.

"As long as he ain't white or over twenty then we

good." He sat down on the couch. Dad looked nice in his Burberry track suit.

I laughed at what he said. "Daddy you cannot hate him if he's white."

"Shitttt yes the hell I can, you ain't about to fuck up the blood line." Laughing himself he winked at me to let me know he was playing. "Jurnee as long as he ain't a sleazy ass guy then we all good.

The doorbell rang and he stood up.

"No. No Daddy, let me get it you just stay here." I ran to the door and opened it.

"My Yin, sup baby." He hugged me so tight and I hugged him back.

I gave him a quick kiss, "Hey my Yang."

Grabbing his hand, I walked him through the hallway and into the living room where Dad was. My heart was beating and I said a quick prayer to myself one more time. When he looked at Audrey he hurried up and looked at me.

"Daddy, I know you know who this is already but—"

"Jurnee go upstairs and let me talk to Audrey for a minute." He said with his eyes on him.

I wasn't expecting him to say that and I heard the

seriousness in his voice. "D-Daddy—"

"Now Jurnee." He said sternly.

Letting go of Audrey's hand, I went upstairs and immediately cried once I reached my room. Hurrying up and taking my phone out, I called my girls. Coya didn't answer, Toni was sleep but Brinx came through.

"I think my Dad is about to kill Audrey." I said as soon as she answered wiping my tears.

"Oh my goodness, what happened?"

I told her and tried not to cry again. I couldn't even hear what they were talking about.

"Well, let's not jump to conclusion. Maybe they are having a man to man conversation and you don't need to be a part of that. I mean of you haven't heard any yelling, cussing or guns cocking then it's all good." Brinx told me making me feel a little better.

"I did all that talk to Toni about her Dad and mine is tripping to. Brinx I don't know what I'm going to do if this becomes a problem."

"Stop boo, don't think the worst. If you do then that's what will happen, relax and think positive."

We both heard my Dad call my name.

"Call me as soon as you can, love you."

"Love you too." I told her hanging up and going

back downstairs.

I looked at Audrey as soon as I got down there. He was standing by the fireplace looking the same as when I left him. When he saw me he smiled and I felt relieved. Looking at Daddy he rubbed his bald head.

"You have my approval to keep dating him. All I want you to do is keep what I have always instilled in you. If your grades or anything academic wise are affected, then it's a wrap." He told me with that same stern tone.

I couldn't help but hug him and cheese at him. "Thank you Daddy, I love you."

"I love you too Fuzzy, y'all can go hang now, curfew still the same."

With that, me and Audrey left outside. "Oh my goodness I feel like I can take a deep breath now. What did he say to you?" I asked Audrey after we got in his truck and pulled off.

"That's between us men baby but it's all good." He kissed my hand and kept driving.

I didn't even care, as long as everyone got along, I was happy.

**

Me: Have a good first day of school my sexy college guy.

Yang: Thank you baby. Make sure you kill that shit today and all year.

I read his message smiling and then put my phone in my crossbody purse. Today was the first day of school for everyone. Summer was so good that I knew senior year would be all of amazing. We were in Indian summer which means high 70 degrees. I had on a pair of slightly ripped jeans, with a short sleeve yellow and black flannel button-up crop top.

My pair of yellow and black Nike Air Max went perfect. Mom came over yesterday and did a treatment on my hair. I put a part in it and left it hanging down. Taking my phone back out, I sent Audrey three selfies. I put my purple glitter bookbag from Aldo on and head down the stairs.

"Look at my beautiful senior." Dad greeted me with open arms when I walked in the kitchen.

"Good morning Daddy, thank you." Hugging him I sat down at the table where he had breakfast made. It was a tradition with him every morning since I can remember. Breakfast would be laid out and we'd eat together. This morning he made homemade waffles, bacon and eggs.

"So, let me hear the rules for this year." He said as he sat down and say grace with me so we could eat.

I had to put a piece of waffle in my mouth because he made the best. "Summer is over, so curfew is ten on weeknights and midnight on weekends. Nothing below a B, make sure I stay on track with SAT and ACT prep. Boyfriend cannot get in the way of completing my senior year strong. Use good judgement and if I ever need you, I just call and you'll come to fuck shit up." The both of us laughed at the last part because he's had me say that since I was little.

"Good girl and also remember. That car is a privilege that can be taken away." He gave me that forbidden expression.

"I know Daddy and I won't take it for granted." I assured him. We continued to eat and talk about the school year.

"Ayyyyyeeee senior year!" Toni and Coya yelled acting silly when I came to pick them up. Brinx stayed next door to me so of course I already had her.

My girls looked so bomb today. Brinx took it back old school, she had on a complete copy of Cher black and yellow outfit from the movie *Clueless.*

I blew my horn and rolled the windows down getting excited with them.

"Oh my goodness summer flew by and now it's our year!" Toni was so geeked when she got in putting her seat belt on.

As I drove we didn't even turn the radio on like we normally did. All we could do was talk about our expectations of the year.

"Damn, it looks like more seniors than last year." I told them when we got inside the lunchroom.

This year all the seniors had to meet in the lunchroom to get their schedules. If you had all your credits then you had Ms. Smith for a counselor. If you were off even by a little, then you had Ms. Collins who was evil as hell. No matter who you had though, the goal was to walk across that stage with your class in June. Whether you had to have a 1 to 7 hours or you had to go to night school.

"I know it's crazy and is it just me and does it look like all the niggas got finer?" Coya said and she wasn't lying.

"Why would they do this to me the year, I get a boyfriend." I admitted laughing.

"Well that's you mami, we're still single." Toni

teased.

"I second that." Brinx added laughing.

"And I'll be the third to put my foot in yo' ass if you talk to any of these lames." August came behind her, scaring all of us. "And you, don't make me tell my big bro." He pointed at me then kissed Brinx on her cheek.

We saw Adrian and Austin walk in the lunchroom next. Coming over to us. We were all in line waiting to see who had who for the year.

"There is nothing to tell because I didn't do anything." I stuck my tongue out at August.

Austin was whispering in Coya's ear and Toni had her hand on the end of Adrian's dreads. It made me miss Audrey and wish he was here.

"Don't let a little loneliness get you in trouble." Austin said to me joking.

I smacked my lips laughing and just waved him off. The room got more crowded, I was ready to get my schedule and leave. Once the lines had to break off in alphabetical order so me and my girls had to separate. Once I got my schedule in my hand I squeezed out the lunchroom and waited for them.

"Over here!" I called out to them when I saw them get out.

They ran to me and we synced of schedules. We were satisfied with what we saw. We had first through third hour all together. Then the other two hours we had separate. We all didn't have one class without a Legend in it. Now, it was time to get your locker. In Cooley, you could pick whatever locker you want. As long as you have a combination lock and you are not allowed more than one locker.

Once you pick, you have to give the locker number and combination to your second hour teacher so they can keep it for records. Our school was three floors with a new building attached to it. Over the summer we got a new black gate put around the whole school. It was high and protected so no outsiders can get in. Now, if you want you can have lunch outside on the bleachers.

The worst thing in the world about going to this school were the three flights of stairs. Do you know how irritating it is to have a first hour on the first floor to the left?! Then your second hour is on the third floor all the way on the left! On top of that you have five minutes to go to your locker and head to class before the bell rings or you'll get caught in a hall sweep.

That means a write up which give you three warnings. After three detention, three warnings again, then its suspension.

"This is the perfect locker spot. The bathroom is over there and the doors to the stairs are right here." I told Brinx who picked our spot for the year. I laughed because Coya was already putting her star stickers, Angela Bassett picture, plus pictures of us and herself up.

"When you gon' put my picture up?" Austin came over to her locker messing with her. The guys lockers were across from ours.

"When you stop being ugly." She joked back, closing her locker.

"You got a lot of jokes but you hung with this ugly nigga all summer." It was cute when he put his hand around her neck.

All of us were headed to first hour when the Talbert sisters walked past us. Today was not the day for them to try shit. It was the first day of school and I knew fighting wasn't on our mind. We already got they ass in Myrtle Beach. When they walked past us all three of them rolled their eyes and scoffed at us. We just laughed and talked shit.

"Oooo chile I never seen so much bitterness in my life." I said out loud.

"Oh yeah oh, we'll see who's bitter by the end of

the day." Regina said and her sisters laughed and high fived her.

"Bitch what is that—"

"Nope! No!" August stepped in front of me. "Them hoes ain't going nowhere in life but to get some government assistance after we graduate. You better than this shit in-law, come on now it's the first day."

"But your brothers fuck with us so-called hoes tough as hell!" Regina yelled with her sisters pulling her back.

"Bitch that don't mean shit, y'all was only as, strong as ya gag reflexes! Bop ass bitch!" When Adrian said that the whole hallway laughed.

We went on to class still laughing and talking about it. I don't know what Regina meant by her comment. But if she comes at me at the end of the day I'm smacking her in the face. First day or not.

"Good morning and welcome to the first day of school. Most importantly, welcome the first day of your senior year." Ms. Allen, the writing comp. teacher greeted us.

Her class was specially chosen for seniors only. You had to have passed your English classes with a B or higher. Also, you must be looking to major in English, journalism or any form of writing in college. I was more than excited she picked me, Ms. Allen has written for The New York Times and Detroit Free Press.

"Who-Ho!" The class clapped and got excited after she said that.

I was in this class alone but it was ok. What I did notice was the storyboard she had on the wall. It was from the site me and Audrey met on. I saw three stories on the board by SwagWordz and I just smiled. While Ms. Allen talked I texted him teasing him and telling him he was famous. First hour went great, her class wasn't a joke but I knew it would be worth it.

"Should I be offended that I have Spanish for first hour?" Toni said to us while we all walked to second hour we had together.

"Girl no, that's an easy A." Coya answered.

"Exactly. Count your blessings because Mrs. Allen writing comp class is no joke." I told her moving my hair out my face. I saw Eddie at his locker, he winked at me and I gave him a half smile still walking.

"Uh, since when does Ms. Lane teach English 4?" I asked them shocked to see her when we walked in the class. Usually Mrs. Crowder teaches that, and Ms. Lane teaches English 3 (11th grade English).

"I guess she missed us from last year." Toni said playing around.

"Hello everyone, happy first day of school." Ms. Lane spoke to us when the bell rang and everyone came inside. She was gorgeous and looked like she may have had some good luvin' all summer. Her skin was glowing, she had on a long pencil skirt. It showed her curves and her short sleeve blouse was tucked in her skirt. It wasn't shocking that all the boys drooled over her.

"Ok so I will be passing out the year syllabus and a classroom agreement that needs to be signed by your parents. Also, I will be passing out a card with your name and another student's name. Who you see will be your partner on all projects the whole year." As she talked she was passing out everything.

I saw Toni held her card up showing Adrian and they both were happy. I saw mine and it had August's name on it. Brinx was sitting next to me and when she flipped hers over and it said Erika, I poked my lip out to her. Erika was cool but of course we wanted each other or at least her have August. I felt bad so I raised my hand to see if I could help.

"Yes Jurnee." Ms. Lane answered my hand raise while she stood next to me and Brinx.

"Is it ok if we switch?" I whispered it because I didn't want anyone else to hear us and it makes others copy.

Ms. Lane looked at my card and then at Brinx's. "Is there a real problem or are you trying to be your friend's hero? I assigned everyone together for a reason, your friend is just going to have to live with it." She gave me a fake smile then sashayed off to the front of the class.

"Bitch much?" I whispered in Brinx's ear, chuckling.

"It's fine, thanks boo I don't mind working with Erika. Plus I'd prefer August being paired with you instead of these other hoes." She laughed and said.

The rest of the day flowed well. Even though it was senior year it still was work that needed to be done. We all had to prep for testing next year, college counseling and a lot to prepare us for June. The final hour came and this was Physics class with just Adrian.

"Aw shit, I know I'm getting an A+ this year." He laughed and joked when we were paired.

"Oh my goodness, everywhere I turn it's a Legend on my left and a Legend on my right." I played back with him because I was just on the phone with his brother during lunch. He was having a good first day as well.

"Ain't God good." Adrian was so damn silly.

Mr. Kimbro started the class telling us what Physics was and what he expected. Everyone was taking notes because he wasn't to be played with. Pop quizzes, projects and weekly progress reports. The good thing was we would be watching a lot of movies and documentaries. That was always better than listening to the teacher talk. It was finally about eight minutes until the bell rung to go home.

Phones started vibrating and I didn't pay any attention to it at first. Mr. Kimbro was at his desk with his head deep in a book. The door to the classroom was open and I saw some students walking by. When they would see me they would laugh and whisper. Then the class started doing the same thing. Only they were looking in their phones and then eyes went to me and Adrian.

"Tha fuck y'all looking at?" Adrian asked with his nose turned up mad.

Hell, I wanted to know too. Me and his phone went off the same time and it was a tag on Facebook. I hit it and it was from that bitch Regina. It was captioned 'Best Friend Goals or Nah'. When I pressed play on the video it was a white wall. The camera moved and I recognized the house as the beach house at Myrtle Beach. A door opened and the camera went to a bed.

When I saw who were laying in it my damn ears felt like they popped. I wanted to throw my Gucci glasses because they had to have me seeing things. It was Coya sleep and Audrey was laying next to her. Then the camera showed the floor and their clothes were all off. The video jumped to another part where they were obviously up talking. I know both of their voices so I knew it was them.

This all just looks foul. This is all fucked up, but no one is up yet. You stay here, I'll ease out. Find my girl and we put this behind us. Deal? Then I heard Coya say. *Please don't play me Chaos, this will destroy everything if it got out. With your brother and most importantly with my girls.* The video was jumpy but I didn't care, all I cared about was the two of them naked and in the bed.

I don't know what I was feeling because it was so much running through my mind. To narrow it down into one word wasn't happening. But I trusted my eyes and ears, I know what I saw and what I heard. I looked at Adrian and he had his phone in his hands tight looking like a demon. He looked at me and it was like he transferred that anger into me. Fuck the tears, I was livid.

The bell sounded and we shot out of class. Everyone in the hallway was looking, snickering, shaking their heads. Some were even looking like they felt sorry for me and Adrian. We both saw Coya at the locker and she ran up to us before we could. I thought Adrian was about to lay into her. But he walked right passed her and through the double doors that led downstairs.

"Jurnee please let me—"

I ended her sentence by slapping the shit out of her. "I can't fucking believe you! Why Coya!? Why would you do me like that!?" I was yelling so loud and I didn't care about the crowd.

Coya held her face with tears in her eyes. "If you could just listen I swear—"

"I guess you were just living up to your words! If I wasn't giving him some then you were the someone else who would!" I don't care what kind of scene I was making on the first day. This was all over school, the two of them did this.

"Jurnee let's go, come on before you get suspended." I don't know where Toni and Brinx came from. But they both were grabbing me and pulling me out the double door.

"Guys please—" Coya cried out.

"Coya just don't, ok! Don't!" Brinx shouted at her then we got through the door.

I was heated, I saw red and even when we got outside. I just needed to get away from school. I needed to see Audrey and fuck him all the way up. Toni snatched my keys out my hand.

"Toni give me my keys so I can go to Audrey's house!"

"No, I can't do that Jurnee. I know you wanna beat his ass, hell I do too. But not now, it's not smart. Let's go to your house and cool down."

I had no energy to fight her right now. Everyone was still staring, pointing, laughing and giving me that pity look. I jumped in my front seat, let her drive and Brinx got in the back.

What a great fucking first day.

BRINX

"Thank you so much for coming with me today. I know we are not official to be dealing with family drama." I gave August a sincere look.

We were on the way to meet Soo-Yun at Ruby Tuesday restaurant. I finally picked a time and day. I just wanted this out the way, I wanted her gone and to hear me tell her that. August was going with me and I really appreciated him for it.

"Didn't I tell you to stop thanking me? I fuck wit'chu hard, Brinx. You're the one who wanna move all slow and shit with our relationship. You can't even do single shit anymore so you might as well give me the title." His smart mouth butt drove his truck as smooth as he said his words.

"August you don't know what it takes to be my man. I'm high maintenance and spoiled, my Dads can barely handle me." I playfully flipped my hair at him.

"I know why you won't make it official."

I folded my arms turned my body towards him in my seatbelt. "Oh this I gotta hear."

August pulled into the parking lot of the restaurant. When he found a space he parked and then looked at me before he turned the car off.

"Because you know you wanna give me that pussy. And as long as you're officially not my girl then it's your excuse not to."

I wanted to kick him in his nose. Because he was so blunt but mostly because he was right. "You're full of it." I told him rolling my eyes and getting out.

"You know I'm right, that's why you not about to speak on it." I like how he grabbed my hand with confidence.

We were a little early so I knew she wasn't here yet. He sat next to me so Soo-Yun could sit across from us.

"So, what a good first day of school huh." August said to me.

I knew he was talking about the video that was posted on Facebook. I couldn't believe it, I was in computer class when I got the tag. The first thing that came to my mind was it wasn't real. I kept saying stupid shit to myself like it was photoshop. But listening to them talk, my heart broke as if I was Jurnee.

All I saw was our friendship in flames. There was going to be a divide, a side that had to be chosen. I saw

Toni first after the bell rung and she was about to cry. All we did was try to hurry and find Jurnee before she saw it. When we heard yelling and saw a big crowd on the second floor, we knew what it was.

"It started at the bottom then dropped all the way down. That's why I keep thanking you for coming. I know you have a lot on your plate with Chaos and Play." I told him then crossed my legs. I loved my Cher outfit I had on because *Clueless* was one of my favorite movies.

August rubbed his hands on his wave fast three times. He looked stressed about the whole thing. "I don't even know how to handle the both of them. We don't do shit like that to each other. Adrian didn't go home like I thought. Austin went to Wayne State to make sure Adrian didn't go there. I hit up Chill and he told me him and Audrey saw it. I called him but he didn't answer. How is yo' girl?"

"A mess. Toni is with her and they knew I had to do this today. We are going to spend the night at her house tonight. Coya has called me and texted, I'm just really disappointed in her right now."

August nodded his head. "That's understandable, I feel the same way about Audrey. I mean we were all drunk, me and my brothers were high. But damn, I don't even recall them being near each other."

"Me neither. I—" When I looked up, I saw Soo-Yun come through the doors.

August looked where I was looking and he grabbed my hand. "You got this my One." Kissing it, he put his phone in his pocket.

I waved my hand so she could see where we were. As she walked over here, she was all done up like she was at the mall. Black long hair straight and down, her slim body was in some tight jeans. Her vest like shirt was tight as well, she also had some heels with a Prada purse. Whatever it was she did for a living, she had money. I just hope she wasn't about to think that means anything to me.

"Oh, I thought it would be just the two of us." She looked at August like he was a problem.

"We'll I'm not doing this to make you comfortable. He's here for me." I answered with the same attitude she gave towards him.

After she sat down and put her purse in her lap. She flagged down a waited and ordered a drink.

"I didn't know drug addicts can still drink." When I made that sarcastic remark, August hit the side of my knee under the table. I didn't care.

"As long as it's not drugs, I'm fine. I have been clean for two years and married for six months." She held up her big ring.

I gave her a non-genuine smile. "Oh, well isn't that nice. Can we just cut to the chase, why are you here?" Sitting back, I folded my arms and waited for her to answer.

"I'm your mother Brinx, I have the right to want to see you and Brooke." Her voice was light but there was a know it all to it.

I chuckled and looked to the left when she said that stupid shit. "You may have birthed us, but you are no mother to us. I don't understand why you are here. The last time I saw you, you shoved a baby in my face and took off. We have been fine for a long time and will continue to be fine. Just go away, leave us alone." I have been waiting to say that since she came in here.

August didn't say a word, he just kept rubbing my knee and letting me know he was right here.

Soo-Yun blinked her tears away and wiped the corner of her eye. I don't know if she was trying not to cry or not.

"I have a lot of regret Brinx. I have done drugs and prostitution since I was twelve. When I had you, I knew I didn't want you. Not because you weren't beautiful, or worth it, because you were. But because I knew I couldn't be the mother you needed. I couldn't protect you or provide for you. It was the same when I had Brooke but not a day went by when I didn't think about you both."

Now it was my turn to fight back tears. I don't like showing emotions when it comes to this woman. I didn't like to talk about her or admit my abandonment and trust issues because of her. But her words were making my heart feel sympathy and I couldn't control the words that came out my mouth.

"You could have at least tried." I spoke lowly, but I knew they both heard me.

She gave me a small smile and said, "I know, and I intend to now...with Brooke."

Immediately, wrinkles came to my forehead. "What?"

Her expression was like she felt embarrassed for me. "Brinx, you are a grown woman now. I missed everything but I am glad you turned out good. However, I do not plan to do that with Brooke. In fact, I plan to be in her life permanently and have full custody of her. Although I appreciate Robert and Bryant for all they have done, I never signed over my rights. My husband paid for me to have the best lawyer. I plan to fight for her."

"Wait, how the fuck you come up here, build her up and then tear her down again? What the hell kind of person are you?" August cussed her out.

I was in shock at what she said, my feelings were hurt and I felt worthless. Tears fell and I didn't care, I looked at her.

"I hate you, you're a selfish, selfless bitch. You want everything to be easy, you fuck up with one daughter and think you can make it up with the second one. You'd rather act like I mean nothing than take the time and build a relationship with me." I stood up, pushing the chair I was sitting on to the floor.

"Fuck you, your husband, your money and your lawyers you have. My Dad's will never let you have her!" I picked her drink up, threw it in her face and ran out.

"I hate her! I hate her!" I was so loud, and people were looking at me.

August came and hugged me, and that's when I broke all the way down. Now, I have to go home and tell my Dad's what all just happened.

TO BE CONTINUED....

I HOPE YOU ALL ENJOYED PART 1 OF THIS SERIES. BEFORE YOU GET UPSET ABOUT THE ENDING. PLEASE TRY TO REMEMBER IT IS NOT THE END IT IS A SERIES AND THE WHOLE POINT IS TO LEAVE A CLIFFHANGER. PART 2 WILL BE OUT SOON! THANK YOU SO MUCH FOR THE LOVE AND SUPPORT.

---LONDYN LENZ

Made in the USA
Coppell, TX
14 January 2022

71576014R00246